Such Pretty Toys

Just as Professor Neil Kelly, first encountered in *By Frequent Anguish*, is about to depart for a sabbatical in England, he receives word that a bomb explosion has killed his close friend Morgan Lacey and injured Morgan's wife, Barbara. From her hospital bed, Barbara prevails on Neil to fly to Santa Fe and try to find out who had hidden the tiny, lethal explosive in the jack-in-the-box she had sent her husband for an April Fool joke.

At the start of his search, Neil is amazed to learn that the wealthy, over-achieving Laceys are involved in the activities of the CIA. And 'The Firm' is not his only companion — or rival? — in the search for the killer. The FBI also has some unexpected agents in the area, who appear to be working against the CIA operatives.

At the heart of the mystery is Barbara's beautiful niece Linn, who runs the computer system at her father's successful construction company and is engaged to a brilliant engineer of shadowy background. Linn's family nickname has even inadvertently supplied the code word for a treasonable computer operation. How much is she involved in what is going on?

Before Neil Kelly can unravel this grim puzzle he has to augment his expert knowledge of 17th-century English literature with a crash course in computer technology.

S. F. X. Dean once again demonstrates the delightful wit, deft characterization and graceful prose that marked his debut in crime fiction.

by the same author

BY FREQUENT ANGUISH

S. F. X. DEAN

Such Pretty Toys

A Neil Kelly narrative

COLLINS, 8 GRAFTON STREET, LONDON W1

William Collins Sons & Co. Ltd
London · Glasgow · Sydney · Auckland
Toronto · Johannesburg

All the characters and events portrayed in this story are fictitious.

First published in the UK 1983

British Library Cataloguing in Publication Data

Dean, S.F.X.
Such pretty toys.—(Crime Club).
I. Title II. Series
813'.54[F] PS3554.E1734

ISBN 0 00 231799 0

Photoset in Compugraphic Baskerville
Printed in Great Britain by
T. J. Press (Padstow) Ltd

To Anne, Mary, Rose and Eileen
and in memory of Em

Love (having found) wound up such pretty toys
as themselves could not know:
—E. E. Cummings (from *No Thanks*, 1935)

CHAPTER 1

It was already April fourth, and Neil Kelly finished his packing savagely. He resented the fact that he was not yet in England. If his original plans had been taken into account by anyone else, he would have been settled there three weeks ago. Now that April's there, I'm here, he thought bitterly, cursing the college and his own scrupulousness about his students. If he had just handed his Elizabethan poets class over to the nincompoop Hatterley . . . he growled disgustedly at himself and checked the clock on the Congregational church, just visible over the roof opposite. He had an hour. He stood looking for what would be the last time for five months over the town of Oldhampton and the campus of Old Hampton College. The pale spring sun was encouraging a few student ball-players to loosen up, and two Frisbee tossers were skimming their toy with insolent skill. All the pedestrians over twenty-two that he could see were prudently buttoned and zipped into coats.

His plane would leave in the evening from Boston, which meant that he had a ninety-mile bus ride ahead of him; he had no intention of driving his old Volvo to Boston just for the privilege of paying parking fees for almost half a year.

He buckled the third and final canvas suitcase with a sigh, half grunt, of relief and lugged all three bags downstairs to the front hall. Bradley Oakes, his student tenant, who had demonstrated in the last three weeks of unanticipated joint tenancy that one of them was not as smart as the other had hoped, was standing grinning by the library doorway.

'You got a call.'

'I hope you told them I left.'

'You haven't left, basically, so I said you'd call back.'

Neil set the bags into an orderly heap, tight-lipped.

'Should I have told them you already left, you mean?'

'Who?'

'Who called? I couldn't really tell. Not a student, though. Someone older.' Bradley grinned wider: his only indoor skill. He was vastly amused by the fact that there were—on this very campus where he was enduring the rigours of undergraduate education in football, hockey, baseball, squash, disco, and beer—a number of inexplicable middle-aged presences designated as professors who insisted on carrying out their activities in the midst of his strenuous programme of R & R. 'That all you're taking to England, three bags?'

'Right. Did you get the number?' Neil had been quite explicit about his inaccessibility to further callers when he had briefed Bradley at breakfast. He needed that secretarial screen partly because he *was* so damned scrupulous. If a call reached him, it nagged him until he dealt with it.

'Number? Oh. No. He said he was coming over. He said he was an old friend of yours. He said he was just visiting Oldhampton and wanted to say hello personally.'

'Is there any possibility he gave you his name?' Neil walked to the kitchen and put on water for a cup of instant coffee.

'Name? Well, like I said, not exactly. He said to tell you Danny Boy called. Is that his name? It sounds like a song or a racehorse or something.' He spread his arms and sang, 'Oh, Danny Boy . . .'

'Dan Boyd?' Oh Christ, another old college classmate with a son he wanted to get into Old Hampton where acceptances usually went either to the very bright or very rich. Neil had discovered long ago that when old college friends realized they knew a distinguished professor at a famous college, not to use the lever of friendship was as sinful as having an expense account and not eating well—was, in a word, unthinkable. He hadn't seen or heard from Danny Boyd since they had graduated and gone their separate ways, Neil to a postgraduate fellowship in literature at Oxford and Dan off to some cultural attaché desk in a remote corner of the State Department.

He settled himself grimly into the leather chair, sipping his final cup of coffee and listening to a bit of 'Morning Pro Musica' on the college FM station. Bradley hung about uncertainly in the doorway.

'Listen, Professor Kelly? I might not be here when you actually leave, so listen, good luck over there and have a great time, okay?'

Neil roused himself for a final grudging courtesy to his cretinous house-sitter. 'Thank you, Bradley. I expect I will. Are you off to the library then?'

'Well, no, not exactly.' He grinned and scratched his nose. 'Basically, I usually play baseball on Saturdays.'

'Ah, of course. Well, take good care of the house in my absence. Please try to remember our agreement about no parties. You have my forwarding address in Devonshire.'

'Hey, don't worry about a thing, Professor. No one will touch your books while I'm here.' He offered his hand for an embarrassed, restrained shake, holding Neil's hand with the care one would give to something really old and fine, looking away as they shook. 'Hey, there's someone getting out of a car out front. That your Danny Boy?'

Bradley's departure through the front door coincided with the visitor's arrival, so all three had a flurry of meeting and parting on the small porch. It was indeed Dan Boyd, heavier, redder of face and thinner of hair, but with the same rotund, rather bloated good looks, and acting the hearty old classmate to the hilt.

'Neil, you old son of a gun, how are you?'

'Hello, Dan. Surprised to see you here. Oh, goodbye

again, Bradley. Dan, this young man is my lodger, Bradley Oakes. Bradley, Dan Boyd, an old, old classmate of mine from Old Hampton.'

'Jeez, you make me sound a hundred, Neil.'

'Really, Dan? O.H.? What club?'

'Knights all the way, Brad, and you?'

'Hey, that's great. Knights here, too.' They beamed at each other with the sureness of mutual recognition. Heart, as Cardinal Newman had once observed, speaketh unto heart. 'It's great to meet you, but I gotta run, okay?' He ran.

'Nice boy, Neil. Your lodger, you say?' They entered the hall, and Dan stopped by the bags and raised Groucho Marx eyebrows twice. 'Making a getaway, are you?'

Neil groaned inwardly. He and Dan had never been on these old-buddy terms. 'Yes, I'm on my way to England. Tonight, out of Logan as a matter of fact. I only have a short time before my bus, Dan, but if you'd like some coffee, I have some.'

'Great. Had breakfast over at your inn. Coffee was instant, couldn't drink it.'

'So's mine,' Neil said.

'Still okay with Dan. Has to be better than theirs.' He looked around the house as they went to the kitchen, shamelessly estimating and cataloguing how well his old classmate had done for himself. 'Isn't it amazing, you back here at Old Hampton as a famous professor? I guess if I thought about it, I could have predicted it. Remember tutoring me for the Shakespeare final? Jesus, those spot passages.'

Neil spooned out the freeze-dried and poured the water. 'How did you do?'

'Well, I passed, let's leave it at that.' He sipped the brew. 'Perfect.'

Neil led the way back into the library. 'I don't want to be rude, Dan, but I am going to catch a bus in half an hour. I'm off for some sabbatical research in England.' He looked Dan squarely in the eye. 'I honestly expected you to have a son or daughter in tow. Old classmates often do.'

Dan Boyd guffawed with needless exuberance. Still acting. 'You mean use my influence with old Neil to sneak my kid with the lousy College Boards in under the admissions requirements? Sorry, Neil. Look, no kids.' He opened his coat. 'Well, a stepson who lives out in California, but he's a rock musician and wouldn't be caught dead on a good college campus except to play a concert or something.' He set his cup carefully on the end table and looked solemn. 'I can see you still don't like to bullshit around, Neil. Same old guy.'

Neil winced inwardly for the second time. Heartiness was one thing, but this offhand dissembling was something more. If Dan Boyd didn't want a dumb child admitted to Old Hampton, he wanted something else. Probably something Neil was even less likely to want to provide.

Dan Boyd took another swig of coffee, washed his teeth with it, made eye contact with Neil and held it. 'I've come to ask your help, Neil. And to bring you some unpleasant news, I'm afraid.'

'Dan, it's not about the Alumni Fund needing more money, because I've already got that news, and there's no news about seventeenth-century literature any more, so it must be something I just don't care enough about to respond.'

Dan Boyd smiled and held up a hand he supposed was reassuring. 'Listen, about your bus, don't sweat it. I'm driving you to Boston myself.'

'Sorry, Continental Trailways is, Dan. All ticketed and planned.'

'No, really, hey, it's no trouble. I have to go to Boston myself, honest, no lie.'

'Dan,' Neil began wearily, 'I have just had the roughest year of my life. A girl I loved very much was the victim of a sordid, ghastly murder, and I spent several months under medical treatment because of it. I have been forced to endure publicity I didn't want, and praise and blame — neither of which I deserved — '

Dan Boyd made his traffic-cop gesture. 'Neil, hold it, old buddy, hold it. I know everything you're going to tell me. The murder of the Lacey girl, the scandal for the college, your part in solving it — all that stuff. And, believe me, I know how burned out you must feel, how much you must be looking forward to this sabbatical in England. But I think — I know, Neil — that when you hear what I have to say, you'll change your mind.'

'No.' Neil stood up. 'I won't. So don't even bother, Dan. Just let's say it's been nice meeting you again, but please go.' He was feeling less inhibited by natural courtesy every second.

'Does the word "patriotism" mean anything to you, Neil?' It was obviously the salesman's trump card, and sweaty, sincere Dan Boyd played it with maximum solemnity.

But Neil had been getting rid of importunate salesmen and students for too many years to be embarrassed. Intellectual crudity he could deal with. 'There are three words, Dan, which no adult who wants to be taken seriously ever uses: patriotism, piety, and sincerity. Whatever you're selling, a tour of western Europe in support of American cultural exchange — whatever, forget it.'

Boyd made no move to leave. Rather, he settled an inch deeper into his chair and shook his head sadly, injured but understanding.

'You're a lot tougher than I remember, Neil. You used to be kind of soft. I remember you bought a magazine subscription from some jerk who came around the dorm and gave you a song and dance. We need that new toughness in you, Neil, it's a fact.' He sat bolt upright now and looked what Neil imagined he imagined was both pious and sincere. 'Okay, fella, no bullshit. I work for the federal government, you know that?'

'That's wonderful, Dan.'

'I'm not supposed to spell this out, Neil, but I'm not really with the State Department. Haven't been since way back when. It's an intelligence problem, Neil.' His eyes widened and his mouth performed an involuntary grimace, as if the admission had been wrung from him against his will.

'Dan, I honestly don't care if it's World War Three. I gave at the office. My energy, my tolerance for old friends out of the blue, my time, and nearly my sanity—all gone. I need this sabbatical and I'm going to take it, starting out by bus, on my own, and without another word from you. I might just never be any good again as a teacher, Dan—and I was very, very good—unless I take this time off now, in a lovely English place called Ottery St Mary, and think and write my way back to something approaching seamless sanity.'

Without raising hand or eyebrow, Dan Boyd spoke just once more.

'Morgan Francis De Sales Lacey.'

Neil snapped at him, 'What is that supposed to mean? That you know he's paying for this leave? I'm not ashamed of it; it's public knowledge. It was De Sales's girl who was killed here this past year, right on this campus. And it's his foundation that's paying my way to England for this research.'

'He's dead.'

'Not when I talked with him by phone last Tuesday. What do you mean, man, what's going on?'

'De Sales Lacey, your old classmate and mine, too, Neil, remember, chairman and trustee of this college, was killed last Wednesday night in his home in Santa Fe,

New Mexico. His wife was with him. A bomb did the killing.'

Neil sat down in a wash of horror and nausea. All the pain of what he had been through in the past year went through him again in a hot rush. He stared at Dan Boyd incredulously, waiting to hear the rest through the beating of the blood in his ears.

Dan Boyd stood up. He was emotionally in charge of the moment, and he knew it. He walked towards the window and looked out towards the campus, letting Neil get his composure back. Without turning, he started to speak again. 'I knew this would come as an awful shock to you, and I wanted to give it to you a little slower, more gradually.'

'A bomb? Not an accident?'

'No, not an accident, we know that much. Murder, Neil. Killed when he opened a package with a small explosive device in it. His wife was apparently standing just behind him. Some kind of booby-trapped toy.'

Neil was dry-mouthed and felt stupid, as though Boyd's words were coming from too great a distance to be heard clearly. 'Toy?'

'Apparently a little jack-in-the-box. Except that, instead of a funny face coming out, there was enough explosive in there to blow their eyes out. Died instantly. It started a small fire.' He paused significantly. 'My people heard right away, of course.'

'Why?' Neil croaked the word, almost beyond caring what else Boyd was saying, but needing to hear the story out to its grim conclusion. 'Who are your people?'

'Central Intelligence Agency, Neil. That's who I work for. Whom.'

'But why didn't I hear about this—'

'No one but the immediate family has yet. No one else. They sent me to tell you. We were afraid you might even have already left.'

'Did De Sales work for—with—whatever, the CIA?'

'You know I can't tell you that, Neil.' Boyd sounded wounded, almost prissy, like a man who'd heard an obscenity in mixed company.

'Did he?' Neil shouted hoarsely at him. 'Goddamit, it's obvious he did, Dan. Don't you know a rhetorical question when you hear one? Do you think I'm an idiot? If he weren't working for you people, why would you be here, doing this ghoul's work?'

'Isn't it obvious that my answer was as rhetorical as your question, Neil?' He eyed his old classmate and tried to get the tension back down to a manageable level. 'It's Barbara who wants to see you—I mean—'

'Babs? Is she alive? You said—'

'No, I didn't say that. Listen, Neil. Old Morg is dead; his wife is in the hospital in Boston. She was blinded by the explosion, and burned pretty bad. She's the one who asked you to come. My people just took responsibility for telling you.' He looked away miserably. 'I'm sorry I said she wanted to *see* you, that was a dumb slip.'

Neil felt a new shock, a mixture of hope and pity. 'She's alive in Boston? My God, which hospital? I should be there now.'

'You'll get there faster in my car than by bus, Neil.'

'Wait. Slow it down for just a minute, Dan. Tell me exactly where Barbara Lacey is.'

The agent answered him evenly and slowly. He knew that Neil Kelly would be going with him to Boston now and that he had plenty of time for the rest. Inwardly, he felt immense relief. He wouldn't have wanted to report back to Langley that he had failed to carry out even this simple errand. He knew the rest would be easier.

He spelled it out without elaboration. Barbara Lacey had been badly injured in the blast that killed her husband. She was apparently leaning on his shoulder; they think she must have been watching him open the package. The explosion blinded her and burned her face badly. She was rushed by private jet to Mass. General on the orders of a specialist. She woke up for the first time yesterday, and the first thing she had said, four hours after the doctors had told her what had happened, was Neil's name. 'She asked us to call you and get you to come and see her, please.'

'Insane.' Neil was thinking now entirely of Barbara. He had known her before her husband did. He had dated her first in college; they had all eventually become close friends. More than twenty years later, he had, against all reason, fallen in love with her daughter, whose brutal death it had taken him so long to get over. He could understand De Sales getting involved in politics or spying or whatever else came along. He was a man of what they had always laughingly called 'Large Affairs', from multinational corporation president down to college trustee, always with a dozen newsworthy commercial and political connections. But Babs? It was impossible to imagine her blinded and burned simply because she was Morg's loyal wife. He could see the scene with terrible clarity in his mind: Babs standing in the one place you'd expect her to be—at her husband's shoulder, an evening drink in hand, sharing a relaxed cocktail hour before dinner—watching with bright, amused eyes as he opened his surprise package. *Enough explosive to blow their eyes out*. He groaned and shook his head savagely to exorcise the picture. All the old gestures of despair and anger get called up by true, sudden grief. He knew he looked idiotic and ghastly sitting there, and he did not care. He put his face into his hands and wept.

Dan Boyd returned to the window and watched the Frisbee players on the fraternity house lawn across the street. He silently admired their skill at catching the spinning disc on the tip of a finger. He had always longed for grace.

Neil spoke again, dully, as if speaking to the room. 'Now you are Talthubios.'

'I didn't get that, Neil. What'd you say?' Dan Boyd turned away from the window.

Neil stared at him out of hollow eyes, suddenly shrunken in their wells, as though he were in shock. 'Talthubios is the bringer of ill tidings. That's you. This past winter, against my better judgement, I let myself be persuaded to read the part of the messenger in the college winter Greek play. An aged errand boy, he brings news to the captured and enslaved queen of Troy that changes the whole play and the fate of all the characters.' He was almost musing now, and his voice trailed away softly, staring at the framed poster on the wall, which Dan Boyd could see was an announcement for *Hekabe*. 'In Euripides, you know, Dan, the messenger's speech is a fixed, formal thing. The telling of his news always leaves him drained and transformed.' He looked at his old classmate with the shrewdness Dan Boyd remembered. 'You not only don't seem drained, Dan; you don't seem the least little bit transformed. Perhaps you just don't care. Or maybe you're just a lousy actor, Dan.'

Dan Boyd was out of his depth. He floundered for a few seconds, waving his hand as though he had a denial to present, but swallowed it. He recalled, without any sense of having forgotten it, what it had felt like for four years to walk along with Neil Kelly through the quad when they were in college together, and to sit beside him in class and know—know in his miserable bones—that what he himself had learned after the hardest studying was what Neil had known after glancing at the problem for the first time. 'It—it's my job, Neil. There's a lot of tragedy in it, sure, and I don't have the, I guess, luxury for, you know, emotions. Like doctors or priests, I guess.'

Neil laughed and sobbed at the same time, wiping his hand across his face as he hiccupped and spoke. 'Oh

Christ. Doctors, priests, and spooks. And dear Babs Lacey blind and burned. And you have a job to do. Don't make me puke, Dan. For Christ's sake, show some simple human decency and say it's a lousy, awful, shitty thing or something, but don't stand in my house and salute the flag to show me how tough you are.'

'Okay, Neil. I'll show you something. You have me pegged, and that was always a pain in the ass: brilliant Neil and slow Dan. But you have the other thing all wrong.'

'What are we talking about? What other thing?'

'The murder of your friend. And the complications. We were called in right away. Our man for that area. That tells you your friend was CIA-connected, but it wasn't the way you obviously think. It wasn't Morgan De Sales Lacey; he had nothing to do with us. It was Barbara Lacey who worked for us. That's the big bad news they sent me to tell you, but not to tell you.'

Neil stared at him for a long, uncomprehending moment, then sank his head into his hands again.

He had known Babs for thirty years, and what Boyd was saying was clearly impossible. He felt shock, bewilderment, and a kind of embarrassed rage—felt, he realized, just the way a colleague whose wife had betrayed him had described feeling. In the daily traffic of the inevitable ordinary, so few events short of tragedy can finally move us until pride is offended; then shame and some twin of guilt mock us. He knew there was little point in saying how incredible it was. He knew intuitively that Boyd had gone beyond his instructions to tell him this, out of some need to one-up him, and that it was the least credible fact and also the one he was surest was true.

'I'll go with you to Boston.' His voice was a low croak now. He cleared his throat noisily. 'I have reservations . . .' He could not focus his mind, but he knew dimly that he would have to cancel his flight, call people . . .

'I'm authorized to say that we'll take responsibility for cancelling your present outstanding arrangements, Neil. If you'll keep careful account of what it costs you: airline, even any advance deposit on a place over in England, we'll see you're reimbursed. We have forms I'll give you.'

Neil slowly rose to his feet, like a wounded man. The feeling of spiritual numbness and sharp, marginal shame was receding now, and he thought of Barbara, alone and blind and in real pain in Boston. 'There's nothing to keep us here any longer. Let's go.'

Dan Boyd preceded him onto the porch, carrying two of the bags. Neil mechanically locked and tested the door behind him, lifted the other bag, and followed Boyd to the grey Buick at the curb.

'I'll ride in the back, Dan. I need to think.'

Boyd seemed a little hurt again as he stacked the bags together in the seat. 'Really? Okay, Neilo, sure. Why don't you just put your head back and leave the driving to us? Boy, this old town has changed a lot since you and I were students, eh? You know, somehow I never got around to coming back to a reunion . . .'

His voice droned on, supremely worth ignoring. Neil shut it firmly out of his consciousness and stared sightlessly at the streets and buildings of Oldhampton.

They edged past one of the town's pale yellow trucks, from which men in blue hard hats hauled their orange sawhorses and black kerosene bombs to set up another barrier.

Neil closed his eyes and let the curtain of blessed numbness descend, let his thoughts drift back over thirty years.

Barbara Lacey, who had been Barbara Murrow then, had been his first serious date in college. They had sat side by side in a Lit. class, and it seemed to Neil that she was the most breathtaking girl he had ever seen. Breathtaking physically and intellectually—as bright as himself. After an agony of undergraduate indecision, he had finally got up the courage to ask her out after class for coffee, and by some miracle of instant mutual understanding they had become promptly inseparable.

In those distant days that meant lunches, movies, studying together in the library, endless hand-holding walks, and eventually good-night kisses at her dorm, nothing beyond that. It had been for Neil, the perpetual student, a time of bliss and the wild, joyous awakening of first love. Then, in confused tears, explanations, rages, and reconciliations, Barbara had met his best friend, Morg Lacey, and they had all gone through the merry-go-round of falling out of love, falling into love, and trying to save the friendships. De Sales had ended up engaged to Babs, after melodramatic meetings and handshakes and kisses and hugs and a hundred relatively sincere protestations that no, hey, it's okay, he understood completely. It had taken him the better part of a year to get over it before he realized that Babs's ambitions for her own future life far exceeded and, in some important ways, contradicted his own. She was to be the perfect wife for Morgan De Sales Lacey, giant of industry. She understood his hard-driving, ambitious style because it was her own style; they both had an eye for wealth and an old-fashioned power that comes only with corporate position of the first rank. Neil had survived, a trifle wiser, and had gone to England, where he had met a modest, gifted, gentle Devon girl, Georgia McCabe, a classmate at Oxford, whose idea of the good life was twin to his own: a life of scholarship, teaching, small college towns, and marginally shabby gentility. He and Georgia had had twenty-five years of genuine, deep happiness together, most of it in this small town ninety miles west of Boston, and had raised a family of girls, grown now and moved away, before their steady joy had been crushed by her lingering death from cancer.

In the most bitterly ironic of circumstances, Pril Lacey, his own godchild, had come to Old Hampton and become his student. Knowing every moment the idiotic psychological readings his colleagues would put on it, and against every instinct of his own, he had fallen in love with her, and she with him. Their love was cut short before it was ever consummated, by her murder last spring term. The anguish of that shared loss had bound him, Barbara, and De Sales together with new ties.

Now De Sales, the man of Large Affairs—whose torrents of energy often wore out second-level managers and secretaries in less than a year—the legendary chairman of one of the great multi-nationals, perennial head of a dozen fund drives, confidant of three American presidents, was simply dead. And gentle, brilliant, iron-willed Barbara, the perfect wife-hostess who made him possible, was hideously injured.

He opened his eyes for a moment and saw the back of Dan Boyd's head, his bald spot showing thinly through the carefully combed-back screen of dark hair. Boyd was still in his monologue about something from a long time ago; Neil shut him out again ruthlessly. If Dan Boyd was telling the truth, Barbara Lacey had some significant connection with the CIA. Significant enough to be the target of an attempt to kill her? Mad and awful. He felt completely helpless when he tried to imagine what he could do for her.

'Do you people know who sent the bombs?'

Dan Boyd had been in the middle of analysing the failures in security around the President when he had been shot the previous week. He broke off, puzzled, glancing back over his shoulder in the mirror. Apparently Neil hadn't been listening. 'You say?'

'Who sent the bomb—do you people know?'

'Oh. Well, yeah, but—'

'Oh, for Christ's sake, Danny, don't start that again. You came to get me, and you got me. I know what happened and I know that Barbara Lacey has some connection with your agency—'

'Yeah, well, listen, Neil. About that. I wouldn't say anything about that right away in Boston, you know?'

Neil pushed the suggestion aside with a weary gesture. 'Of course I won't say anything about it. Now who sent the damn bomb?'

'Well, I was starting to say, Neil, it's a little complicated.'

'You mean you don't know? I should think you people and the FBI and every other damn police force would have people all over Santa Fe tracing the delivery.'

'Yeah, well, gosh, Neil, that's just it. I mean it only took about fifteen minutes to trace the thing back to the toy store where it was bought.'

'Well, did you get a description of whoever bought it?'

'You're teaching your grandmother to suck eggs, you know, Neil. We aren't complete boobs. Yeah, as I say, it was easy. Listen, don't mention this to anyone in Boston, either, see, because, well, I don't know if the director wants the details out even to you, you see what I mean?'

Neil wanted to hit him. 'You do know.'

'Yeah, Mrs Lacey sent it herself.' He paused to let that piece of information sink in. 'Bought it, paid for it with her charge card, and had it gift-wrapped and sent to her husband for an April Fool's present.'

'Oh my God.'

'So you can see it's a little complicated. I can't really go into it any more than that, Neil; I'm bound by the book on this.'

They were passing through the Worcester Hills. These foothills of the White Mountains were putting on their first spring cover of yellow willows and the haze of red buds that meant maples. Now that April's here.

Neil didn't speak again until forty minutes later, as they drove up the short, narrow street approaching the Massachusetts General Hospital in Boston. His mind had almost stopped functioning at all. He had gone in an hour from the happy anticipation of his vacation trip to shocked horror to wild incredulity to this leaden mental torpor. It was almost an effort to open the car door and get out.

'Listen, Neil,' Boyd said, leaning across to the right window, 'I'll take your stuff over to the Park Plaza, where I'm staying, and check you in there. Mrs Lacey's up in Intensive Care unless they moved her already. A woman from the regional office is there somewhere, waiting for you. Mary Dowd.'

Neil shook his head to clear it. 'Mary Dowd.'

'Right. You okay, buddy? Anything I can do you for, like calling the airline or anything?'

Neil grasped at the sensible suggestion, which at least broke off one of his practical problems from the mass and made it manageable. 'Would you, Dan?' He took the sheaf of tickets and reservation slips from his jacket. 'Would you call TWA and explain, and so forth? Look, Homes Abroad is the place I rented the English house from—' he fumbled through the slips clumsily. 'Oh Christ, you can figure it out. Just cancel everything.' He thrust the handful of papers at Boyd.

'I'll see you later. What hotel did you say?'

'Park Plaza.'

'Where is it? I never heard of it. You sure you don't mean the Copley Plaza?'

'Used to be the Statler. In Park Square.'

'I'll be damned. Oh; thank you, Dan.' An adult lifetime of habitual courtesy was beginning to manifest itself again. He turned and entered the hospital, thinking in a daze, what on earth am I thanking him for? Nobody thanks the messenger in a Greek play.

CHAPTER 2

The fat, white-haired woman in the tight blue dress beamed at him presbyopically over her glasses and told him yes, Mrs Lacey was a patient here, but no, she was not permitted any visitors in Intensive Care. Neil distinctly heard her pronounce the capitals. He ran his hand wearily through his hair and tried the name Dan Boyd had given him.

'Mary Dowd?' She rotated her files efficiently and looked at him again above her spectacles, as though he had said something rather shameful. 'Are you sure you have your party's name right? We don't have any patient named—'

Neil cut her off brusquely. 'She's not a patient. She's—here from the government. I was told she was here especially to meet me, about Mrs Lacey's case.'

Light seemed to dawn on the cheerful face before him. 'Oh, oh, I know the party you mean. Let me see. Would you mind giving me your name, sir?'

'Neil Kelly.'

She checked a card she took from a desk drawer. 'Would you mind awfully much if, just to make sure someone else isn't claiming to be you, I ask you to show me some identification, sir?' She was in an unfamiliar role now, and it made her sweat along her upper lip. 'I'm sure you understand.'

'Of course.' Neil pulled his passport from his jacket pocket and stood for inspection while she read it and looked up from the picture to his face.

'It's a very good likeness, thank you, Mr Kelly.' She handed the blue folder back to him. 'Just wait right on that sofa over there, and I'll call up.'

Neil blew out a sigh of frustration, but saw no alternative. He sat on the plastic red sofa. The woman busied herself with the phone, and then with other details of her job. After fifteen minutes had passed, Neil walked back to the desk.

She tried to forestall his question. 'I'm sorry, Mr Kelly, I truly am. They said someone would be coming down in a few minutes and they'd tell her you were here.' Her sorrow appeared sincere, confused, and a little frightened. God knows who she thought he was. He sat down again and endured another blank ten minutes before a businesslike, square woman in a tweed suit came over to him, put out her hand, and announced that she was Mary Dowd. He rose and shook hands; she had a hard grip.

When he stood, he was eye-level with her. She had unmitigated, thick, black eyebrows.

'I came as quickly as I could. May I see Barbara Lacey?'

Mary Dowd was one for holding eye contact. 'No. Not for a while.' Her voice was educated, but abrasive. 'She's awake and, God knows, she keeps asking for you, but they're doing something with her bandages now, so you'll have to wait. I'll get you a cup of tea in the lounge.' She turned and walked away towards the elevators without waiting for a reply. Mary Dowd, leader of men, he thought, trailing after her because there was nothing else to do.

They rode with two white-coated interns and a black orderly up to a floor where Mary Dowd held the door for him, walked down a hall busy with laundry carts and juice carts and orderlies talking *sotto voce* in Spanish, and entered a small staff lounge furnished with a rectangular table and six moulded plastic chairs.

'All the comforts of home. Sit and I'll get it. Tea okay?'

'Fine. A little sugar, no milk.'

She was back in three minutes with two mugs of tea,

red tags hanging from them. 'Give it time to steep; I've already used the bags once.' She looked disgusted. 'All they have here is supermarket Brand X, so these are my own Twinings bags, but I'll be damned if I'll only get one use out of them.' She dunked her own teabag up and down patiently and then pressed it out against her spoon with her thumb. When in Rome . . . Neil did the same.

'When will I be able to see Barbara Lacey?'

'How much do you know?' She sipped her tea and appraised him across the rim of her cup.

'Babs Lacey is here with severe injuries sustained in an explosion. She is apparently blind. Her husband was killed in the same explosion. This all happened in Santa Fe this past week.'

'Not surprising they brought her here, you know. One of the great places in the world for her kind of injuries. Ever since the Coconut Grove fire forty years ago. People come here from all over the world.'

'Are you also with the CIA, Miss Dowd?'

She sighed. 'Danny Boy. God, what a klutz. He really a friend of yours?'

'We went to college together.'

'Well, at least he remembered to call me from the hotel. The dummies up here never told me you called, you know. I don't know who's less efficient, these Spics or the cops in this town. Anyway, Danny called and said you were downstairs, so I went down.'

'I'd have worn a red carnation if I'd known you'd have to search for me.'

'No problem. Middle-aged English teacher. Besides, you look like my father; he was a teacher too. Social Studies.' That observation seemed to disgust her mildly.

Neil was getting increasingly disconcerted and uncomfortable at this housemother-receptionist they had assigned to him. His good manners, having surfaced briefly, were submerging again fast.

'Really?' There was a long pause while they both drank tea and looked out the dirty window at a grey wall. 'Is Barbara's face—will she be badly scarred?' The question wrenched itself from him almost against his wish to know the answer.

'No idea. She's completely covered in bandages, except for her mouth. They do wonderful things with plastic surgery.' She grinned toughly at him. 'Wigs, dark glasses; they take skin off the legs sometimes. She almost had her head blown off, Professor. Are you ready for that?'

'No, Miss Dowd, I'm not ready for that. I was once on a ship which exploded and burned, and I saw a lot of people I knew cooked to various degrees of roast meat. I was not ready for that then, and I would still not be ready for it now, but I will not faint dead away. Are you vetting me, and if so, why?'

'Just for myself. I guess I'm curious. Maybe you'll do.' She paused fractionally. 'Maybe.'

'How I do and what I do are really none of your damned business, Miss Dowd, are they? Now if you're through playing whatever little sadistic game this is, would you mind going over there and finding out if I can see Barbara Lacey now?'

She stood, almost languidly, not in the least put off by his anger. 'Oh, they're ready. They told me when I went to get the tea that you could go in.'

'I thought only the Russians had women like you working for them.'

'That's all right, Professor. I thought the British colonial type went out with the empire.'

Neil stared at her coldly and brushed past into the hall. Two doors along, a young, bearded doctor raised a hand to him, asked him if he was Mr Kelly, and gestured him into the room.

'It's your friend Mr Kelly, Mrs Lacey,' he called softly. Then he withdrew, giving a thumbs-up sign to Neil.

The mummified figure of the woman in the bed lifted her hands as he came toward her. The right hand was partially bandaged, and Neil took it gently, her left hand strongly. From the aperture in the beehive of bandages covering her head the whispering, croaking ghost of Barbara's voice spoke his name.

'Babs. Dear Babs. I'm so sorry.' The tears came and brimmed over.

'Neil. Rea'y you?' The words were blurred and thick.

'Yes, Babs, it's me. I'm sorry I took so long. You almost missed me completely. I was on my way to England—'

'Your poor leave.' It sounded like *Yo po lee*. She squeezed his hands tighter. 'My 'tupid tongue go' cut. So'ry.'

'It's fine. I can understand you fine.' Should he talk louder? Her left ear was completely covered, but her right was unbandaged.

As though she were reading his confused thoughts she said, 'I' partly deaf, too. Lef' side all bur'ed. They te' you? Oh, Nei'!'

He shuddered within himself, trying desperately not to communicate it through his hands to her. Inside her bandages, she seemed to be weeping. Could she still cry real tears? Images from old horror movies—ghoul faces, empty mouths, empty eyes, punctures in hives of bandages—flooded his mind.

'You mustn't talk too much. You must rest.'

'Wou'n't let 'em make me. Not till you came.' *No' ti' you ca'*.

'Well, I'm here, and I won't leave.'

'Kee' holding my ha'. Talk abou' old times. Don' say anything' abou' this.'

He rummaged his mind desperately. 'Remember picnics on the lake? Can you remember the wine, the famous wine?'

'Boo Nu'.'

Was she smiling under her cocoon now? It had been an infallible tickle for her once, any mention of their first picnic date by the campus lake. He had brought a bottle of Blue Nun without having the foggiest idea about wines, had forgotten a corkscrew, had tried to break the neck of the bottle in debonair fashion against a rock, and had smashed the whole bottle, bleeding profusely on the two bologna sandwiches and generally bringing the picnic to an early end in gore and humiliation.

'The maple buds are bursting everywhere. The redwing blackbirds are back. Even I can tell them; the hill is full of them behind my house. I guess it's going to be an early summer.' God, did everything have to sound dumber than the last thing? Idiot, idiot, talk to her. You love her.

'Hhhn'—She tried again. 'Hhsnow las' week in Sanna Fe.'

'Really? I thought they'd be having high summer out there by now.'

She sagged away from his hands, back against the pillows. 'Morg's dea', Neil.'

'I know, Babs.'

'My faul'.'

'No. No, Babs, listen—' What did he think he was going to say? She gripped his hands again.

'My faul'.' She beat her left hand and his right hand weakly against the covers. 'Tell you how?'

'Yes. They told me what happened, Babs. It wasn't your fault.'

'Know I' blind?'

'Yes, I know.'

'Godda' killed him, Ne'—Apri' Foo'.'

'The toy, I know.'

'You know. 's people donno. You do. Met on Apri' Foo's Day. Ever since dumb presents, silly toys 'chother. Pretty toys.' She struggled against some pain in herself. 'Jack inna box. Lissen—' a moan? a laugh?—'look' jus' like Father Dopey.'

Neil almost laughed aloud, then let himself. Father Dobie was a priest they all knew from years back, full of his own importance, his huge beaked nose always thrust into everyone else's business, a born inquisitor, always hunting imperfections in others and totally oblivious to the multitude of his own, including giving the dumbest sermons they had ever heard.

'Old Dopey.' Neil leaned close to her ear. 'Not just dumb—'

She finished for him: '*Dam'* dumb.'

'Nose and all?'

'No' 'nall, I swea'.'

He lifted her unscarred hand to his lips and kissed her tenderly.

'Just tell me how I can help you, Babs. If there's anything in God's world I can do, just ask me.'

'Member we met?' Her bandaged hand made a motion of scribbling.

'You thought I was deaf and dumb.' It was an old joke, their first. Neil had sat next to her day after day in lecture, unable to get up courage to speak, and had finally written in his notebook *Will you go out for coffee with me after class?* and showed it to her. She had always claimed she went because she thought he was a deaf-mute. Was she suddenly asking to say something she couldn't say aloud?

'Me now,' she mumbled. ' 'cept blind, too.' Her hands kept gesturing frantically for something.

Neil took his ballpoint from his pocket and put it into her hurt hand, which was the one she wrote with. Gently into her other hand he put the small notebook from his side pocket.

'Say som'pin funny.' She urged him with her hand to keep talking, and she began painfully to print on the page.

Neil blathered on about nothing and everything, college places they had walked together, promising that he would take her to them again when she was well. The first word she wrote was SLATER in shaky capitals.

'Rotte' bassad,' she croaked vehemently.

'Well, it wasn't my fault you fell in the lake,' was the best he could improvise. She started another line. CIA ME. 'If you had agreed to marry me that first week we met, when I asked you, I might have taken that job with the *New York Times* and been famous by now.' She printed EM'SLINN, the apostrophe curving wildly down into the M. In spite of himself, Neil half blurted the word out. Could she mean it?

'Em's Linn?' She quickly put her hand up over his mouth clumsily.

The pen slipped from her hand and bounced to the floor out of sight under the bed.

'Lissen—dam' mou' droolin'—yuk—lissen.' Her voice sank. 'Tired. Ol' fifty-four—'

Neil recognized both references with no effort. Babs had a half-sister Emily whom she adored. The four had double-dated years ago on a sailing date off Orleans. It was wonderfully pleasant. They had all got mildly drunk on a case of cold beer, but the apparently planned-for spark between Neil and Em just hadn't ignited, to Barbara's great and obvious disappointment. After that, Em was just permanently a good friend. She had later married a contractor out west and given birth to twins, who were her pride and joy, and then another son. Among the members of the family and the close 'uncles' like Neil, the twins had immediately become Em's Linn and Em's Tim, the first an irrepressible gamine, a whirling dervish of a little girl with startling eyes, all curls and dancing, the second her quiet, dark-eyed shadow of a brother. Em's husband, who, in his own phrase, had 'unsucceeded' at a baseball career, still had his uniform shirt from the Cubs, with a big 54 on it, hung up over the playroom bar. When his wife wanted to make him wince, she'd nudge him in the ribs and say, 'old fifty-four here—'

'Find ou',' she whispered brokenly. 'No' them—' She jerked her bandaged hand in angry gesture toward the door. 'You.'

She slumped back into the pillows and released his hand suddenly. The monitor connected to her from the bedside stand began a regular red blinking. Neil went quickly to the door and almost bumped into a nurse on her way in, thumbing him out brusquely as she came.

The corridor was empty. Neil rather expected to find Mary Dowd and perhaps a few other agency types clustered outside the door, ready to pump him for details of his visit.

He took the elevator down to the lobby and walked out through the main doors. Regular visiting hours must be starting; a cheerful throng of flower carriers and fruit-basket luggers were waiting for permission to deliver themselves and their gifts somewhere upstairs.

Boston had changed its shape, its habits, and its contents since Neil had known it as a graduate student thirty years before. He tried to remember the skyline as he walked, but what he knew was gone. It had become a mild spring day, and he wandered aimlessly away from the hospital down past the Hatch Shell, along the river in the general direction of Park Square. Students swarmed everywhere. They now constituted almost the whole population of Boston and Cambridge, some quarter million of them, having come from all over the map to study in one of the great academic enclaves of the modern world. The Latin Quarters of medieval cities must have been like this, he thought, buzzing with languages, pulsing with the quick laughter, the quick anger, and the easy rudeness of a swarm of unsophisticated, unlaundered kids trying to be men and women of the world. Neil remembered Back Bay as streets of elegant hotels and immense brownstones fronting wide avenues shaded with wineglass elms, through which one could wander in spring out to tiny, green Fenway Park. Now every ex-hotel was a dormitory, and where there had been flower shops in the basement doorways there were now countless pizza joints and sub shoppes. Newbury Street was holding out, an aloof strip of expensive art galleries and boutiques. But from Ipswich, back alphabetically through Hereford, Gloucester, Fairfield, to Arlington, the student army with their junk food, junk music, and secondhand clothes owned the streets, their serape'd vendors ready to supply Neil with whatever he needed in the way of belts, chains, or pipes.

It was Saturday, and small commercial traffic was moving, although every parking place along every curb, legal or banned, was jammed. A short-bodied, spotted bird, the sort of bird that might have been drawn by a child, hopped on cold twigs of feet between a green Pinto and a white Maverick on Commonwealth Avenue. Figures for a new bestiary.

Babs and Neil had tried learning the names and calls of birds when they were first courting in spring. She had become quite good, but to Neil it was still news that the red flash across his yard was definitely a cardinal and, except for owls, they all sounded much alike. When his birdwatching friends shook their heads at that sort of ignorance, he provided reminders about how few of them could sort out the gerunds from the participles if the occasion arose, at which they usually subsided into rude mutterings.

He should have been aloft over the Atlantic by now, being fed and cosseted by girls young enough to be his students, provided with magazines he never read and champagne he had no intention of drinking. Somewhere over in Devon, a British couple waited innocently to hand over their house keys to him, having already pocketed a three-month advance which he supposed the Lacey Foundation would never get back. A hotel room in a modest tourist place in Queen's Gate, also paid for, would not be occupied by him tonight, although by six o'clock they would gladly relinquish it to an importunate German from one of the endless line of gleaming buses lining the street back to Hyde Park. A long-anticipated meal in the best seafood restaurant in London, next to the skin diseases hospital in Leicester Square, of all places, would go unordered and uneaten, but not unmissed. That made him realize that he was only a block from the Ritz-Carlton, which has the best bar in Boston. He resolved to break his peripatetic journey and mourn his friends and losses in befitting style.

The bar of the Ritz is a splendid bar, the only one in the world built 'to the Pope's specifications', as the friends of the architect, the great Earl Pope, better known for his massive public structures, liked to note. They provided him with a martini dry enough, cold enough, and deep enough to stimulate that instant euphoria he had wanted induced in order to rest in it. He had two. The olives only reminded him, as his tension melted, that he was hungry. He tried to review what had happened in the speeded-up time since Dan Boyd had walked into his living-room, rather than think about food yet.

Morgan De Sales Lacey was dead. Old Morg to his intimates, but you can't be intimate with the dead. He had died because his wife had sent him an April Fool's love token, an annual joke between them, a jack-in-the-box toy which had blown up in his face and killed him.

Obviously, Barbara had not known it would be booby-trapped when it arrived at their house. She had been leaning over his shoulder when he unwrapped it, as a result of which she now lay, a mummified horror without eyes, perhaps without any real face, in Mass. General.

Someone who wanted to hurt one or both of them had got to that toy after she ordered it, rigged it, and made it deadly. Presumably the FBI, and with them or in addition to them the CIA, as well as local police, would have begun an investigation.

The CIA was surely involved somehow, at least they thought so. Barbara Lacey had been working for them on an unspecified assignment. Simple spooks' paranoia? Assume for a moment that Barbara's connection with the Agency was entirely beside the point. Assume further that the bomb was in fact intended for De Sales. He had a thousand interests: commercial operations from oil drilling to boat building, political connections from the White House to several state houses, and personal enemies of the kind men like that make. And finally, Em's Linn. What on earth could a twenty—twenty-one?—year-old girl who, the last time Neil had seen her, was a student at Dana Hall School for Girls in Wellesley have to do with any of it? Yet it was her name Barbara had scrawled with such urgency before she collapsed.

The police and the FBI would obviously be mounting an extensive investigation into the domestic ramifications of the killing. When a hired terrorist had walked up to the golf cart of an Oklahoma industrialist the previous month and shot him dead, Neil remembered, the same kind of operation was news for weeks, finally pointing to problems in the jai alai rackets, involving frontons that the man had owned through umbrella corporations. De Sales's interests and holdings went at least as far, and the same sort of underworld contract was not unthinkable. If Danny Boyd and his present company were any evidence, the CIA was taking the whole thing very personally, which meant that they were unwilling to accept *prima facie* that the killing was as simple a matter as corporate or gang violence.

That left Em's Linn. And Neil Kelly. Bereft of his friend,

now witness to the agony of his friend's wife, and feeling more witless and tipsy every minute. The second martini had not been a good idea. The sole idea he could generate was to walk carefully back to his hotel and take a shower.

He left the Ritz by the Arlington Street door. By a commodious vicus of recirculation, as some Irishman might have said in some mad book, he had come back along the Public Gardens and was just a minute from Park Square. He blinked at a Park Square whose low, human-scale buildings had been mostly demolished except for a row of sleazy delis and strip bars and the nailed-up doors of the old Playboy Club.

He checked into his hotel, which, except for some kind of palm garden court at the back of the lobby, was still the old Statler to the half-life, no matter what it was called now.

Boyd's people had not exactly broken the bank for his accommodations, he noticed: a cramped studio room up on the west wing of the eleventh floor, where traditionally airline crews with a quick, regular turnover schedule are booked. The bellman apparently suspected that Neil was neither a pilot nor a stewardess. He opened the door and let Neil into the cubicle ahead of him, eyeing him professionally.

"You with TWA, Mr Kelly?'

'Me? No.'

'Oh. I saw on the card, so I thought—well—'

Dan Boyd was apparently playing games. TWA yet. 'No, actually,' he said, giving the slab-faced man a half dollar, 'I'm with the CIA this week.'

'I get it. Thanks.' He winked and pocketed the coin almost as though he were satisfied. 'Listen, you got any questions, call me. Ask for Frank. If I don't know the answer, we'll figure it out between us, okay?'

'Right. Okay.' He bolted the door and dropped on to

the small bed to get his thoughts together. Some echo of a song pounding out of a window over on Berkeley Street reminded him that the correct expression was 'get his head together', and since it was starting to split slowly in two with a headache, perhaps their phrase was apter than his. But then that music had at least contributed to producing it. And the brief euphoria induced by two fast drinks on an empty stomach was crumbling fast.

He unzipped the bag with the toilet kit and towel in it—realizing that he was mildly surprised to find his three bags right there—stripped, and went to shower. Twenty minutes later he was stretched out asleep on the bed.

The phone, then Danny Boyd's voice, then his watch, woke him and told him an hour had passed. Dan was saying that he wanted to give him time to get organized, but that he probably wanted lunch anyway, right?

Lunch with Dan Boyd was unthinkable. His head started to hurt again at the idea.

'—not with me, Neilo; Mr Slater would really like to meet you. Listen, Neil, I—uh—think you better make a point of it. He's the one who has to approve your expenses, and all. Oh, listen, I took care of cancelling your ticket. And of course you know I already booked you into the hotel, I guess.'

Poor Dan Boyd, the natural-born lackey, sweating out his next gofer assignment already probably, never understanding that he wasn't a big-time operator just because he was allowed to run errands for big-time operators. The CIA, the Mafia, and even the Church and the Kremlin probably couldn't exist without third-string dons and monsignori and commissars like Dan Boyd.

'Who is Mr Slater?' Barbara had certainly known.

'Well, call him the regional administrator of this problem, Neil. I think it's important you meet with him.'

'Which region?'

'What do you mean, Neil? I don't get it.'

'This—problem, as you call it, Dan, occurred in Santa Fe. We're now in Boston. That's a region?'

'Well, we don't exactly mean a geographical region, Neil. More of a problem region, like an area of responsibility.'

Talking nonsense only made the headache worse. 'But where?'

'Not really a place at all, Neil. Do you get the concept of a region of responsibility? We use that—'

'I mean the restaurant. Where?'

'Oh.' He chuckled and said the inevitable. 'I got you. Not in the hotel. Mr Slater—' he lowered his voice to say it, an acolyte's reverent tone—'doesn't like hotel food. He's something of a gourmet. Locke-Ober's. You know where that is?'

'Unless they've torn it down and moved it to Brookline. When?'

'Well, gee, now, really, Neil. Can you get over there right away?'

'No.'

'Soon?'

'Soon only if I go naked. Not so soon if I dress and catch a cab right away. Tell your boss in half an hour at the earliest. Best I can do.' Neil hung up before Boyd could explain any more of the demanding mysteries of his commander's style.

CHAPTER 3

Locke-Ober's is one of the few remaining great places to eat in Boston. In Neil's graduate-student days it had boasted a men-only bar on the ground floor, and the city's best food, along with the best waiters, upstairs. He had sprung once for a private dining-room for four when he had won a modest literary prize for scholarship, and he remembered that it had added fifty cents per person to the bill. Entering the familiar dark entrance from the grimy alley below Tremont Street and thinking about current menu prices, he wondered what a private dining-room would add to the bill these days.

Yes, Mr Slater was waiting for him at his table. Yes, he should come right this way. The waiters were obviously still professionals, not college kids in open shirts who handled food as though it insulted their dignity.

Slater stood and shook hands with Neil, calling him Professor, but introducing himself as Jack. He was a head taller than Neil, and had thick, black hair and a Guards' moustache, both recently shaped. Slim, probably forty-five, Neil guessed, wearing bespoke tailoring and a Union Rugby tie, of all things. His hand was hard, but his nails had been professionally manicured.

He offered to order a drink to let Neil catch up with him, but Neil told him he was too hungry and that he'd wait for the wine, knowing Slater would choose something fine and make a production of doing it. The agent expanded his Dewar's Profile smile at the implied compliment.

Neil had lunched, dined, or drunk cocktails with perhaps a hundred college presidents or senators or corporation types, some or all of them trustees or foundation executives in the past decade, and he knew that the ritual was as stylized as ballet. And he knew immediately that Slater had learned the style and made it his own. The spy who intended to own the store.

They began with the pawn to king-four of such lunches, deferring like mad to each other's taste in wine.

'Actually any old plonk will do for me,' Neil said, smiling broadly. Translation: I know more about wine than you do, friend, so why don't you just take your best shot and let's see what turns up.

'Oh-oh! That means you're a world-class oenophile at least, and I'll probably insult your palate. Well, I don't think we can get into much trouble with a nice, gentle seven-year-old Bordeaux—assuming, of course, that your appetite wants something substantial, like beef.'

'Steak would be perfect.' If he translated that as meaning that Neil had really been planning on Coquilles St Jacques but was only going along out of elementary good manners, so be it.

'You're sure?'

'Positive. A salad first, then just steak rare and a baked potato.'

He ordered brilliantly for both of them, as Neil had known he would.

'First of all, Professor Kelly, let me say that I'm honestly sorry about your friends. I knew Mrs Lacey because of our professional connection, of course . . .'

That was smoothly done.

'. . . but I realize that you are perhaps the best friend the two Laceys had in the world. You all went to school together?'

'Yes. Thank you.'

'Dan Boyd tells me you're a scholar of the classical drama . . .'

Dan Boyd would.

'. . . there's something I'd call Sophoclean about this, some dimension of tragedy far beyond the immediate circumstances. You know *she* sent the toy that exploded?' He left the question hanging in the air between them while their salads were brought.

Neil simply nodded. The hard-eyed spook was beginning to appear from behind the mask of connoisseur and educated, worldly fellow. He wondered what required text from the Great Books would pop up next.

'Did you enjoy your stroll through Back Bay?'

Neil did not miss the implication. 'Moderately. I hadn't

realized the extent to which it had become a student ghetto.'

'Almost entirely. Boston isn't what it was, I'm afraid, even in the reign of good King Curley. This mayor seems determined to cover it all with either parking lots or skyscrapers. A great loss of a human place.' He shook his head philosophically. '*O tempora, o mores*.'

Neil ate his salad hungrily and said nothing.

Slater tried again. 'Did you notice that the magnolias along Beacon are coming in a little early this year? That January thaw, I suppose.'

Mmm. I didn't notice, no.' Neil ate half a roll greedily.

'I find natural beauty deeply soothing. Do you like landscape painting, Professor?'

Neil managed to swallow and answer at the same time. 'Yes, I do.'

'Any particular painter or period? I'm an amateur collector myself.'

'It would be the Sung Dynasty of China if I could afford it. Since I can't, I try to see them in a museum whenever I can.'

'I collect Samuel Palmer. Do you know him?'

He really wasn't that good at this form yet. 'Yes.' Neil had conducted enough tutorials to know how to manage this level of gamesmanship. He knew Palmer, but he didn't want particularly to be drawn into an extended discussion of him so that Slater could shine.

'Actually, I traded a rather nice little Friedrich for a Palmer just a few months ago. Kenneth Clark thinks Friedrich the better painter, you know, but his remark that Palmer is the last true Virgilian is the whole point, don't you think?'

'I certainly can't think of one after him. Do you feel nostalgic for a lost golden age, then, Mr Slater?'

The tailored and barbered agent grinned ruefully and ate his salad in dainty cuts. 'I suppose I do. Not so much an age of heroic willing, though, as one of endless, perfect contemplation.'

'Is my next line supposed to be, "what's a nice fellow like you doing eating rare meat," because I'd suppose you should be a vegetarian?'

'Oh, excellent. I don't suppose the sport's question to the educated whore has ever been better put. Do I translate you accurately: what's a smart bastard like me doing in the trade of international thuggery and buggery?'

'Not quite. I know exactly what you're doing.'

The waiter cleared the first course, put their entrées on the table, and showed Slater the label on the Bordeaux before pouring him a sample. When he had approved and dismissed the waiter, he looked back at Neil expectantly.

Neil finished his observation. 'You're showing off how well you've read up on George Smiley. The spirit of Le Carré is hovering over us at least as much as that of Samuel Palmer. And if this conversation gets just one degree more oblique, I'm afraid we'll have to finish our meal sitting at right angles to one another to be understood at all.'

Slater laughed, but seemed fractionally off balance. 'Some of you college professors play a mean game.'

'I'll tell you a couple of things about us, Mr Slater, so you won't have to intuit them and you don't have to guess. We sit down to food and drink with a lot of different kinds of people. We play little social games just like everyone else, with foundation people, political people, other academics who want our jobs and our grants, publishers who want our books. If we are good, we get wooed a lot, and I have been wooed a lot. Some think I'm easy game, or will be, because they have something I want, perhaps a literary prize or an endowed chair. Those who think they know our ambitions always think they know us. People who need us to serve their purposes know us by the quality of our desperation, and turn that to their advantage, just the way politicians promise farmers subsidies to get their votes. Honest and otherwise prudent citizens often exaggerate to themselves what they imagine to be our intimidating intelligence and come all over goose bumps and forget their own accomplishments – which are often quite intimidating to us.'

Slater was rallying. Enough to try to turn the argument against his opponent. 'Is it all games to you? Are you really that cynical?'

'Not at all, Mr Slater. Only cynics think games are cynical. We are always playing for life and death stakes if we are serious adults, Mr Slater. Our reputations, our dignity, our careers – even sometimes our old-fashioned sacred honour. For those stakes I have learned to play what you call a mean game. Only playing offhandedly would be cynical.'

'Then I shouldn't expect that your next suggestion will be that we cut out the games and level with each other?'

'Would tennis without the net really be any pleasure at all?'

Slater wiped his hand across his brow in a mock gesture of exhaustion, laughed, and shook his head. 'Time out. I think I need to visit the locker room and sit in the whirlpool for a few minutes. Be right back.'

Neil watched the retreating slim figure make a one-man parade of his progress through the tables towards the rest room. Slater's absence provided an opportunity to relax his own attention and sip his wine while he rubbernecked around the elegant old dining-room, quietly humming with the sounds of contented eating and efficient service.

The room appeared to be just about half full, with more than half the occupied tables taken entirely by men. The only identifiable celebrities he saw were an actress whose play must be trying out in Boston, chipping away at her dessert while she harangued her male companion about something, and the Speaker of the House of Representatives, in quiet colloquy with someone who could have been a TV anchorman or a political fund-raiser. That look of transparent sincerity, never to be confused with intelligence. By eavesdropping hard on their exchange, Neil managed to hear the Speaker, a rumpled giant whom Breslin had once described as a fine spring rain of a man, say with the calm assurance of a sinless seminarian, 'But John, we *aren't* wrong. If you're on the side of right, you're never wrong.'

While he was mulling that piety, he noticed Slater, making his triumphal return, stop first at the table of the actress, bow, and say something to the nervous woman that made her smile radiantly for at least five seconds, and then pause with beautifully calculated casualness at the Speaker's table, put his hands on the man's big back, and inject some comment into that conversation, getting a meaty handshake in return.

He seated himself, knowing Neil would not have missed anything. 'The play really is hopeless, as your namesake on the *Globe* so unkindly said, but her performance is really quite fine.'

'And did you cheer Tip up with some good news about the Democrats probably coming back strong in the off-year elections?'

'How could I?' He smiled thinly. 'They're not going to. No, I simply congratulated him on his remarks on the budget in the House last week. Do you suppose he didn't make any?' He tackled the last cut of his steak jauntily, pleased with himself.

'And here I was congratulating myself on holding you to a scoreless tie, and it turns out you were playing the entire room. I've been sitting here just doggedly passing the ball back at you, imagining myself testing your skills to the limit. With all the different games you are handling simultaneously, you may not even remember that we were talking about toys that kill and a woman in a half world of grief and darkness.'

This time Slater rose with quick grace to the moment. He permitted himself one wry twist of the lips, then said quickly, 'We are dealing, Mr Kelly, with a woman who is balanced precariously on the edge of reality.'

'Which is to say, of sanity?'

'Exactly.'

'Are you implying that if I leave here now, and resume my interrupted sabbatical trip to England, writing a simple, honest letter saying that I see no earthly way I can be of use to anyone in this . . .' he fumbled for a word sufficiently serious, but rude enough '. . . *fricfrac*, that there is some danger you'll hold me responsible if she does slip over the edge into madness or catatonic silence?'

'Yes. But worse, from our point of view, we should be left in the dark, as we are now, frankly, about who and what are behind all this.'

'That's brutal enough to be honest.'

'It is. The larger, more impersonal aspects of the matter have priority in our thinking. We are not insensible to our colleagues' fates, to Barbara's fate in this case. But it is far more important, in the long run, what's going on behind all of that.'

'Beyond that and beyond your investigators' ability, apparently, to interpret the evidence.'

'There are two answers to that, Neil. I may call you Neil? Two answers. The absolutely crucial link we have connecting the few bits of evidence is lying up in the Mass. General with her eyes gone and her mind in the balance, deep in grief for her dead husband. She is telling us, in effect, that you must be let into this matter or she will sink into silence and stay there. We don't like that, but it is a fact we must deal with. Two, someone in your field, not mine, once observed that fiction is truer than history because it goes beyond the evidence.'

Neil waited until he had paused expectantly, and completed the quotation for him. ' "And common experience tells us that there is always something beyond the evidence." '

Slater inclined his head to acknowledge the point. 'That's just one of the reasons why, when I am the director of my firm, we will hire more English majors and fewer social scientists. A little literacy might be a dangerous thing, but none at all makes for a stony mind.'

Neil continued to chew thoughtfully. It was excellent beef and the feeling of eating well at leisure was deeply satisfying. Slater filled both their glasses with the last of the Bordeaux. Neil lifted his glass to look at the light through the dark wine.

'I need to talk with Babs again. Perhaps I can convince her that I'm relatively useless in this case.'

'Sorry, that won't be possible.'

'Don't be ridiculous. If she's too tired today, I'll go over there tomorrow and see her again. It should only take fifteen or twenty minutes. I have to understand a lot of things much better—'

'Barbara is in surgery. I spoke to Mary Dowd by phone when I went to the john. She suffered some kind of minor stroke about a half hour after you left her, and has apparently dropped off into a coma. The doctors think there might be some brain damage they failed to detect, and they have to perform surgery to relieve the pressure on the right side of her brain.'

'Then she might never recover.'

'That's possible. Of course that team of doctors is first class. One of them was consulted on the surgery for the President's press secretary when he was shot last week.'

Neil drained the wine. The strain and fatigue seemed to have returned suddenly.

'Besides,' Slater continued evenly, 'just before Barbara

passed out, Mary Dowd told her that you had agreed to work with us. That was the last thing she heard.'

Neil boiled with sudden fury, the adrenalin of simple anger wiping away the momentary weariness he had felt. 'What the hell do you mean Mary Dowd told her? Who in God's name gave Mary Dowd permission—'

'I did. Before I left the hospital.'

'How dare you presume?' Neil was close to shouting now, and slammed his napkin on the table, clattering a cup.

'I told her that if Mrs Lacey showed signs of slipping into a coma, which the doctors had said was a distinct possibility, Mary was to tell her you agreed. She apparently just smiled and let go of some . . . grip she had on the world, and passed out. Five minutes later, the monitor showed her brain functions were slowing and they rushed her to surgery.'

'Dear God, poor Barbara.'

'The last thing she heard made her happy, because it meant her wish was granted; you would be doing whatever it is she thought you could do in this. Comfort her family, I suppose. None of us expects, realistically, Neil, that you are going to be able to do any more than that, but for her sake we're willing to say you're cooperating with us.'

Neil glared at him. The captain, who had edged to a nearby station, glided away. 'And if I pack up and go to England now anyway?'

'I'm relying on your conscience to preclude that possibility, Neil. I might have none left, but I know one when I see one.'

'You bastard.'

'Let's get you back to your hotel, Neil. You're bushed. As for me being a bastard, maybe. But why don't you wait till you've had a chance to get beyond the immediate evidence on that too?'

'I think I need to get back out into the fresh air.'

'Just one more thing.' Slater had an advantage at last, and he wasn't about to let Neil so easily off his hook. Neil could feel the weight of his assurance compelling him to sit and wait, even though he wanted badly to get up and leave.

'What on earth is an emslin?' He smiled in what appeared to be genuine half-embarrassed puzzlement. 'Am I pronouncing it right? Emslin?'

'I don't know what you mean.'

'You disappoint me, Neil. Of course you do. Toward the end of your conversation with Barbara in her hospital room she began whispering, and you blurted out a word that can only have been that—emzlin? Would you mind telling me what that was all about?'

'You were listening to us, you bastard.'

'The monitor was in plain sight. The nurses wanted to know her vital signs, so did we. Words can be vital signs, too, know. Surely some romantic poet has already said that.'

'Did you listen to her confession when the priest came in, too?'

'There was no need. She was unconscious then and he anointed her without verbal confession.' He tilted his head and lifted his hands as if to say, 'So what?'

'If you must know, Emslinn is an old joke between us. Barbara and I used to date in college. I used to—then, this is all thirty years ago—get terrific headaches from studying. Actually, I simply needed reading glasses, but I tried out every headache remedy in the drugstore before I went to an optometrist. Once when Barbara was with me I asked the pharmacist for a bottle of Emslinn. Someone had told me to try Empirin, and that was the closest I could remember the name. It became our private name for any panacea, a cure-all. She was asking me if I had any Emslinn for her. Satisfied?'

'How often one's suspicions are unfounded. I thought, you see, that it might have to do with the circumstances of her accident.' He made a sketchy gesture of breast-beating. '*Mea culpa.*'

'Do you know what a "Claude glass" is, Mr Slater?'

'No, I don't believe I do. A *Claude glass*, is that it? Something to drink Emslin from?

'As you surely know, Claude Gelée was a great landscape painter, who, after his death, became, in the eighteenth century, so much the absolute authority that often the natural landscape was compared unfavourably with his pictures. Much of Europe was held in contempt for not being "up to Claude's standards". Sophisticated travellers then often carried with them a small instrument called a Claude glass, which enabled them to look at the landscape in a brownish haze, so that they saw nature as though it were properly varnished. As the master would have painted it . . .'

'You think that men in my profession have learned to prefer the world overlaid with our assumptions, and that therefore it is *we* who are out of touch with reality?'

'It happens in my field, too. Sometimes it is the critical tradition piled on top of the great book which becomes the object of reverence and attention, rather than the work itself.'

'Your students are lucky to have a teacher, Neil, who can sort out the real thing from the pile.' He signed the check and credit slip with small, tight strokes, and nodded his thanks to the waiter, who whisked it all away as the two men vacated the table and went out the door and down the steps together, not talking.

They walked together out of Winter Place and up across Tremont.

'How,' Neil asked, genuinely curious, though still angry, 'can you possibly expect me to work for you or with you, or however you prefer to describe it, and at the same time not trust me enough to tell me what I'd need to know in order to act intelligently? Surely if you value my co-operation, that evaluation is based primarily upon my intelligence.'

'I have my car under the Common. Mind if I walk you as far as Boylston?' Slater's interpolated question was purely perfunctory. 'You're right about your intelligence, of course. Although people like you generally like to say that our kind of intelligence is an oxymoron, we respect the individual real thing. But that could scarcely be our sole motive. Frankly, if Barbara Lacey hadn't insisted, you'd be winging your way towards Heathrow right now.'

Neil watched a gaggle of Hari Krishnas defying the sharp April wind, clicking their tiny tambourines and swaying to their own chant along the edge of the Common. Those thin orange dresses couldn't possibly keep out the cold; he wondered idly if they wore longies underneath. One of them darted forward and offered him a luridly coloured pamphlet, but he indicated that the boy should give it to his companion.

'Mr Liddy is interested in your movement; give it to him.'

Slater took the pamphlet with a gentle smile and threw it in the air, saying in a pleasant voice to the skinny boy, 'Moron.' He turned to look at Neil.

'Smiley and Liddy, the twin nemeses who haunt my passage through the workaday world of thuggery and buggery. It's all need-to-know, you know. I'm authorized to tell you exactly what I think you need to know to be useful to us. Are you afraid of danger?' He asked the question with friendly interest, as he might ask 'would you ever hang glide?' Implying that his own timidity was being revealed in the question itself.

'I was in the war. I have been shot at and missed and, as a Rabelaisian friend of mine likes to say of college politics, shit at and hit. I have not enjoyed either experience and would never willingly undergo either again.'

Suggesting that you wouldn't avoid either if it were necessary.'

'Suggesting nothing beyond the evidence.'

'Your original question was carefully couched in the subjunctive, I noticed. You didn't say "what I'll need to know," but "what I would need to know." Do I infer correctly that you are still unsure of your moral obligation to help here?'

'I've never been unsure of my moral obligations to my friends.'

They had arrived at the entrance to the underground garage, where Neil turned to leave Slater and cross Park Square to his hotel. 'I simply don't accept as given that I have any to you or yours.'

'Neil, a pleasure, honestly. Among other things, I'm the guy you give your bills to so that I can get you reimbursed. Why don't you just stay in Boston a few days, see some Sung landscapes at the Fine Arts, get your equilibrium back, then we'll talk again. I really think you might help us find out some things we'd like to know about who did this to your friends.'

Neil shook the proffered hand firmly but tried not to convey any enthusiasm, just good manners. Slater's grip was believably sincere.

'Thank you for lunch, Mr Slater.'

'Hey, Jack. After all we've been through together, call me Jack.'

'I shouldn't think so, Mr Slater.' Neil turned and walked away first. If he could catch the subjunctive, let him get the person right, too.

As he crossed the wide triangle through the rubble of the old square to the Park Plaza, a wan seventeen-year-old girl asked him if he wanted to party and called him Pop. He said no thank you and why wasn't she in school.

She laughed after him and yelled, 'It's Saturday, asshole.'

He pitied her teachers.

CHAPTER 4

Leaving the hotel was simply a matter of putting his few garments back into the open suitcase. Best things about canvas luggage was that, if you had no packing system, you could always cram something in somewhere; it was all nooks and crannies. And thank God for no-iron shirts.

He picked up the three cases and walked out of the scarcely-used room, leaving the key on the bed. Dan Boyd hired it; let Dan Boyd settle for it. He rode down and walked through the lobby, giving Frank the bellman a silent wink. If that minion thought he was a secret agent for TWA, nothing Neil did was going to surprise him. He walked across the street and got into the airport limo.

Boston's greatest advantage for travellers is that the heart of the city is just ten minutes from the airport. In half an hour, the van had completed the swing of hotels, sped out through East Boston, and dropped Neil at the American Airlines terminal at Logan.

In ten minutes he had a ticket for Albuquerque, which he discovered he didn't know how to spell, through Dallas, which he could. To his astonishment, he found that he could not fly directly to Santa Fe, which, even though it was the capital of its state, was simply a medium-sized town. The cheerful, blue-suited woman who sold him his ticket told him he'd have no trouble once he got to Albuquerque, since there was a regular shuttle-bus service between the two places every hour or so.

'You are a pysychologist?' she asked candidly.

'No, why, do a lot of psychologists go to Santa Fe?'

'Like Jews to Miami. I was there last summer. I think, except for Indians and psychiatrists and other divorced women, there isn't anyone there at all.'

'Ah. What tribe?'

'Jungians, mostly.'

He waited for her follow-through. Perhaps it was a lonely life, selling tickets to strangers.

'Oh, you mean Indians. Pueblos, the ones who live in those apartment buildings they build out of clay or whatever.'

'Ah. And the divorced women, what tribe are they?'

She ripped off the flimsy of his ticket with a sad smile. 'Those are rich, thin, and younger mostly. And they live in condos.'

'Sounds to me like a great place to visit.' Let her wait for his punch line. 'If I start chasing rich, thin, young divorcées, I can always go and get my head examined.'

'Good luck. Your plane will be boarding in forty minutes.' She pointed to where his departure gate number was written on his boarding pass. 'You're all checked in. Have a nice flight.'

Did he expect the forces of federal pursuit to come charging down the corridor, led by an inflamed Jack Slater, and followed by a red-faced, bellowing Danny Boyd?

He went to his gate, got inspected and X-rayed, and sat on quietly reading a *Globe* someone had left on the seat until they called his flight. The Red Sox had beaten Texas in an exhibition game, but were still having trouble finding a catcher. The psychic who said she had predicted Reagan's shooting now admitted she had faked the TV interview after the fact.

Fifteen minutes after he had patiently read every filler in the paper, they were airborne, and he was on his way to a place in the exact opposite direction from the place he had been aiming for eight hours ago, for a purpose he was entirely unclear about, motivated entirely by his brimming rage and horror at what had happened to Barbara Lacey and her husband and his disgust at Slater's old-boy acting and ruthless probing for leverage to move him toward whatever errand the CIA would like him to run for them. He hoped his calm exterior wasn't too transparent.

He had exactly one clue. Em's Linn. Somewhere in Santa Fe there had to be some trace of her connection with the bombing. To find that trace he was simply going to have to go back over what he could of Barbara's steps there. Which meant, perhaps, intersecting, as she had done, with whatever international terror or malice had sent her into darkness and near-madness. He kept that thought in his mind, revolving it slowly, like a dream which had to be examined from every side to be teased into yielding up its metaphor, until he realized that they were above the Mississippi River and someone was trying to feed him. He took coffee and then went to sleep.

Dallas isn't one airport, but an interlocking web of mini-airports, and if you land in one you are pretty well trapped within it, forced to patronize its bars and souvenir stands—assuming your notion of memorabilia runs to wall-size portraits of the Cowboy cheerleaders in their hotpants sitting on the corral fence waving—until your connecting flight from Los Angeles or Atlanta shows up. Neil dozed again.

The flight from Dallas to Albuquerque gives everyone a chance to understand both how large the Southwest is, and how empty of people and water is it. All these factors are connected causally. When the Sangre de Cristo mountains appear, you are approaching your goal, a sprawl of half a million people, all apparently working and living in one-storey buildings. Perhaps only the Indians built apartment houses.

On the ground, Albuquerque puts you into a clean,

human-scale airport where the information givers are polite and careful in answering your questions, and the skies really are apparently not cloudy all day.

Neil bought a shuttle-bus ticket for thirteen dollars at the counter and put his name down for a reservation on the next one out to Santa Fe. Then he went back to the arrival area just in time to catch his three bags as they spilled off the delivery roundabout.

Since he knew nothing of the area, he went to the airport newsstand and bought a small paperback with some essays about the history and geography of Santa Fe and a section of coloured photographs. Neither his quick scan of the booklet nor anything he had learned from the woman at American Airlines prepared him for the empty beauty and unassuming charm of the country.

The minibus took six passengers in its nine seats on his trip. They were a nun and a crisp widow in jewelled spectacles—who together formed an instant bond and told each other the stories of their lives in an audible dialogue for the rest of the ride—a Japanese lady who was reading a Harlequin romance without looking up, a businessman who checked order forms by himself in the last seat, and a burly, bald fellow with thick glasses who sat next to Neil and chatted in the predictable clichés of an experienced traveller killing time.

The fat man was named Michaels, but asked to be called Dan. He was clearly an academic of some sort, and Neil was pleased to have one modest guess prove correct when Michaels said that he taught psychiatry at Columbia to medical students.

'I was told that Santa Fe is inhabited entirely by Jungians and Pueblo Indians, with a population of rich divorcées added for spice,' Neil told his companion, laughing.

'No, no,' the burly man insisted with mock seriousness, 'it is we psychiatrists who are the spice. Some of us are a bit confectionary, but most of us pride ourselves on being spicy.' He asked what Neil taught.

With a politely inward sigh, because he didn't really want to talk shop, Neil found himself explaining his book in progress on Donne, and the fact that he'd been diverted from an English sabbatical to visit some friends out here who'd experienced a tragedy. It struck him as he spoke that although he prided himself on two things—being an excellent listener and rarely boring others with his special interests—Dan Michaels was one of those rare persons who was a better listener than himself, and who was, furthermore, really interested in John Donne.

'I should explain why I am asking all these foolish questions about Donne,' he said. He had only asked three, each giving evidence of already extensive knowledge about the poet. 'At Columbia Med. I lecture on sexology to young doctors. You would be astonished to learn what they don't know, those boys and girls. Or perhaps you wouldn't be astonished. I use a dozen different literary texts, from St Augustine to Walt Whitman, to make them think about their own sexuality intelligently, and the one that invariably produces the most puzzlement among them is Donne's elegy "To His Mistress Going to Bed". To me it's the most nearly perfect expression of sensuous intelligence in English, but I have never been able to get that across to them. Can you explain that?'

Neil was enchanted, as we all are when what we take seriously is taken seriously by others. They began an animated exchange over the male and female genital images in the poem, which ranged from Petrarch back to Ovid and forward to Freud. Both of them noted without comment that the Japanese lady, although she was still staring at her Harlequin romance, had not turned a page for ten miles.

At one point their colloquy was interrupted when the nun in front pointed excitedly out the window, and they all leaned to see a ragged line of six brilliant hot-air balloons strung out above the red hills, their sides great lozenges of yellow and scarlet, circles of blue and green, chequerboards of white and orange, and huge block gold-on-black lettering advertising beer, all blazing like fantastic floating cathedral tops upside down in the empty sky.

'Albuquerque is the hot-air balloon capital of the world, you know,' the businessman remarked, and returned to his figures.

'Shakespeare called them unearthly, lovely toys, and you can see why,' the nun said.

Neil raised his eyebrows to Dan Michaels, but kept his peace. He at least knew that Shakespeare had done no such thing. He went back to an uncompleted thought and the two men continued their explication of Donne's famous poem.

With convincing bashfulness that made him look like an embarrassed schoolboy peering through magnifying spectacles, and with apologies for presuming to talk outside—way outside—his competence, Michaels asked if Neil thought that perhaps—just perhaps, mind you—Donne might be interpreted as conforming to the psychological archetype Jung called the 'trickster'.

Neil looked with astonishment at the beaming, red-faced psychologist. 'It never remotely occurred to me. Could you possibly amplify the question? I don't want to say it's wholly incorrect without being sure what I'm rejecting.'

They both laughed at that. Michaels, however, immediately became earnest again, explaining that he might never have such an opportunity to pick the brains of a captive Donne expert again.

'The trickster is one of the classic archetypes of the unconscious mind, you know. He appears in fairy stories, in the folklore of every known people. The American Indians have perhaps one of the best-developed conceptions of the trickster. He is a shape-shifter, a shameless joker—the poltergeist phenomena, all those pranks, Jung was sure, emerged from a kind of adolescent psychic energy in the collective unconscious. The god Mercury was certainly a trickster figure; some think Jesus was—I hope I'm not offending you? Shamanism, with all its changes from animal form to human form—Casteneda was a shaman—is deeply rooted in the archetype. Now consider Donne. The wild, sensual Jack-of-all-beds, man about town: a typical, oversexed adolescent unable or unwilling to grow up. Brilliant, gifted, a poet whose literary influence extended over the lives of other great poets, but never taken seriously by the establishment. Shall we say he was dismissed as some sort of a joker? He compares himself to a flea, to this, to that—' He interrupted himself to dig into his side pocket with a gleeful grin. 'What do you make of that?' He produced a tiny enamelled gold box, covered with an engraved design of coloured wildflowers.

'It's a seventeenth-century flea box,' Neil said unhesitatingly, touching the lid of the exquisite piece.

Michaels pocketed it again. 'Correct. Almost anyone else would have said a snuffbox, even many antique dealers. In fact, I use it for something entirely different, but I think Donne would approve. But it is, as you immediately observed, a flea box, of the sort Donne and his pretty girl-friends and their crowd would have carried on dates so that when they picked fleas off each other, as everyone did in those lousy days, they could have a place to put them.'

The Japanese lady moved ever so slightly closer to the door and away from the bulky gentleman with the box of fleas in his pocket. What a country. Perceiving her discomfort, Michaels took out the box again and held it to his ear, shook it slightly, smiled, and put it back in his pocket.

'I should be ashamed of myself,' he said to Neil *sotto*

voce. 'You see, there's a little of the old trickster, the old Adam, in all of us. It comes out in our silly antics and demonstrates that we are far from fully civilized. Memory, as Papa Freud noted, is itself a trickster, plays terrible tricks on us – is, in fact, a most dangerous form of fiction which we often mistake for history. Like our Sister's remembrance of Shakespeare on the subject of hot-air balloons,' he added dryly. 'And we like to be fooled. I have seen perfectly solemn colleagues in the faculty room reading comics – not Doonesbury, mind you, but Spider Man and Superman and that crowd.'

'It never seemed a significant element in any literature to me, with the obvious exception of fool figures and so on.'

Then perhaps that's significant. Perhaps only sub-literatures have it, take it seriously. Much spy literature, you can see, is based on disguises, James Bond supertoys that convert cars into airplanes at the push of a button, on what even historians now call "dirty tricks", eh? Was that, then, why Donne was outside the establishment? Isn't his whole career shifty, ending up as a saintly cathedral dean posing in his graveclothes, mind you, for his final portrait, explicable in just such terms? My God, maybe he was a spy for Elizabeth against the Catholics!'

Neil rose to the bait. It was too delicious to resist, and he wasn't about to let the rotund psychologist think it didn't matter what metaphor one laid over the work of a great writer. They argued like old friends and suddenly found themselves looking up at the hills in which Santa Fe nestled, just ahead of them.

Since the psychiatrist was there to read a paper at a convention of Jungian scholars out at St John's College, they made hasty plans to continue their conversation over a meal or a drink if their respective schedules permitted, and agreed to exchange addresses. That was a quick reminder to Neil that he didn't have the foggiest idea where he'd be staying. He didn't want to just barge in on Emily Mitchell and her family with his presence as a guest to go with the bad news he was bringing, and he had left in too great a hurry to make reservations.

Michaels solved that for him with a recommendation. He himself was staying at La Posada, in something called a casita, which he described as a small, perfect house-keeping apartment. He suggested that Neil get off there with him and see if he couldn't luck into one. La Posada was the last stop of the shuttle around town, and as soon as Neil saw the rambling, landscaped old grounds with the low, wide circle of adobe casitas, he jumped at the chance.

Dan Michaels checked in without any hitch, and they parted with a handshake and renewed expressions of their intentions to talk again before he went off waving a key, saying, 'I'm in seventeen. Call.'

Neil's luck was good; there was one casita in the north corner available because of a no-show, and he took it with a sense of relief. It turned out to be a tasteful, three-room apartment, decorated in neo-Navaho, but reasonably, with a tiny, complete kitchen and a corner fireplace with a free supply of the local piñon in a wicker basket.

He emptied his bags into the closets and drawers of the bedroom, took a hot shower, and lay on the bed trying to imagine what he would do next. The time difference from Boston meant that it was only late afternoon, although his stomach kept insisting it was past dinner-time. Since his little refrigerator was empty, except for a bottle of pimentos the last tenant had left, he reluctantly dressed again, in suntans and a button-down shirt, adding a madras jacket for the cool evening air.

The simplest thing to do again turned out to be wise. If this kept up, he would become a Tolstoyan. He went into the dining-room in the Staab House on the grounds, apparently the original ranch house from which the inn was developed, and had a satisfyingly well-cooked Veal Oscar and two cold Heinekens.

While he sat alone in the enormous room, no one else apparently being ready for dinner yet, he thought about what he knew and did not know about Barbara's half-sister, Emily Mitchell, and her family.

CHAPTER 5

Emily Mitchell was one of those women invariably described by anyone meeting her for the first time as a 'dynamo'. She was barely five feet tall, and she wore her mop of red hair like a battle flag, cut short and brushed back without any effort at style. Her face was plain and cheerful, and only her mouth was remarkable—a wide, expressive smile her best feature. She was as different from her half-sister as New Mexico is from Philadelphia; one woman tailored, coiffed, and cool, unlikely to respond to any situation until she was intellectually sure of it, the other rough-cut, outgoing, and most likely to plunge into anything first and try to understand it afterwards.

Her husband, Doan Mitchell, who liked to consider Emily a typical easterner, was as fascinated by his wife of more than twenty years as he had been when she was his bride. Doan had been a baseball player when they met in Philadelphia, and they started dating because he had walked over to the box where she was sitting with friends at a Phillies-Cubs game and asked her for her autograph.

'Isn't this supposed to be the other way around?' she said, signing his scorecard.

'Not unless you want to know my name too, ma'am,' he said.

'It's on your shirt. Turn around and I'll read it to you.' She turned him around briskly. 'You're—you're sure a tall one, and you're Mitchell. Didn't they tell you?'

'I'll bet you don't know my first name, though, because it's not on there and I'm not famous yet.'

She lifted a scorecard from the lap of the girl sitting next to her. 'Mr Number Fifty-four Mitchell, would you sign my scorecard for me?'

'Why, I'd be pleased to, ma'am, he said solemnly, and so she found out his name was Don. 'See,' he said, 'Doan.'

'Either you can't spell right or you can't talk right, Mitchell.'

He looked honestly hurt. 'What do you mean? D-O-N, Doan.'

'If you're going to call yourself *Doan*, then you should spell it that way, not Don.'

He looked at her as if she were crazy. In his world, where more than half the working population were southern country boys, his accent was scarcely a matter for comment. She told Neil years later, when the six were having dinner in New York, that he grabbed away his scorecard and stalked away, genuinely crushed. There he was, a star rookie pitcher for the Chicago Cubs, trying to pick up this cute little redheaded thing at the ball park, and she tells him that he doesn't know how to pronounce his own name. Or spell it.

The next time they had met he had been up in the big leagues for six weeks, had won just one game and lost three, and had an ERA of 9.50 and looked as if he was on his way back to the high minors or to the Giants as the player named later in a deal for a utility infielder. But by then he had managed, at least, to get his name spelt DOAN MITCHELL in the regular roster on the scorecard. He walked over to where she was sitting and showed it to her.

'Now are you satisfied, darn it?' he said.

'Wouldn't it have been simpler just to ask me for a date the first time?' she said.

'Well, darn it, do you want a date?' he yelled at her, ignoring the hundred or so people in adjacent boxes who were enjoying his red-faced discomfort.

'I certainly don't want to wait another six weeks,' she yelled back at him. 'You might be pitching for Sioux City or Pawtucket by then.'

'Well, we'll just see about that, won't we, Emily,' he hollered at her. That was her description of it: 'He stood there pounding his glove and just hollered at me, "We'll just see about that, won't we, Emily!" '

For good or ill, he was brought in to relieve in that game and gave up a double in the bottom of the ninth that lost the game for the Cubs. Their post-game date had much more of a wake about it than young love's first springing. But Emily used the occasion to convince him that he'd probably be better off going back to college and getting himself another profession before he was too old to do anything but coach high school or drive a cab. When the Cubs sent him down a week later, he promptly quit and went back to the University of New Mexico, where he majored in engineering and eventually turned himself into a solidly successful contractor at just about the time Albuquerque was starting to boom and expand into a metropolis.

After a hectic correspondence and three or four cross-country visits with Emily's family, they were married in the Murrows' home parish in Philadelphia and immediately moved into an adobe house Doan had built for them out on the Old Santa Fe Trail.

Emily quickly found out that she had been living just to discover the Southwest, like half the population of their new home city. The region around Albuquerque has the absolute highest density of Ph.D.s in the world, not excluding the brain belt around Boston and Cambridge, simply because it is the centre of a vast complex of nuclear and related research facilities. One only has to remember that the atomic age began a short distance from Santa Fe, in Los Alamos, and nothing has been the same there, or anywhere else, since. Doan didn't think the sixty-mile commute each way every day was any problem, and after he made his company big enough so that his helicopter took him most days, it wasn't. Albuquerque, like any city, has plenty of honky-tonks and urban tensions, and he wanted his kids to know a little more about the hills and their history.

The twins were born that following year, and the youngest, Will, five years later. Along with their parents, they seemed to make up one of those prosperous, cheery American families of bright, active parents and healthy, interesting kids, But, as Neil was well aware from raising children of his own and watching them change before his eyes from little girls in smocked dresses into sloppy teenagers in hideous army fatigues and then into young married women in saris, designer jeans, and sandals, a lot can happen.

One of his own daughters had married, but divorced right away, then remarried the same summer, apparently determined to make someone a wife, then left that undealt with while she moved to Sausalito. She dressed in unironed Indian prints, worked in bookstores, read her own poems at gatherings, and seemed to be dying at twenty-five of a self-inflicted life. The other had for a long time lived alone, loved a writer for a while but feared his wit, which she found wounding, having only earnestness at the service of her own passions; she worked for causes, tried to keep up but started drinking, pulled herself together, married a rather childish assistant professor of linguistics, and seemed happy.

Em and Doan had sent their children east to secondary school, assuming that would enhance their chances at getting into a good eastern college—the twins to Dana Hall and Andover, Will to Milton Academy. If Barbara had encountered Em's Linn out here in Santa Fe during the school year, perhaps there had been some changes in the arrangement.

As Neil ate his dessert and drank a cup of satisfyingly strong hot coffee, he knew that his next step had to be a visit to Emily and Doan to ask them what they knew. And to tell them what they probably didn't know yet.

There was a cab right outside the Staab House letting off three men in wide-brimmed black hats and checked shirts. He signalled the driver, got a nod, and climbed in, giving the address he had copied from the phone book in his casita. To his mild astonishment, one of the black-hatted men held the cab door for him, shut it gently behind him, and said, 'You okay now?' Apparently the identification of bad guys in New Mexico was more complicated than the old westerns would lead one to believe.

In the late evening light, the landscape was every spring colour but green. Red hills, grey scrub, wild, brilliant flowers he couldn't name, and a sky so gaudy with reds and violets that it seemed false. He had often thought there was no spectacle in the world so fine as the light at this time of day in the Connecticut Valley—what's left of it so late—pouring through slate-blue clouds on to the pearl and smoky masses opposite. But this sky of indigo and blood red went past the eyes somehow and made itself felt in the bones and the roots of the brain; the drama of the sky became an inner drama, not simply something witnessed.

Crossing the Plaza through that blaze of late light, Neil shivered. He was about to tangle more threads together than already were knotted, and anything he might do could make the tangle worse, not better. The local police had been shut out, if he understood Slater correctly, so there could be no help for him there. That would mean the fire department report would have been treated by now with the same lack of concern for the public's right to know, tied up in 'pending further investigation of suspected arson' proceedings. The FBI would have had to be notified immediately, which meant that the FBI would have its own jealously guarded inquiry going, and anyone remotely connected with the CIA wasn't going to be welcome. Those two agencies had been feuding about jurisdictional questions for a long time, and not just since Watergate.

Neil had to know several things quickly if he was to make the slightest advance in answering the questions about his own concerns. Was the bomb aimed at De Sales or at Barbara or at both? If it was De Sales who had been the target, then the likeliest possibility was that a rival in business, pushed aside or broken by the Lacey corporate interests, had hired a professional killer to get his revenge. If it had been for both of them, it was likely to be connected with their multifarious political causes and activities, including, Neil knew, active and generous support for anti-pollution and anti-dumping legislation that would severely cramp the profitable practices of some big, wealthy New Mexico corporations. De Sales's companies were always being held up in the media as models of enlightened management in their disposal and pollution control techniques, and the Laceys had both appeared on television to debate the matter in the past six months.

If the bomb was really intended for Barbara, then her work with the CIA was clearly a probable motive. But what was the nature and scope of that work? And how could Em's Linn be involved? As for himself, he supposed that he must be prepared for the wrath of Jack Slater when he found that Neil had taken off on his own without waiting to be told what to do.

They passed a signpost out on a long hill which directed them to MUSEUMS, but just then the driver turned off to the left and pulled up in the spacious yard of a massive adobe ranch, with huge beams projecting from under the roof of the house in the classic regional architecture, and enormous windows, through one of which he could see a fire burning in a domed fireplace. And, as he paid his fare, he saw Emily standing at the window, grinning happily and waving madly.

She raced out through the front door and hugged him fiercely. 'Neil Kelly, I don't believe it. Welcome to God's country, you old stick-in-the-mud.'

'Emily, you look wonderful.' He walked with her, his arm still around her, through the wide door into the deep, brilliant living-room glowing with red and black Indian hangings against white walls. Every chair and the gigantic sofa had obviously chosen with her six-foot-four husband in mind. 'Em, this is just gorgeous.'

'Well, it took you long enough to get out here for a visit, but you made it. Oh, I wish Babs and Morgan were here. Did you think they were out at their place? Aren't you supposed to be going to England? Isn't this a funny route to take? Because they apparently came, but went back again the same day. I haven't heard from them since.'

She bubbled along like an unquenchable fountain of energy, tossing pillows onto the sofa to make him fit, wheeling the drinks table over, and talking the whole time.

'Babs called me last Wednesday and said they were in town to open the house up for the season. She was going to do some photography, then bam, not another word, and when I called them they didn't have their phone connected yet . . .' She was watching Neil's face now, and what she saw slowed, then stopped her.

'There's been a terrible accident, Em. Babs is in the hospital. They flew her to Boston.' He reached out and held both her hands. 'Morg was killed.'

Her beautiful mouth turned itself into a mask of

sorrow, and tears welled and spilled from her eyes. 'Oh God, Neil. Car crash? Their plane?'

'Let's have a drink and I'll tell you the whole thing slowly.' He could tell that she was not immediately registering, was still trying to absorb the first shock of what he had said. 'Doan out?'

'Doan? Yes. Work. Some big job up in Gallup—' Her voice broke into a squeaky cry. 'Where, Neil? When?'

Neil poured two glasses of the *fino* sherry and handed one to her. 'It wasn't an accident. It's a terribly complicated story, and I want you to just sit and listen while I try to explain it, even if parts sound incredible. First of all, Morg was murdered . . .'

She sat back and gulped at her drink and let her eyes widen. Her face shone with new tears, but she did not speak, watching him every second. Neil was conscious of the stillness of the evening out on this lonely hill, the sweet perfume of the piñon wood burning, the dry bite of the sherry, and the last red, theatrical flood of light coming through the west window. The moment seemed frozen, yet it was only a moment, while he set the stemmed glass with great deliberation on the coaster before him, reading in a glance the motto printed on it: *Every calculation based on experience elsewhere fails in New Mexico—Lew Wallace, Territorial Governor, 1880.* Then, as carefully as he could, he told her about the April Fool's toy, the explosion, the terrible injury to her sister, and the decision to fly Barbara to Boston as fast as possible—even about the cloak of government secrecy which had been thrown around the case. He omitted only what Babs had said about her daughter Linn. When he had finished, it was night outside and the fire was burned down to the grate.

Emily rose in a daze when he stopped, almost absentmindedly put wood from the basket on the fire, blew her nose, and threw the tissue into the blaze. Then she turned to face Neil. 'What in God's name is going on, Neil?'

'I don't know, Em. Whatever it is, they had absolutely no right not to inform you and Doan. That is the kind of stupid, inhumane, bureaucratic, unfeeling act that makes my blood boil. Sooner or later, they'll decide you are entitled to know, and they'll arrive full of explanations and justifications. You'll probably hear plenty about national security, but it seemed to me that the first requirement was that Babs's family know where she is and how she is.'

'Oh Neil, poor lady, blind.' She put her hands over her face briefly, as though trying to imagine the world gone dark, and wept again.

'It's only fair to tell you, Em, that I'm probably causing trouble right now by doing this, by telling you.' He thought of Barbara's shaky scrawl, EM'SLINN, and suppressed a shudder of self-disgust at what he had to find out, and at his own final lack of candour. God forgive me, he thought, but what the hell else can I say?

'You mean you can get in trouble for this?'

'Don't worry about me. Just don't explain anything. Make them tell you. Tell them the truth this far: I was here, I had seen Barbara in the hospital, and I told you about the explosion. Then let them worry about it if they choose to.'

'If I go to Boston in the morning, can they keep me from seeing her, Neil? Will they—' Her angry question was cut off by the door chimes. Neil had almost simultaneously realized that a car had pulled up out front, its sound on the gravel muffled by the thick walls of the house.

'Doan?'

'He never rang in his life.' Emily moved swiftly to the front door and opened it. Neil stood by the sofa and waited tensely. If it was simply a friend or a neighbour, she wouldn't need him glowering over her shoulder. She turned abruptly back from the door and re-entered the room, followed by a barrel-chested man in a tan suit and green tie. He was no more than thirty, black-haired and black-eyed, and handsome in a bony-faced, hawkish way.

He didn't wait to be introduced, but walked over to Neil and stuck out his hand. 'I'm Agent Russell Cady. I'm with the Federal Bureau of Investigation. Who are you?'

Neil could feel the force of that direct approach, the intensity in the man. He took Cady's hand and looked him right between the eyes, lying on instinct. 'I'm John Huffam.' If Cady could recognize Charles Dickens's two middle names, more power to him. 'Am I supposed to tell you whom *I* work for?'

'Only if you're here on official business.'

'I'm a friend of the Mitchells.'

The man grunted and turned back to Emily. He was apparently used to hostility. 'Mrs Mitchell, as I told you a moment ago, I have unpleasant news for you. You might want to sit down.'

'Oh my God. More bad news? Is it about Doan? My husband?' She collapsed onto the sofa, her hand over her mouth.

'No, it has nothing to do with your husband. May I ask what you mean by *more* bad news, Mrs Mitchell?'

'My kids? Is one of my kids hurt? Oh God, Timmy?'

Cady sighed impatiently. At his own gaucherie, Neil hoped. 'No, ma'am. It's about your half-sister, Mrs Lacey. She's been injured.'

'But that's just what N—I just heard that five minutes ago.' She glanced at Neil and back at the agent. 'Barbara was hurt in an explosion right here in Santa Fe.'

Cady glared at Neil with new interest. 'Mr Huffam, I know you aren't local police; are you from the State Police office?'

'No, Mr Cady, I'm not. I told you, I'm just a friend.'

He growled with angry disgust. 'Well, there's only one

way you could know about Mrs Lacey's injury, Mr Huffam, and both of us know it. So now we both know who you work for, don't we?'

'As a simple matter of fact, Mr Cady, just so you won't go leaping to any breakneck conclusions, I know Barbara Lacey is in the hospital in Boston, badly burned in an explosion, because I happened to be in that hospital this morning and saw her.'

'And you want me to believe that was pure coincidence, is that it?'

Emily looked on, stricken and dismayed, from one to the other of the two men sparring in her living-room while she tried to swallow the sense of what she had been told. Neil saw her take a long, shaky breath.

'John happens to be a friend of the family and a doctor, Mr Cady.'

Neil wondered if a Ph.D. in English Literature would hold up under a quick quiz on medical facts. He felt like a smuggler watching the customs inspector give him a cold eye. In for a penny, in for a pound: 'Let's be precise, Emily. I practice psychology, Mr Cady. I thought Emily might need my help.'

Cady was almost convinced. The manufacture of instant fictions and compounded lies, the common coin of any faculty club any weekday lunch hour, was obviously not a form of counterfeiting he was competent to detect without forensic equipment.

'Would you be, by some extension of coincidence, Dr Huffam, a psychiatrist working for some federal agency?' The black eyes glittered, but this time he smiled. His teeth were square and perfect, but the smile was feral.

'Mr Cady, I hate to insist, but let me say two things quickly, whether they disturb you or not. One, I don't work for the federal government in any capacity. The idea is repugnant to me. Two, since you say you do, it is you who must provide identification to us, not we to you.

May I see your card?'

The agent deftly produced a wallet and a blue and white card from his pocket. 'I showed this to Mrs Mitchell at the door.'

Neil read it with a smile. 'Well, now that we all know each other, can we talk about what you came to tell Mrs Mitchell?'

'If you actually saw Mrs Lacey, you may know more than I do. The evening of April one, about eight p.m., there was a small explosion, followed by a fire at the home of Morgan De Sales and Barbara Lacey, off Mt Carmel Road in Santa Fe. Mr Lacey was killed, and Mrs Lacey was badly burned. The fire department notified the police, who called us.' He interrupted himself to look hard at Neil. 'Then a strange thing happened. Strange, at least, in my experience. Maybe you, Dr Huffam, are more used to strange things in your business. The patient, Mrs Lacey, was immediately flown by private transport to Boston, where, as you have personally verified, Doctor, she is being treated by burn specialists. *And* our regional office and these poor local yokels who were just trying to do an efficient job of police work were told in no uncertain terms to sit on the case, because someone in Washington had taken over. Since the only ones who might tell the FBI, in effect, to go play with their hoops would be the National Security Agency, Doctor, you'll understand if my mind catapults to the unremarkable conclusion that you might be from them.'

'Mr Cady, I'm sorry you had your case taken out from under you. I didn't do it. But the most obvious and painful fact is one you continue to ignore. This woman has had a terrible shock. Her brother-in-law has been killed and her sister severely injured, permanently blinded, and might die. That happened here in Santa Fe three days ago, but someone with an interest in keeping the matter from her own family moved her to Boston without even the courtesy of a call to Mrs Mitchell, her sole living relative. Do you think *we*—Mrs Mitchell and I—care one iota about your pretty internecine rivalries in the federal law enforcement merry-go-round?'

Cady bit his tongue, but apologized forthrightly. 'I'm sorry, Mrs Mitchell. Dr Huffam is right to this extent at least. I shouldn't have put my own concerns ahead of yours. But it was a shock to find that what I had been told was a confidential—indeed, a secret—message for you from Washington had already arrived when I got here. I'm just the messenger. Well, I can say you got the message, I guess, and leave you with Dr Huffam.'

Emily rose, still shaky, but anxious to be rid of the hawk-faced agent. 'Thank you, Mr Cady. You only did what you had to do.'

He turned to leave, but looked back at Neil. 'I wonder if you'd be good enough to walk me to my car, Doctor?'

Neil touched Emily's arm. 'Be right back. Glad to, Mr Cady.' He followed the broad shoulders out into the yard.

Cady turned to him at the door of his black Ford. 'Will you be here long, Doctor?'

'Hard to say. I'm actually on my way to England, in a roundabout way. I'll certainly stay until the Mitchells are ready for me to leave.'

'Do you know this part of the world well, Doctor?'

'Not at all.' They looked together out over the edge of the hill at the partially moonlit view of Santa Fe. 'It reminds me of El Greco's view of Toledo in this light. It's a beautiful country.'

'My people were Navahos several mixtures and several generations back, Doctor. This was a lot more beautiful place, believe me, when the Navahos had it.'

'I read in a book just today, Mr Cady, that the Navahos took it away from the Pueblos. Was it even better when *they* had it?'

He cocked an eye at Neil appraisingly. 'The old people

call this season Thunder-Sleeping. Perhaps this year the thunder awakened early; that's supposed to be a bad sign.'

'Jung has already explained that to my people, Mr Cady.'

Cady opened the door of his car and got in, speaking through the side window. 'Jung didn't know the half of it. I'll bet he didn't know that the Navaho have a hunting song guaranteed to bring in the game. It says among other things, *they will hear my heartbeat, and they will follow my thoughts*.'

'An Irishman, though, once wrote a poem about his sweetheart. In Irish, you know, "sweetheart" is *macushla*, which means "beat of my heart". It says, among other things, "Macushla, macushla, if my mind were yours, you would love me." '

'Yes,' he nodded, completely serious. 'It's like love. And it's my game, Doctor.'

'Maybe, between us, we can get them to tune in one of us.'

'Watch out. There's always the chance we'll start hearing each other. Now that could get messy.' His black eyes weren't wavering an inch in the direction of good humour.

'Just remember, mine is the one with the Boston Irish accent.'

'Is that what it is? Mine will be the one saying *may your soul rest in peace*, Doctor. I don't intend to lay off, no matter what Washington says. I have a personal and a professional stake in what happens out here in my back-yard. So keep an ear cocked, and if you hear an Indian heartbeat on your stethoscope, stand very still.'

The black car moved smoothly out into the road and away down the hill toward town. Neil watched it a moment and went back into the house. The season of Thunder-Sleeping had a cold edge to the evenings at seven thousand feet.

After Cady had left, Emily seemed to lose even more of her natural energy. She poured herself a large gin-and-tonic. 'If this keeps up, I'll be drunk by morning,' she sniffled. 'Oh Neil, what is going on here, anyway, what is going on? Come on in the kitchen. If I'm doing something, I won't be so nervous.'

They moved out through a gleaming, dark dining-room with a massive wrought iron chandelier into a butcher-block and stainless steel kitchen that Locke-Ober's would have been proud of.

Emily tied a red checked apron around her and said, 'Sit, sit. I'll scramble you some eggs western-style. Don't say you're not hungry because that's not the point. The point is to keep Emily busy while you explain what in hell is going on with the FBI and you and all this crazy stuff.' She moved back and forth between the ceramic-topped range and her work counter and the refrigerator with the ease of frequent practice.

'I don't know what I can tell you, Em,' Neil began. 'Only a little more than twelve hours ago, I was innocently packing to go to England to finish my book on John Donne. Now *he* might have understood all this. I met a fellow Donne freak today, as a matter of fact, and we were talking about the times Donne lived in—he came from a family of distinguished Catholic martyrs, but he ended up as a priest in the Anglican Church, after being a pretty famous rake about London. This other fellow was trying to convince me Donne was probably a Protestant spy. I think the times we're living in perhaps have more in common with that time in England than we sometimes think in our historians' zeal to compare ourselves with the decline of the Roman Empire.

'Barbara was doing something—some job or other—for the Central Intelligence Agency.'

Emily stirred the eggs in her pan more vigorously.

'Jesus, Mary, and Joseph. Now did she actually tell you that?'

'She didn't tell me much, but she told me that. And she asked me to find out what I could about this whole tragic mess.'

'Was that what Cady was chewing nails about? You two were talking right past me for a couple of minutes there. Does he think you're working for the CIA too?'

'That or the National Security Agency, or some other bunch.'

'God, it's a real mess. Not the eggs, don't worry.' She skilfully slid the eggs from the pan on to two plates, acquired four slices of toast from somewhere and buttered them, and handed the plates over to the counter. 'Hold on, I've got some really good Mexican beer instead of this old gin.' She lifted two Carta Blancas from the refrigerator door, uncapped them, and set them beside the plates.

'Hmm.' She tasted her own cooking. 'Turns out Emily's hungry too. I don't eat awfully regularly with Doan away nights. Eat, eat. Keep talking, but eat.'

The beer was icily marvellous. Neil preferred his beer English-style, about the same temperature as a good red wine, but the Carta Blanca was perfect with the paprika'd eggs. 'You did know that Barbara had done some sort of errand for the CIA once before?'

'That thing at Yale? I always thought that was some kind of inside joke I never understood. Babs certainly never said much. Didn't a whole bunch of CIA come from Yale—William F. Buckley and God knows who else?'

'Well, Yale didn't have a monopoly on it, but there was certainly a string of old-boy connections through which the CIA recruited and directed agents. That goes all the way back to the OSS and Final Clubs and a lot of other Ivy League flummery of the sort effete easterners dote on.' Neil smiled at his own mild irony.

'That other thing Babs did is certainly old news now.' He thought for a moment. Five years ago? Six? Although God knows there's probably someone at some desk in Washington sitting on the bundle of relevant documents, trying still to keep it a secret. As far as I know, all she did was tell De Sales that some Italian count had tried, in the process of making a slimy pass at her, to get her interested in telling him about a missile contract some company of De Sales's had got. For a couple of months after that—I assume De Sales told the right people in Washington—the CIA asked them to let her meet the slimy count whenever it was socially reasonable and to pass along what they called "any hard information", an unfortunate phrase I can believe they actually used. However, the count seems to have broken his neck that winter skiing in Gstaad. That seemed to be that for the CIA and Barbara.'

Emily looked as though she tasted something bad. 'Doan got a taste of that whole dumb secrecy business last year. His company got a little teeny sub-contract for some new facility on the Tonepah Range up in Utah where they fire the test missiles that land over here in White Sands, and they about questioned him and investigated us to death before he got clearance to build the old thing. Little old two-and-a-half-million-dollar project; he told me it wasn't worth all the trouble and paperwork. But he figured there might be some bigger ones later, so he put up with their silly old stuff—do you know they even checked on me back when I lived in Philadelphia? Emily Murrow, girl spy.' She moved back to the stove and lifted a pot of coffee over to the counter. 'Get two mugs from that cabinet up behind you, will you?' She produced a small carton of cream. 'You mind if we don't bother with a pitcher?'

'Does Doan's company have any federal contracts now?'

'Yes, I think. I honestly don't know what they've got anymore. We finally agreed that, unless it seemed important for me to know—oh, you know,' she made a face, 'there's kidnapping and extortion attempts and God knows what else for people in our bracket—sometimes I wish we were poor again—well, he doesn't tell me and I don't ask.' She stirred her coffee glumly. 'I guess I have to ask now, if someone's going around killing people in my family, don't I? Oh, stop weeping, Emily, you'll weaken the coffee.' She wiped her nose angrily and drank, holding the cup firmly in both hands.

She heard Doan's footsteps in the carpet before Neil did, jumped up and ran to the door, and threw herself into his arms as he stepped through the kitchen door.

'Hey, great, whoa—Neil Kelly, you old son of a gun!' The big man, now a good forty pounds heftier than when he was a fastballing rookie pitcher, encircled his wife with his left arm and reached out to shake Neil's hand. 'What brings you in this direction? Hell, Emmy—is something wrong, honey?'

She blurted out the few raw facts of her sister's injury and De Sales's death without letting go of him. He stared down at her face unbelievingly.

'Neil—?'

'It's true, Doan. Sit. Here, have some of this good coffee. It's all crazy, but it's true.'

Obviously dog-tired after a long day, Doan Mitchell sat his wife on one stool and eased himself on to another and took a long gulp of the black coffee. 'Heck, I can't sit on these little things with my big behind; come into the living-room and tell me what's going on in there.'

They trooped back into the front room, and Doan sprawled with a sigh of gratitude on the vast sofa and eased off his boots. Neil, after a pleading look from Emily, repeated the horror story of the bombing briefly, then added, as logically as he could, all the other things that had piled on top of it since nine that morning. He glanced at his watch as he spoke and realized that it was now Sunday morning, even in Santa Fe, and had been Sunday morning in Boston for several hours. No wonder his own energy was beginning to seep away to zero.

When Neil had finished, Doan rubbed his face and said, 'Jeekers Crow.' It was as close to swearing as Neil had ever heard him come. 'You told me,' he said to his wife, who had curled herself into the crook of his arm, 'that Babs called you last week and said they'd be over as soon as they got the house open. Wasn't she going to photograph birds this year? She's crazy about birdwatching when she comes out here, Neil, you know, just crazy about it. And then we didn't hear from them, so we figured old De Sales got himself called back east suddenly, they'd be back, you know?' He squeezed the tiny woman against him in a protective bear hug. 'You mighta been right when you said big business wasn't worth all the hassles, honey. It sure isn't worth getting your goldarn head blown off.' He sat upright suddenly, ready to act. 'You going to Boston in the morning, see Babs, Em?'

'I thought I better call Jane first. Find out if she's conscious. Neil says she's in some kind of a coma and they had to operate on her brain. I don't want to go all the way there and just sit in the lobby for three or four days.' She turned to Neil. 'Jane Wheeler? Doan's sister? You know her? She lives right on Beacon Hill, and she's a doctor, even if she's not at Massachusetts General, so she should be able to find out, shouldn't she? Don't they tell each other things they won't just tell civilians?'

They talked for another half-hour about what they knew and what needed to be done. When they returned to the subject of the federal agencies involved, Doan groaned.

'Shoot. I knew I never should have touched that first little government contract. Now they'll be buzzing around the office like goldarn vultures.'

Neil knew then the answer to his earlier question in the

kitchen. 'Are you involved in some work for the government now, Doan?'

'Involved. I guess. I'm up to my behind in government work now. We did three-fifty last year, Neil, total. I'm not bragging, that's just a fact.' Neil knew he was talking millions, and dollar volume for his company's business. He didn't know if that was gross or net, but to an academic the difference was purely that, academic. His own dollar volume had peaked this past year when he got the fifty-thousand-dollar grant.

Doan shook his head. 'Of that, maybe one per cent is federal money. One per cent. You know what it will be this year, projected? Fifteen and a half per cent of gross. Yeah, you could say I'm involved with them. Mostly up toward Tonepah, but some at White Sands, some right here in Albuquerque.' To an easterner Albuquerque, sixty-five miles south, was scarcely 'right here', but to Doan it was obviously just down the street. 'Give me a real drink, will you, honeypie? I need to relax.'

Emily poured him a stiff measure from the Johnny Walker Black bottle. He took it, leaned over the coffee table, and picked up a framed photograph of a dump truck with himself, looking younger and leaner, standing with one hand on the front fender. He held it out proudly. 'My first fully owned rig. Now I'm so big I can mislay a rig like that for a month and not even know it. Before I bought that, I was borrowing and leasing and driving myself around in a ten-year-old pickup with that logo on the side. Nobody hiring FiFoChi Construction then knew that that pickup was my field office, my home office, and my whole operation. FiFoChi the First.'

Neil accepted the picture from him. 'Old Fifty-four Chicago rides again,' he said, and put it back on the table.

Doan grinned for the first time. 'I knew that number would be a household word some day. Industrial ware-

household word anyways.'

'You've certainly grown since then.'

'That's what Emmy's always saying.' He put both hands on his belly sadly. 'Oh, you mean my little company. Yeah, I guess you could say that. Not just dollar volume either. I've got tax troubles now, union troubles, industrial espionage problems, you name it. Everything in God's great world except woman troubles; I sure must be important.' He took another bite of his Johnny Walker and showed his teeth. 'I'm not De Sales Lacey by a long shot, but I've managed to grow, yessir.'

Em shook her head. Neil could tell she was proud of her man, but she was also afraid he would put his guest to sleep with reminiscences. 'Doan, honey, do you suppose maybe Neil might like to talk about *something* else besides FiFoChi?'

Neil shook his head back at her. 'No, listen, Em; to an English teacher, this is pure romance. I really want to know. Are you international yet, Doan?'

'By golly, yessir. Starting to be, anyway.' He leaned forward with new enthusiasm in his voice, relaxed by the Scotch and genuinely willing to brag a little. 'Fellow came over here last year from a bit outfit in New York, branches all over the Middle East. Got themselves a whopper of a contract to build some air bases in the Negev and God knows whereall else. Recruiter. He's trying to hire my best people right out from under my nose. I said to him, hey, hold on, mister, what are you trying to get away with? He says I'm trying to show these poor guys how they can do the same work for better pay, full living accommodations, faster promotions, and go first class all the way, R & R anywhere in Europe they want to fly, and bonuses at the end of every contract, Doan, he says.'

'Let me guess. You let him.'

'Like heck I did. I was ready to fire him out of here on

his behind until we started in talking. Then I came up with an idea.' He pulled his ear and grinned. 'Well, I didn't actually have it first. One of my managers suggested it to me one night after a foremen's meeting we were having in the office. Irishman named Keeney, heck of an engineer. He says Doan, instead of getting all hot under the collar about these Negev construction people, why don't we work out some arrangement with them to let them use some of our people during our slow months, you know, and let us subcontract some of their design work to do right here. Showed me how we could develop designs and deliver them visually, mind you, by computer, to them on site. Never even saw that technique before that. He says, let's put some of our own people as foreman interns or trainees right into their camps. Like lend-lease. Heck of an idea, especially when construction jobs started to dry up here with twenty per cent interest rates.

'Well, I laid that on this Curtis from New York, and he put out his tongue like a kid tasting peppermint ice-cream and just said, Doan, give me more of that. So I did. Oh, usual goldarn problems with unions and work permits and whatall, but by golly, Neil, we've got a whole generation of top field men training on their sites right now—general foreman for their asphalt plant, assistant foreman for their aggregate plant, one for structural excavation, and three kids assisting on piping—these are engineering students, you see? And they are going to be my people when they're trained. You know why? Because they'll start being family men then. Heck, that's the root problem for these people over in the Negev. You can't raise kids over there, take a wife. Couple of their people are interning with us right here. I might just steal them before I'm through—good men. I'm proud of that deal, Neil. Heck, turns out we've solved half their construction and design problems right here in New Mexico.'

He sat back and forgot his immediate sorrows for a

minute, a man in charge of his life, a successful man. Neil felt it was worth it to let him get away from his family's tragedy, even for such a brief while.

It was almost one-fifteen. They heard a motorcycle blare to a roaring stop outside and the carport door slam.

'Timmy, that you?' Em called out through the dining-room. 'Come in here and meet someone.'

A pasty-faced, slim boy in a leather jacket and black jeans, carrying a dark-visored riding helmet, came to the doorway scowling and pushing his mop of red hair back with his free hand.

Doan was on his feet. 'Know who this is, Tim?'

The young man glanced at him a second without interest. 'No, sorry. Should I?' He seemed to feel his parents' disapproval, and he took three steps toward Neil and held out his hand. 'Are you someone I met before?'

Neil shook his hand. Long, bony hand, but the good grip of someone who could wrestle a heavy motorbike easily. 'I'm Neil Kelly, Tim. I know your parents from way back. I actually saw you and your sister together when you were about six years old, when your dad brought you to Boston on a trip. I wouldn't expect you to remember.'

'Oh. Yeah, well, it's nice to see you, Neil. Listen, Em,' he said, abruptly turning from the visitor to his mother, 'I gotta be out of here early to meet some guys in Taos, so if you hear me leaving about five, it's just me. I'll eat on the road.'

Doan, tight-lipped at Neil's having heard the boy using his mother's first name and at his plain rudeness to a guest, put his hand on Tim's arm. Without bothering to shake it off, the boy moved casually away toward the mantel.

'Tim, listen, we got some very bad news tonight.' In as few words as possible, he told his son about De Sales and Barbara.

Emily interrupted him. 'Neil saw Aunt Barbara in the hospital. A man from the FBI was here—' whatever else she was going to say got caught in a flood of tears—'oh God, it's so awful. I'm going to see if I can fly to see her in Boston in the morning.'

Tim shot Neil a look of plain malice. 'You both know what I think about J. P. Morgan Lacey, Doan, so I'm not gonna say I'm sorry. It's too bad Barbara got blinded, but she wasn't exactly uninvolved in that capitalist empire of his, was she?'

Doan took a sharp, audible breath, and Neil thought he was going to hit his son. So did Emily, apparently, because she rushed to Doan and wrapped her arms around his and screamed at her son. 'Tim! Who do you think you're talking about? Barbara is my sister. Can't you get off your stupid, radical soapbox for a minute, one minute, and say something decent?'

Doan was rigid in his wife's arms, a giant of an angry man being gentle with a woman barely five feet tall. He spoke through stiff lips. 'Maybe you better forget about taking off with your friends in the morning and stick around here so we can talk when we're all a little calmer.'

Tim turned almost languidly toward Neil, at the same time turning his back on his father.

'Some family scene, huh? Did they tell you I'm the family disgrace? No ambition, don't want to make a million dollars, not willing to let them ram a capitalist education down my throat, and I don't share my family's awe for that hypocritical old bastard Lacey. I think it's about time he got what he deserved from someone.'

He zipped the cuffs of his jacket as he spoke and fitted his riding helmet back on his head so that his face was finally hidden behind the smoky plastic of the faceguard. Neil thought, how perfect the process they call alienation has become when our children can stand before us as nearly unrecognizable as aliens from another planet, faceless, without affection, and all but empty of the love we pour into them.

Doan spun him around by the shoulder with a long arm. 'Don't turn your back on me, Timmy, I'm talking to you.'

'You think I care?' The voice came flat and toneless and vicious from under the mask. 'I'm getting out of this place. Maybe I won't be back.' He shrugged off his father's hand and walked out the door without another word to his mother. On the back of his leather jacket, in the flowing script of the Coca-Cola slogan, was written *BG&E—The Real Thing.*

'Oh, Doan.' Emily sagged against her husband's chest, and now he held her. 'Oh, I'm so ashamed, Neil. He does that stupid—stuff all the time—' She buried her face in Doan's shirt.

'Goddam that boy. He's my own son, and I say goddam him if he'll talk like that in front of his own mother. He's a carbon copy of every delinquent on every TV show. I told you he got kicked out of Andover for screwing around leading some stupid kids' protest against something they weren't doing right.' He snorted. 'Krikey K. Christ, you'd think he knew something; you'd think he actually knew something the way he goes around spouting that stuff he spouts, but he's as ignorant as a hog, that boy, except for bullcrap and more bullcrap. Does he seem drugged up to you, Neil? You work with students. Could you tell if he was on some drug makes him act like that?'

The big man seemed both bewildered and ashamed; pain and fury were about equally mixed in his face. His language was certainly the worst Neil had ever heard from him, and he could only guess at the anguish behind Doan's profanity.

'I'm no expert, Doan. I know our kids often disappoint us for a long time before they please us. Listen—' he picked up his jacket from the sofa arm and put it on—'it's too late for me to do any more visiting. I probably should have gone home an hour ago. Let me call a cab and let you people have some privacy.'

'Like hell you will,' Emily said vehemently.

'Kind of hospitality's that?' Doan grumbled. 'We'll drive you back downtown, as long as you're too snooty to stay here tonight. You come along too, Em. We'll just leave this old place empty for a half an hour; it won't blow away.' He caught himself, realizing what he was saying. 'Someone wants to blow *us* up, we'll be out.' His wife tossed him a set of car keys from the mantel.

'Don't drive him home unless he promises to stay here after tomorrow. My car. I told him that.'

' 'Course he's going to stay here. 'Course you are, Neil. Wouldn't hear of anything else.

They went out the front door, leaving the house fully lit and unlocked.

'Let 'em steal it if they want to. If a man's goddarn own kids don't want it, what's it worth?'

The sleek Chrysler roared down the old Santa Fe Trail. 'Take it easy, honey,' Emily said, touching her husband's arm. After that, they slowed to a steady sixty.

The big man driving was still tense with his anger. He began talking bitterly to the night at large outside their speeding vehicle. 'When I started this darn business I used to say "suit" for "suite". I didn't know goddarned vichysoisse from Campbell's tomato soup. One lousy second-hand truck, one. Did half the work on that damn house myself; no one would hire me, so I hired myself. Damn storefront office, parked the truck behind the shopping mall. I know I'm swearing, Emmy, you let me get it out of my system. Debts up to my damn bellybutton. Had to insure the rig, but no insurance at all on my family. And that little pissant's too busy being some kind of a damn revolutionary motorcycle cowboy to realize he's got it made in the shade. Gonna save the whole damn world from people like me and his uncle, who built half the damn world he ever saw.' He whispered savagely the country boy's despairing epithet of sheerest disgust, 'Sheeit!'

Emily turned back to half-face Neil, who sat silent in the back, feeling his friend's shame. 'We thought he'd get over all that after he got thrown out of Andover and got back home. Linny was so sweet about it. She finished Dana, and she was accepted at Smith and Wellesley both, but she said maybe she should come back here to live. I know she talked with Tim dozens of times. They were so close when they were children. I could hear them arguing up in their rooms, with both their stereos going full blast. Good grief, if two kids living in one house sound like that, what does it sound like in one of the college dormitories?'

'Does Linn go to college out here now, even part-time?'

Emily scowled. 'Oh, it's so maddening. She's the bright one in this family. Like Babs was, you know? But now she doesn't want to go to college at all. First it was just take a year off to work at a regular job. Daddy gave her a job at FiFoChi, and I guess she's pretty good at it, too, if I do say so—'

'Darn right,' Doan interjected. 'I'd be glad to hire her again, darn it, but I don't want her in that office as a clerk. Go to college, I told her. Go to the goldarn Harvard Business School if you want to, and I'll make you director of business operations or whatever, or sales, or whatever she wants. Emmy thinks she's in love.'

'I know she's in love. With Barry Keeney. That engineer Doan told you about gave him the idea for the Middle East interns programme. It's as plain as the nose on her face; Doan just won't admit it. They sort of live together, I'm pretty sure. Linny has her own apartment, up near the Sheraton, Los Piñones.' Doan snorted again, but said nothing.

They were pulling in through the archway at La

Posada as she was saying, 'Here now, we've got you back home and all we've done is complain about family problems. I suspect they're not all that different from anybody's else's. Honestly, Neil, if you'll stay with us the rest of your visit out here, I promise you we'll avoid the whole dumb subject. I didn't even ask how your girls are. What a night.'

She laughed mournfully and leaned back over the seat to kiss him on the cheek. 'You get a good night's sleep now. Come back up about twelve or one, and we'll give you some lunch, okay? You can meet Will then. He should be back from his old bike trip with that outing club he thinks is his home. Oh, there I go again.'

Neil got out of the car and thanked them both. He wanted to add that they shouldn't worry about their kids too much, but he didn't want to sound like a hypocrite, even to himself. 'I look forward to meeting Will,' he said as a compromise. At fifteen, their youngest shouldn't be too hard to take yet.

As he let himself into his casita and prepared tiredly for bed, he wondered just how many affluent families like the Mitchells there were in this wide country, where so many millions of immigrant and country-boy dreams had turned to the sour insomnia of alienated children and rancid hopes.

CHAPTER 6

It was strange to wake to a morning light he had never seen and to mountain air as soft as silk on his skin. Neil went into his living-room, lit a kindling fire under a little tepee of piñon wood, and watched the light fuel catch and burn quickly. It was as light to hold as oak was heavy, and so resinous that he had a fire instantly. He squatted on the Navaho rug and stared into the little fireplace, which he had learned from Emily to call a kiva. He tossed into the blaze the page from his notebook that he had been holding in his hand, with Barbara's blind, shaky lettering on it.

Fire is the force in wood set free, a minor New England poet had said, and a still pond can be live steam; hot lava was raw rock. Everything in the world can be transformed some way. The wide red country he was in seemed to him somehow closer to the old gods of wood, rock, water, and wind than his own classical God whose name was Word, *Logos*. Yet it must be the case that logic would yield the same results here that it had always given elsewhere. His own sense of culture shock and old Governor Lew Wallace notwithstanding, there was, at the heart of this mystery wrapped in an enigma, some simple truth that would explain De Sales's death and Barbara's blindness and pain.

He was going to have to accept the hospitality of the Mitchells so that he could destroy it by betraying it. He was going to have to enter their house as a welcome friend, but one who had come to spy. There was no other way of observing Linn close up, and Tim could certainly bear watching if he returned. If he could vindicate Barbara's apparent faith—he thought *blind faith* for a moment—in Linn's innocence of connection with the explosion, that would be a happy discovery. Because Barbara must not have believed, before she was blinded, that Linn was connected with whatever she was investigating for the CIA, or she would have simply given them the girl's name. Given Slater her name. Neil had to keep an open mind, against all instinct to protect Emily and Doan, or he knew that all the inquiry in the world would only be a journey from false premises to prejudiced conclusions.

The telephone on the chest in the hall rang twice. He

answered it, expecting the desk to be asking whether he was checking out or staying for the one night still available on the rental.

'Professor Kelly, I'm happy to tell you that Jack Slater is madder than hell at you.' It was Mary Dowd.

'Good morning, Miss Dowd. If you're still in Boston, you're up early.'

'Still here. Our leader was rather pissed off to discover that you aren't. He asked me to tell you to stay put there at La Posada now that we've located you, because he will be arriving in Santa Fe just before one.'

'Are you chortling, Miss Dowd?'

'No, I'm gargling, Professor Kelly. Even as we speak, I am seated in my john accomplishing a variety of matutinal tasks with discreet but efficient simultaneity, at least until you asked and interrupted the sequence.'

'Why do you hate me, Miss Dowd, and feel this need to insult me? Am I entitled to ask that? Is it my taste in ties, or my wishy-washy politics, or the church of my choice that offends you?'

'I'm off your case, Professor, so it's really nothing at all any more. I do think you're a pansy of that academic hothouse kind who have contributed so much to the national malaise we all breathe in along with so many other pollutants every day. I know the type well; my dear daddy was one—but that's a matter for pity, maybe for contempt, not a rich satisfying emotion like hate. This is the last time you'll hear from me, Professor. I won't say it hasn't been cathartic meeting you.' There was the sound of flushing on the line, then silence.

Neil hung up the phone, then picked it up again and told the desk he would be leaving before noon. He wondered vaguely as he packed if all the romantics and extremists who did not join cults these days went to work for the government. He assumed that his apparent capacity to annoy them all must be grounded in some way on his preference for a life of small decencies over one of heroic single purpose. Or *was* it his taste in ties? He meticulously knotted a navy challis with a small paisley figure and went out to Sunday Mass.

The Royal City of the Holy Faith of Saint Francis of Assisi is a miracle in one respect only, perhaps; it is a walkable American city, centred on a quiet, small plaza, and with its commercial and domestic architecture under control.

Santa Fe is also a decade older than Boston. It was a sizable Spanish colonial capital when the local Indians briefly confederated and captured it in 1680, the only Amercian city ever held in war by Indians. It was better built and better defended after the Spanish retook it twelve years later when the Indian confederacy fell apart.

Neil strolled the three blocks to the Plaza, past the portico of the Palace of the Governors, which formed the north side of the Plaza. He circled the small square once in the Sunday morning quiet before returning east one block to enter the Cathedral of St Francis. Over the main doors, the name of God was written in Hebrew.

Mass was in Spanish, as were the sermon and the songs, led with robust energy by a group of dignified men with guitars standing to the left of the altar. For Neil, it was almost like celebrating mass in Latin again, and he gave the responses in the liturgical language of his boyhood. No one seemed to mind.

The morning air outside was still sharp enough, with a wind blowing up from the east and bringing some cloud with it, that he was grateful he had worn his tweed jacket. Seeking to prolong the calming effect the lovely little city had on his mind, he walked in no particular direction for twenty minutes and found himself outside a tiny counter restaurant out on Guadalupe from which irresistible breakfast smells were coming. The eggs he ordered were fried perfectly, the ham was crisp and thin, and his coffee was refilled twice without asking. Morning food like that made the missed meal in Leicester Square less of a painful memory.

He sighed over the empty dishes, paid for his good meal, and left, knowing that there was more painful talking to be done not far away and, beyond that, perhaps much more painful acting.

When he returned to La Posada to pick up his bags and pay his bill, Jack Slater was seated in his casita reading the Sunday *New York Times*.

'I see here in the *Times* that the well-known entrepreneur De Sales Lacey died in a tragic accident in his Santa Fe home just this weekend. Too bad. Paper says a fire, probably resulting from the careless disposal of smoking materials. When will people learn?'

'They should have bothered to find out that neither De Sales nor Barbara smoked.'

'Ah, but you see, that indicates a visitor. They should have watched whom they invited more closely.'

'Since the Securities and Exchange Commission takes a dim view of the suppression of evidence which might affect the market, I assume that the ghouls you work for were forced to allow that much news before the market opened again on Monday. I should imagine that De Sales's death would cause a pretty sharp drop in De Lacey Corporation shares. Was that the reason? Surely compassion for the families had nothing to do with it.'

Neil went right to his packing without any trivial courtesies.

'Drop about eight to ten points before it's through, I'd say. Second-level management just won't be up to the standards of your old pal Morgan. At least that's the opinion that a very interested investor in Beirut indicated when I discussed it with him. Awfully grateful for the inquiry, too, since it gave him a chance of Friday to avoid being caught holding a large portfolio of DLC.'

'Well, Slater, at least there's a biblical name for it. It's called making friends with the mammon of iniquity.'

'Oh, I know the name for it, Kelly. And speaking of names, are you by any chance going around telling certain people that you are Dr John Huffam?'

Neil searched the tabletops and upper drawers for stray belongings and shoved his bags out the door, saying as he went, 'Why would I do a thing like that, Slater?'

The agent's voice called him back with a laugh. 'Hey, Kelly, or Huffam or whoever you are, you left your pen next to the phone.' He walked over to the door and handed Neil the familiar silver ballpoint.

'Thanks. I thought I—' Then Neil remembered where he had actually left the pen. Under Barbara's bed in the hospital room in Boston.

'It was funny,' Slater said conversationally, picking up the bag Neil had put down and taking it down the short flight of steps outside, talking back over his shoulder. 'On the tape I could hear this click, and I couldn't think what it was. Did Mrs Lacey write something down for you?'

'You're a victim of your own devious mind. I just dropped my pen, nothing more complicated than that.' They swung along like old friends across the flowered grounds of the big estate toward the office.

'Now that makes twice you've lied to me, Neilo, that I know of for sure. That crap you gave me about Emslin and headaches was nicely done, but I kept asking myself why, the first time I asked you, you said, "I don't know what you mean, Mr Slater, sir." That was just to give yourself a few seconds to think up the headache story. I realize that now. You're fast, Kelly, but you're not perfect. I'm slow, but I remember everything. Everything.'

He stared at Neil with cold eyes. They were at the archway to the street, and Neil took the extra bag from him.

'Sorry I can't continue our chat, Slater, but I have to pay my bill and call a cab. No doubt you and I will meet again, since you seem to have the instincts and ethics of a burglar.' Neil went in through the door to the office.

A young girl came out from the inner office and showed him the bill for his casita and meal in the restaurant. He paid it with traveller's cheques, since he had left Oldhampton with five hundred dollars' worth in his pocket. Then he went around the corner behind the little souvenir shop to the public phones. One of the men who had arrived the night before, stil wearing his black Stetson and checked shirt, which was now stained, was complaining loudly into the first phone that he had called a cab twenty minutes ago and was still waiting and could they goddammit get out here and get him to the airport in time for his flight. He hung up disgustedly.

Neil said to him, 'You've been waiting for a cab, too? Is there another number, or just the one?' There was a framed yellow ad for Taxi service next to the phones.

'Goddam right. Hell, drank too much, missed the damn shuttlejack to Abbacue, gonna get my ass in some sling if I miss that plane. Just hope to Gawd I got enough money to pay the goddam fare.' He wandered over to the door to stare out nervously.

'Professor Kelly? Neil? Is that you? It is you!' The young woman running towards him from the big sitting-room behind the lobby could only be a grown-up Linn Mitchell. She was in jeans, sandals, and a white sleeveless blouse, tanned brown, her black curls pulled back under an indigo scarf twisted into a rope. He had forgotten she had violet eyes. She had become a stunning young woman.

'Linn? Hello—how did you know—'

'Mum called me.' She kissed his cheek and hugged him enthusiastically. Isn't it awful about Aunt Barbara? We just tried to call your casita, but we must have just missed you. This is Barry Keeney; Neil Kelly, Barn. We were going up there for a brunch anyway, too, so why not give you a ride? Mum told me about it. Honestly, I'm shocked.'

Barry Keeney came forward and offered his hand. He was a tall, lean, grey-eyed man with a boyish smile; blond for an Irishman, but on the reddish side of blond; full-bearded, and dressed as casually as Linn in sandals, jeans, and a blue polo shirt with an alligator on it. 'It's a great pleasure to meet you, Professor Kelly. I'm sorry for all the trouble you had to bring with you, but I'm sure the Mitchells are glad to have you here.'

The bearded man could have been twice Linn's age, but she was so girlish, and he had so much boyishness in his appearance, that it was difficult to estimate. The older Neil got, the more he noticed that everyone under fifty looked too young to be whatever they were.

Neil shook his hand. 'Please,' he demurred, 'both of you call me Neil. Wonderful, I'll take your offer.'

Barry Keeney picked up all three canvas bags in one hand. 'We thought we spotted you through the window, but it seemed your friend was going to give you a ride before we could.' He gestured with his head out the window towards where Jack Slater was sitting in his parked car.

'Him? No friend, just someone I ran into.' Neil realized immediately why Slater was sitting there. He would be right behind Neil's cab when it pulled out. On impulse, he stepped out into the foyer and spoke again to the grumbling cowboy, who was still sweating out his hangover and his late cab.

'I say, would you be willing to sell me your hat?'

'My hat?' The man took it off and looked at it dubiously. ' 's just a hat.'

'Well, you see, I promised someone I'd bring them a cowboy hat from the States, and now the stores are closed—

I'd be happy to give you twenty dollars for it. Would that be fair?'

'You must be English. You English? You sound it. Well, I dunno. I guess, well, I paid forty-two dollars for this hat in San Antone three years ago.' He made a painful calculation in his head while Linn and Barry watched in genuine puzzlement. 'I guess maybe I got half the wear out of it. Fact is, I could use the money. Could you go twenty-five?'

Neil laughed and produced the cash from his wallet. 'Sold. Delighted.'

He put the stained black Stetson on; it was a quarter size too large. 'Needs a bit of stuffing, eh?'

Turning to his companions, he winked and said, 'Shall we be off then, chaps?' The three of them went out the door and Neil made sure to stay on the inside of the group. Barry's car, a scarlet Trans-Am with 'TA 6.6' printed in gold on the hoodscoop, was parked just inside the driveway. Neil chatted foolishly about how he had always wanted a cowboy hat and hoped that they wouldn't think he was completely insane. He also tried to be nonchalant about riding in a car with blood red leather seats in an all-white interior.

As they were backing to turn and leave, the cowboy's cab pulled in, and the hatless man dived into it, hurling a couple of bags ahead of him and yelling, 'Get this goddam show on the road, boy, haul ass!' The cab accelerated into the street ahead of them and Slater's car made a satisfyingly startled leap after it.

'Do you really want that awful hat, Neil?' Linn finally said.

He took it off and scaled it into the back. 'It does smell a bit sweaty, doesn't it,' he answered lightly. 'Oh, that was just my good deed for the day. That fellow did me a favour yesterday, helped me get settled in, and I knew he was broke this morning and needed the cab fare.'

'Well, we have with us today, ladies and gentlemen,' Barry Keeney intoned over an invisible hand mike, 'the internationally famous Good Samaritan. I understand you're from England, Mr Samaritan . . .'

'You and Barry are going to get along just fine, Neil. I warn you, he's a frustrated stand-up comic.'

'Thank you, koind lady, as the Bishop said to Crazy Jane.'

'Please, Barn, do spare us the comic Irish bits.'

'Linn says you're some kind of detective as well as a scholar, Neil.'

'Oh, Barn, that was private. I'm sorry about that, Neil, but you are kind of unusual. I told Barry about when Pril got killed and you solving it and all that other awful stuff.' She glared at her lover and then looked serious. 'Now we've got an even bigger mess.'

Neil would have preferred to avoid the whole subject of both murders for now. 'What is it, Barry or Barney?'

Keeney nudged Linn. 'Ask her. My name is actually Barnabas, but when I came over here to school I thought Barry would be a good deal classier, don't you know. But she likes "Barn".'

'Where are you from in Ireland, Barry?'

'Ah, the Irish cry acrost the seas and the ages, *per omnia saecula saeculorum*, where are ye from?—Sligo, Belfast a bit, Dublin, bit of school in Germany, bit here.' He laughed. 'Bit of a bum.'

'My people were from Waterford. Well some of them.'

'If the rest aren't Irish atall, sure, what's it matter?' He grinned jauntily at Linn. 'Sorry, darlint, it shlipped out.'

'I love the look of Santa Fe.' They were threading their way through the first thick tourist traffic of the day in the Plaza. 'Now that I have had time to see a few bits of it.'

'Oh Neil, what a shame that it took a death in the family and Auntie Barb in the hospital before we could get you out here for a visit. We love it here. Barry had a chance to go to the Middle East this past year for about quadruple his salary here and a chance to run a whole project, but he turned it down to stay here.

'We turned it down, you mean,' the Irishman said. 'One look was enough. When I described it to Linn, she said, "that's no place for a wife." '

'That was going to be our big news today for the folks. We're going to get married, Neil!' She announced it as all young people do, as though they'd just invented the sacrament themselves. 'Can you keep quiet and pretend you're hearing it for the first time when I tell them?'

'Congratulations. I don't know a thing. When, do you know yet?'

'As soon as possible,' they chorused in harmony.

'Do you think we should keep it a secret until after the family mourning or whatever, this whole thing, is over with?' She obviously wanted some moral support to make her announcement today.

'I shouldn't think so. Your mother and dad can use some cheering up, and from the glowing descriptions they both gave me of your Irish friend here, I'd think your news would make them pretty happy.'

'Daddy thinks Barn is a genius. He's the only one—' she stopped to slap his hand away from her arm where he was pinching her—'who's ever won all the awards in a row that Daddy's company gives out. They have this Rookie of the Year Award, and he won that, then they give an MVP award for the most valuable contribution to a project, and he won that, and then last year he got the Triple Crown, which is so complicated I can't even understand it—'

'It makes me pope,' the driver said drily.

'—it means he did the best work in three project areas or something. Pretty good, huh?'

'For a foreigner,' Barry said solemnly.

They were swinging up the hill towards the Mitchell

house. As soon as the supercar was parked in the side yard away from the driveway, Neil got out, and Linn sprinted past him to hug her mother in the doorway.

At the door, Neil was introduced to Will, a lanky, shy, dark-faced boy with pleasant manners, who looked fit. 'I understand you've been out exploring the West on bikes.'

Will blushed, but looked pleased. 'Yeah, not much of it.' He had his father's big hands and feet, and he hadn't filled out to them yet, so that it seemed difficult for him to know where to put them.

Doan shepherded them into the big, bright living-room and told them that they had talked with his sister Jane in Boston and that she had told them to sit tight until she could find out for them about Barbara's condition.

He also said that he'd talked with a lieutenant in the local police who was a friend of his, and they were as unhappy as he was about having jurisdiction in this case taken away from them cold. The only new piece of information he had gathered was that the toy had been purchased out in a shop on Canyon Road. Neil made a mental note of the store's name, but wondered, if the police were effectively shut off from doing an investigation, what he hoped to accomplish.

They drank Bloody Mary's and waked De Sales and their suffering sister in decent Irish fashion. Neil told Emily that he had offered his mass that morning for Barbara's recovery and Morgan's repose and, for the first time that day, she cried again.

'Maybe I should start going to mass again. I married this darn old Baptist here, and not one of my kids has even a smidgin of religion.' She groaned at her own unintentional rhyme. 'Oh Neil, that's so sweet. I guess I'm glad some people still go to to church and pray, even if they're not going to a wedding or a funeral.'

Linn looked at Barry, raised her eyebrows, and seized the moment. 'Ahem.' Well, I won't say it will be in church, but Barry and I have sort of an appropriate announcement. Guess!'

The mother and daughter were in each other's arms with shrieks of 'Really?' and 'When did you decide?' and 'Isn't that fantastic!' while Doan and Barry shook hands and raised glasses to each other manfully.

Will looked at Neil cynically and asked, 'Does all the yelling and crying mean they're finally making it legal?'

'I guess it does, Will. A gentleman congratulates the groom and wishes the bride happiness.'

The boy shrugged eloquently and rolled his eyes, but went over to his future brother-in-law, gave him his hand and wished him good luck, putting gloomy emphasis on both words, as if it were a very long shot indeed. That seemed to be about the limit to his willingness to try out the gentleman's part in the family drama.

After that, it became much more like a good wake, with talk of the plans of the living far outstripping the fate of the dead.

Will drifted to Neil's side again. 'You a teacher in college?'

'Yes. Although I'm on leave for a while.'

'What college?'

'Old Hampton.'

Will looked mildly impressed. 'No kidding.' He took a handful of potato chips from the bowl. 'Some of the brilliant guys from Milton always went there. I used to go to Milton.'

'Your mother told me that you preferred to go to school out here.'

'Yeah. Well, Colorado. I'm on vacation too; spring vacation ends next Sunday. No place you ever heard of, not like Milton. I'm into rock climbing. You climb?'

'If you mean mountains and great sheer cliffs, no.'

'I'm into biking, too, a little.' He seemed determined to

find common ground with his visitor. 'You ride a bike much?'

'Are we talking about bicycles, and not motorcycles?'

'Heck, yes. Those things.' He made a face. 'Timmy and his stupid friends are all into motorcycles. The great BG&E.'

'What's BG&E?'

'Who knows? They all have it written on their jackets and stuff. Some stupid secret society. They're gonna burn down the world or something, I dunno. They don't make much sense. Like stupid Timmo says to me one day, he goes, "the human will is the one evolutionary tool not yet properly used to build the world." '

'Did he indeed.'

'How about this: they're going to set up "restraints that will compel new millenniums along new paths." '

'I predict an immense traffic jam with a lot of louts on motorcycles at the head of it.'

Will laughed delightedly. Neil watched him catch his sister's eye and react with acute discomfort to her clear, unspoken instruction to get his feet down off the coffee table.

'Are you going to enjoy having—' he indicated Barry with pursed lips and a tilt of his head, 'for a brother-in-law?'

'I don't know. I guess. He's smart, I'll say that for him. You oughta see him do math.'

'Nothing wrong with being smart.'

'He's funny sometimes, too. He's got a million puzzles and jokes and stuff. Like can you think of a regular English word, no names, that has six consonants in a row in it?'

'Sorry, not offhand.'

'He says if I can think of any, he'll give me a buck for each one.'

'And are you allowed to ask someone for help?'

'Sure. He says look in the dictionary, anything, he's so sure I won't get it.'

'In that case, tell him "latchstring" and "catchphrase" for two.'

'Hey, all right!' The boy darted across the room and stood in front of Barry with his hand out, explaining and collected two dollar bills.

He returned to his seat on the sofa beside Neil, beaming and shaking his fistful of money in triumph. 'Boy, I ought to go to Old Hampton and get you for an English teacher. I'd learn all kinds of valuable stuff. Now he says he'll pay half a buck apiece for ones with five consonants in a row, but only if I don't get any more help from you.'

'Well, not all my knowledge is that useful or negotiable, I'm afraid, Will. I promise not to leak any five-consonant ones accidentally. Then when you think of them, they'll be all yours.'

The boy ate more chips. 'I'll say this for old Barndoor: he can get stupid Timmy to listen to him, even if Dad can't.'

'Ah. Is that so?'

'I think Timmy's scared he'll belt him or something, and he knows Dad won't. Barn's the only one Tim doesn't give a hard time to. 'Course Barn rides a motorcycle better than any of Tim's friends, so they probably think that's great.'

'Did you know your uncle and aunt very well, Will?'

'Them?' The change of topic sobered him for a second. 'Not really. You know, they came to visit when they were out here, but we weren't friends or anything, me and them. I guess we're well off, but they're kind of super-rich, like the Rockefellers.'

'You never visited their house, or did chores for them, like cutting their lawn or anything?'

'Are you kidding?' He looked at Neil as if he had

mentioned riding a bike to the moon. 'Those people up there all have contracts with the landscape guy who keeps their grass green and all that.' He slumped back in the huge sofa again. Just as Neil was despairing of finding another topic at random to discover something about the Laceys, Will said suddenly, 'The cops are looking for Jimmy Lathen. That's what my friend Boyd says. He's the one who worked at that toy store out on Canyon, and they think he delivered them some kind of a bomb or something that started that fire up there. Do you know what's going on?'

Neil sat quite still and listened closely. 'I'm afraid I don't know much more than you do, Will. Who's your friend Boyd?'

'The guy I was camping out with on the bike trip. He heard this morning from somewhere, and he called me. Should I tell Dad and Mum?' He looked at Neil across the rim of his Coke glass uneasily.

'I'm not sure there's anything to be gained by passing along a rumour, frankly.' His mind was working furiously, trying to guess how a friend of Will's would have discovered that a toy bomb was delivered to the Laceys. Some teenage bragging across a hamburger? 'Let's say that just between you, me, and the flagpole out there that it would be awfully interesting if you could find out from your friend Boyd where exactly he heard that.'

'You mean it's true? Uncle De Sales got killed by a bomb?'

'Oh, that much is true, but no one's supposed to know it yet. The police have put a very tight lid on this whole thing. Will, and so if there is a piece of useful information like that floating around . . .' He didn't bother to finish, but looked at the boy's intelligent face and widened his eyes dramatically.

'I *knew* you were—' he dropped his eager voice to a whisper—'a detective. I told Linn about fifteen minutes ago, I'll bet he solves the whole case while he's here. That's why you came to visit us all of a sudden, isn't it?'

'May I let you in on a secret with absolute assurance of your discretion, Will?'

'Yes.' Neil liked the short, uncomplicated answer. 'Yes, sir.' He liked that even better.

'Nietzsche.'

'Huh?'

'Nietzsche. It's a proper name, so it's outside the ground rules of your game with Barry. It's the name of a philosopher, and it has five consecutive consonants. They're very common in Slavic languages.' He added absently, 'He wrote a famous book called *Beyond Good and Evil.*'

The boy looked at him, wondering if he thought he had answered the question.

'That's where those quotations from your brother Tim came from. Nietzsche.'

Lunch was an immense antipasto of Mexican foods and raw green vegetables dipped in something so fiery that it made Neil's eyes water. They ate out back, on a broad patio overlooking the town and the mountains beyond it—a view at once both spectacular and somehow calming.

Doan offered him a pair of field glasses in case he wanted to see anything better, but he preferred the broad, unspecific sweep so different from the small-scale, detailed landscapes of his own home valley.

'Do you know how many life zones there are in the United States, Neil?'

'I'm afraid I don't even know what they are, let alone how many of them there are, Doan.'

'Well sir, they're botanic zones, from desert to arctic. There are only seven in the whole country, and New Mexico has six. Heck, we've got five of them between here and Albuquerque. That's why we've solved so many kinds of engineering problems they can use all over the world. You can see we're up in the piñon and juniper zone here, about a mile and a half above sea level. By the way, watch out; you can get a fast sunburn in this thin air if you're not used to it.'

'He has a cowboy hat in my car,' Barry said, sitting himself atop the fence rail with a bottle of Guinness and a glass in his hand. 'Maybe you ought to wear it, Neil.'

'A little sun will do me good. It certainly feels good.'

Doan shifted around uncomfortably, tamping some loose dirt with his boot sole and looking off over the hillside again. 'That was De Sales's lawyer just on the phone—when I went in the house. What do you think, Neil; they're going to release his body tomorrow. Do you think he should be buried back east? They can't reach his brother, and poor Barbara can't decide, and I don't know if we should have him put down here, even if it's got to be changed later, or ship the body back to Philadelphia, or what. Lawyer says there's nothing in the will about it . . .'

Barry spoke, turning away from the women, who were talking about houses, and softening his voice. 'Why not have the remains cremated and stored until they can be disposed of as Barbara would like? It's half-done already, if that's not too macabre an observation.'

'You didn't know De Sales very well,' Doan said without reproof. 'He was an old-fashioned Catholic about some things, and that was one of them.'

'I'm afraid it's a family decision, Doan,' Neil said. 'Anything I could suggest would be beside the point.' Doan kicked a pebble through the fence and wandered back toward the women.

'You're a diffident man, Neil Kelly,' Barry said. 'Not being that myself, I admire the trait in others.'

'Oh, don't let one or two examples be taken as proof of habit, Barry. I often put my two cents' worth in—if I have the money.'

'The boy Will tells me you're a grand man for word games.' He scratched his jaw like a western country boy. 'That cost me more than two cents.'

'We were both making friends with the mammon of iniquity, I suppose. Will's an interesting boy, quite quick.'

'Yes, quick he is. Unlike his older brother. There's a thick one. Make a fine parrot, though. You met him?'

'Yes. I noticed.'

'Anyone who's talked with young Tim for ten minutes has heard all he knows and whatever he's memorized in the last day or so.'

'I understand he's been spouting Nietzsche recently.'

'Nietzsche, is it? Fancy. You should hear him do excerpts from the great IRA speeches, past and present. I won a prize once myself from the Brothers, reciting "Dark Rosaleen" and that sort of stuff, y'know, and he seems determined to impress me with Pearse and O'Reilly and that lot. Ireland Gaelic is Ireland free, and so on.' His eyes danced, and Neil knew with a teacher's practiced instinct that he was being put on somehow, tested who would be testing.

'You're not trying to make the boy into an Irish Nationalist, are you? An IRA terrorist?'

'Well, he's got himself a leather jacket, hasn't he? And he's bright enough—just about—to learn the rudiments of political philosophy as the bold IRA mouths it, isn't he, and he was born a puppet to do other people's bidding, isn't that obvious? Why, running off to Belfast and joining up with those boyos might be just the thing that would bring the man out in the boy.'

'Do you actually think he might? His parents might like to know if there's a real chance he'd do something that foolish.' The man's bemused, off-hand way of talking was beginning to make Neil's high, moral seriousness sound priggish.

'Ach, no, I don't think he will.' The Irishman took a pull from the glass of dark beer in his hand and wiped his mouth across the back of his wrist. 'Trouble with a beard, you're always wiping it off. He and that pack of motorcycle rats he runs around with seem to have some idea of liberating New Mexico first and giving it back to the Pueblos.' He grinned at Neil's polite incredulity. 'Fact. The Apaches rebelled around here back in 1680, you know, and this lot want to start a new Indian consciousness movement three hundred years after that to take back the state back from the Anglos—that's us—they're white and Anglo to a boy, you know, but that's all right. As I told them, the Irish Catholic farmers' emancipation movement in the old country was led almost entirely by Protestant landlords. Tim's lot didn't make it in 1980, so now they've got a five-year plan. Just like Russia. With time out to get high and race their bikes, of course.'

'And do you just tease them about it? Couldn't that be dangerous, letting Tim think you're seriously encouraging him?'

'I tease him to teach him, Neil. He'll never learn any other way. You could be right, of course; there might come a day when he gets his teeth into an idea just beyond the grasp of his mediocre intelligence, and then—who knows—he might either rise to real glory or get himself martyred for Indian rights. Pity.'

'Do they try to work with the American Indian Movement? That at least might give some direction to their thinking.'

Barry roared with laughter. 'Glory be to God, no. The AIM wouldn't give them house room. Or *hogan* room, I guess. Hogan's Heroes.' He emptied his glass and set it meticulously on the fence post. 'What I'm afraid is that the silly little bastards might have made themselves some wee bombs.'

Neil looked at him. Now the Irishman was looking off

across the landscape, as though he'd said nothing important.

'See, if you haven't been over there, you might not be able to recognize it from here, but you can just see the top edge of the Lacey's house over that dark patch there, about four miles out as the bird goes. The big white, toothy thing, that's their solar collector. Look through the glasses. A lovely piece of equipment, made with glass cylinders instead of panels. Much more efficient—'

'Do you actually mean that you think Tim and his friends might have sent the bomb to the Laceys?' Neil didn't mind sounding appalled; he was.

'Oh, I'd never say that to Doan or Emily, would you? Or Linn either, for that matter. She's his twin, remember. But consider this. The one small fact the thick-headed local constabulary were able to establish before they were brushed aside by higher powers is this: the only one besides the shop owner, a harmless woman, who could have got his hands on that toy to tinker with it before it was delivered, was the lad who delivers for them and cleans up the place, and so on. Do you want to guess what local youth activity he belongs to?'

'Ah. BG&E. They know that? Have they questioned him?'

Keeney raised his hands expressively. 'I guess they'd like the chance. If they could lay a hand on him. He seems to have disappeared. Presto, gone like the conjurer's boy up the rope.'

Neil reflected on what the engineer had said, and almost didn't hear when he was asked, if he'd like a slice of watermelon.

'Oh yes, thank you, I would.' The taste of summer from his childhood.

He was handed a thick, cold, red wedge. 'Nice thing about eating watermelon outdoors is that you can spit the seeds out and no one will complain. Will and I had a contest out here one day. My record is nineteen feet, seven inches. With the wind at my back.'

'I don't think I'll challenge that.' Neil took a satisfying slurp and chewed it. 'Do you ever plan to return to Ireland, Barry?'

'I'd think not. A long line of legendary heroes from Kieran and Patrick down to that joyful modern joker Joyce have tried to civilize the Irish and failed. I doubt it can be done at all. Ireland's destined to live out a myth, like Germany, and there's no rescuing the victim of a tragic fate. They'll continue to exile their brightest men and keep their most beautiful women to die virgins.'

'You don't think that Irish Christianity, which after all helped to civilize Europe, and the native intelligence can solve their problems if the British ever give them an unobstructed chance at it?'

'Ah, I like that. "Unobstructed chance". Fat chance. No, Neil, it's part of the mythology that they must have the English tormenting them while they ship their genius abroad to improve the rest of the world, leaving the island homeland to fools. The whole Patrick thing was entirely a fraud—you know that.'

'Overlaid with tales and pseudo-miracles, yes, but a fraud? Come on, now, more blarney from Barney?'

'Well, look at it. Patrick was supposed to have come over in the year 432. That's a magic mathematical number, you know. If you multiply it by sixty, which is the old Sumerian *soss*, you get 25920, presto, the great Platonic year of recurrence. The end and the beginning of the zodiac cycle. Patrick was nothing but the symbolic dawning of the age of Aquarius, the mythical millennium.'

'But of course there was also a year by that number—432, not the other.'

'Bloody coincidence.'

'But Patrick was consecrated a bishop by Pope Celestinus. It's a matter of historical record, and the pope lived, by a curious second coincidence, in the year 432. Shouldn't we apply the principle of Occam's razor here, and choose the simplest explanation consistent with the known facts, and not the fanciest one consistent with our prejudices?'

Barry spat a spray of seeds over the fence and laughed hugely. 'As anyone can see, I'm not a man for razors, Neil. Good-o. I'd hate to have you as a prosecuting attorney if I were up to be hanged.'

Linn joined them with a moue of disgust. 'Don't tell me this overgrown child has hustled you into a seed-spitting contest? Because you shouldn't be taken in. He's got some kind of weird catapult in his larynx or somewhere, and he can just spit farther than anyone else, if that's your idea of a gift.'

'No, we were discussing Irish history, Linn. I turned down the shot at the Guinness book.'

The lovely girl took her man's arm and hugged it to herself, standing on one foot like a child. 'Don't you just love him? Isn't he great?'

'Well,' Neil said, appraising them, 'I don't love him *yet*. Give me more time.'

'Sure, Linny wants everyone to love me, so work on that, will you, Neil? Your Uncle Neil is a lovely disputant, darling.'

'We were over there watching you two go at it, and Mum said, "let them get to know each other." She thinks you're a lot alike in some strange way. I won't say I don't see it, but maybe there's more to both of you than meets the eye.'

'Well, keep an eye on him; he's a slippery man in an argument, Linn. Perhaps in twenty years, after you're an old married woman, you'll know what you should have known back now.'

Barry picked her up, sat her on the fence, and kissed

her nose. 'Watch it, Linny. I think he's saying marriage is just a way of learning slowly what intuition teaches immediately.'

'I've got plenty of time, and I'm ready to learn anything there is to know about this one. No more education out of books for me; plain old empirical knowledge will have to do.'

'That's a painful way to learn some things, isn't it?' Neil asked her gently. 'If you fall off that fence on your bottom, it will hurt, but if you won't take my word for it, you'll have to fall off to learn that.'

'Okay, for *that* I'll take your word. Boy, you two! Mum's right.' She hopped down off the fence, gave them both a sarcastic shake of her head, and went back to her mother.

At that point, Will pedalled past them out of the yard—with a hand raised in apparent benediction to their adult foolishness—and shot off down the hill.

For another half-hour, Neil let Emily take him through her garden and admired Doan's playroom, but declined the chance to shoot pool. His youth hadn't been sufficiently misspent for that.

By mid-afternoon, he had begged off and taken himself for a rambling walk in the general direction of the museums. He was beginning to believe one thing: the psychologists were wrong about memory being the most dangerous fiction—it was experience.

CHAPTER 7

Walking along the skinny footpath bordering the main road, which was itself the original Santa Fe trail of legend and history, Neil harboured the unnerving feeling that he had entered a maze whose walls were invisible and whose centre would have no exit—only a deeper centre within it.

He looked up to watch some soaring bird he supposed a hawk riding air currents. He heard, but failed to see, a lazuli bunting, a horned lark, and a green-tailed towhee nearby, and saw—but realized with chagrin that he could not identify—the blue-purple-red blur of a painted bunting flying past his eyes.

A pointillist blot of tiny birds burst from somewhere, reversed their swoop across the air, and managed somehow to decide their next move in formation without breaking design. Neil admired helplessly; mere humans can only protest the difficulty of Gordian knots and their terrible profusion in life, accepting entanglement, finding themselves innodate, looking about finally for any sharp-edged instrument.

His encounter with Barnabas Keeney had given him the sense that he had entered a tricky magnetic field, or a mirrored fun house, where normal orientation was impossible. The Irishman's manic, almost musical mental energy and his own recent encounter with Dan Michaels both predisposed him to think in 'trickster' terms. The boyish, bearded engineer seemed drawn to taunting everyone—was that some sort of mild sadism?—to playing intellectual hit-and-run games. Neil had seen many students of that type in thirty years' teaching, child tricksters, but the Irishman was subtler, more mercurial, more brilliant than any student of his. He was not surprised that Keeney had listed Joyce among his culture heroes—Joyce, who had made a language of the idea of language and written a novel which was a city which was a sacrament which was the death and resurrection of a man, and who was either a great saint or a terrible sinner.

Where on earth did lovely young Linn fit into the puzzle? Why was it she, of all people, whose name Babs had scrawled in the notebook? Tim he might have understood. A delayed adolescent with an ignorant grudge against the world around him could be capable of any foolhardy action. It had crossed Neil's mind once already, and he let it again, that Tim's abrupt decision to leave the previous night might have been at least as motivated by his mother's mention of the FBI as by his unwillingness to join his family in mourning the Laceys.

Something was deeply wrong with the whole picture. They were not, as Emily had suggested, just another well-off American family going through a crisis of teenage resentment and rebellion. There were a number of other factors here that no other American family could quite match.

He had lived without a family of his own for so long that he felt insensitive to the play and pattern of love and hate and anger in their tensions. Maybe the addition of the mercurial Barry Keeney to the clan would provide a new organizational point, give young Tim an authority figure he could really respect. But when Neil thought about it, those were perhaps just the things he found it hard to associate with the charming elusive Irishman: stability and slow growth. There was, in a way, something both archetypally American and historically Irish to the throwaway quality of his wit and gifts, as though he had them simply to spend. He was surely what the mellifluous Irish themselves would call a devil of a fellow, a playboy of the western world indeed.

When he got back to the Mitchells', there was more bad news. Will was back, and it was he who had told them that the State police had found Jimmy Lathen dead.

The circumstances had caused Doan and Barry to take Doan's pickup and get themselves off to the scene of the grim discovery, just over the Tesuque Ridge, a few miles out on Highway 22. The boy's body was badly mutilated by a bomb blast, apparently in the cab of the truck in which he had been riding. Emily told him, with shock on her face, that it was one of Doan's FiFoChi construction trucks.

'Doan spoke last week about one of their field trucks not being on the job site where they thought it was. That must be it; that must be the truck. That crazy boy must have stolen that truck and taken off with another of those goddam bombs, and it blew up on him. Oh Neil, my God, what's going on? Is Doan going to be involved in this too?'

Linn spoke as calmingly as she could to her mother, asking Neil with her eyes to help get the conversation down to a manageable level. She added an explanation for Neil that Doan's sister had called from Boston, and that there was no change at all in Barbara's condition, and the doctors still didn't know how long she'd be in the coma, but she'd call back every morning and night until there was some change either way.

They finally got Emily to agree to stretch out on the sofa, but that lasted less than five minutes before she was up and getting after the leftovers and dishes on the patio.

'If I'm not busy, I've got too much time to think,' she sputtered, and made them leave her alone at the task.

'I'm frightened for Barry, Neil,' Linn said when her mother was out of earshot. 'Is that foolish?'

'It's a pretty normal reaction, I'd say, Linn. Tell me what you know about the Lathen boy.'

'Well, he's one of Timmy's crazy motorcycle gang, of course, although I think he's younger than any of them. I think he was three years behind me and Tim in school. The BG&E, God, they're so juvenile. Timmy and I have argued this a hundred times. I don't like the shape the world is in any better than he does, but those jerks don't exactly have any great ideas for improving it. I don't know, they think they're a sort of Ku Klux Klan or Hell's Angels or something in their heads—you know, vigilantes. They're going to give New Mexico back to the Indians and put people like Mum and Dad on reservations, that kind of thing. Honestly!'

'Will says Tim will listen to Barry, though.'

'They all will, apparently, for all the difference it makes. Barry's actually gone down there a couple of times—they meet out at some dirt track where they race their bikes—and banged around with them and tried to talk with them. He says it's like talking to the stones on the ground; they just stand around eyeing him and asking if he's got any pot.'

'Is the disappearance of a truck like this an unusual thing for Doan's company? I'd think something as big as a truck would get noticed.'

She shook her head and lit a cigarette jerkily. 'If Mum sees I'm smoking, she'll hit the roof. You'd be amazed. I can remember Dad and Uncle De Sales talking about inventorying their equipment once, how impossible it is. With one job down in Tucumcari and another one up in Taos, and leasing equipment to other jobs, and breakdowns and stuff in the repair terminal, Barry says most big companies are lucky if they can account at any particular moment for eighty-five per cent of their machinery. He says the Army's guess about their equipment is around seventy per cent. One truck is like one needle in a big hayfield. My new computer system cuts the error almost to zero, or it will when I get it updated, but nothing's perfect.'

'You did say *your* new computer system.' He made himself suitably impressed; he knew a cue when he got one from a fundamentally modest young woman who wanted to boast a bit.

Linn coloured nicely under her tan and brushed imaginary motes from her wrist. 'It's only a couple of months old. Dad sent me to take a course from IBM, and now everything's going to be on it. They have software programmes for construction companies, accountants, schools, you name it.'

'Don't tell me; let me guess whose idea it was to introduce computer technology into FiFoChi.'

'Two guesses, and the second one doesn't count. Who else but my brilliant boy-friend? Our inventory programme is named BARNDOOR in his honour. Get it? Lock it before the horse is stolen? He made about fifty improvements in the one IBM sold us.'

'He really is something of a flaming genius, isn't he, your Irishman?'

'Oh God, yes. He'd make a wonderful teacher. He'd kill you if you didn't learn, but he's so good at explaining things anyone could learn from him.'

'I'm glad I don't have him for a teacher. I once had computers explained to me by a gentleman at MIT who had helped invent one and taught it to write poetry—well, verse—and when he was through, I felt I knew just a little bit less than when we started.'

'I thought that's the way I'd be, really. But even I learned.' She smiled and put her hand over her eyes at an embarrassing memory. 'Once when I ran the programme wrong on a sub-contractor's backplan, the computer printed out: I WARNED YOU ABOUT THAT THIRD STEP. RETREAT REPEAT AND REMEMBER. It sounded just like Barry.'

'He must know you pretty well.'

'Honestly, I don't know what he sees in me. Oh, I know I'm gorgeous and all that—God knows boys have been telling me that since I was eleven, so I accept it as a simple fact. My purple eyes.' She blinked rapidly, mocking herself. 'But compared with him, I'm so dumb! I feel like his little girl sometimes. Oh God, he really is wonderful. I am so goddammed lucky you wouldn't believe it.'

'Ralph Waldo Emerson said once that only the weak-minded believe in luck, the strong-minded in cause and effect.'

'There, you see, that proves it,' she said, laughing, not

a bit fazed to be supported in her self-denigration by Emerson. 'Sometimes I just wish he would programme me the way he'd like me to be for the next fifty years and then turn me on and let me run. *He* says that if the government—' She stopped herself with an audible groan. 'Okay, Linny, shut it off. No one wants to hear any more about his nibs. If Mum were here now, she'd say that, so I'm saying it for her.'

Between them, they collected up the last few glasses and bits of leftovers and took them out to Emily in the kitchen, where there was still enough to be done so that everyone got an apron and a job that kept them busy without any serious conversation for the next twenty minutes. The closest anyone came to a tension-making remark was when Emily asked Linn if she had been smoking again, but fortunately her daughter disappeared out to the patio just then with a plastic bag of rubbish, so no answer was necessary.

The two men pulled up in the blue pickup while the chores were still being finished, and all of them immediately went, by unspoken agreement, into the living-room to hear their account of the newest incident.

'That darn Lathen kid killed himself with one of those homemade bombs, at least we know that. Truck's a wreck, blew the whole cab out, started a fire. Time the firemen got there, it was a goner, Boy got blowed out the side door partly by the blast, and they guess he crawled a few yards more before he died.'

Barry added a gentle comment, the Gaelic lilt in his speech accentuated by the cadence of his words. 'He had—he was carrying with him some kind of toy. In his lap, they think. Under his body it was, an Indian kachina doll, you know, sort of a man disguised as a god in the form of a great beaked bird. You see them in all the stores. They think the actual bomb itself was on the seat next to him, not attached to the doll yet.'

Neil asked, as much to relieve the tense silence as for any reason, 'Do they have any idea of where he was going, or what he was doing?'

' 'Course not. Tesuque's a little village, a sort of artists' settlement over there—guest ranch, nothing special, Bishop's Lodge,' Doan answered. 'You get on to 64 just beyond there and go out a ways, you get to the Tesuque Pueblo, little Indian village. Heck, all the highways come together there, 84 and 285. He could have been going anywhere: Los Alamos, Bandelier, you name it.'

'The truck was the one we're missing,' Barry added. 'It was simple enough to tell because we stopped buying those old Fords a year ago and started using these Toyotas like Doan's exclusively for light work. There were only about four of the Fords left in use. A terrible piece of tin.' He shook his head wearily, a perfectionist offended by built-in obsolescence.

Doan waved a hand irritably. 'You tell them, Barry.' He went to the drinks table and poured himself a Johnny Walker.

'Ah, I'm sorry to tell you this, Emily, but the state police are looking for Timmy. Not just him alone, mind you, but the whole mob of his motorcycle friends. They think they have some questions to answer about the truck and the bomb.'

'Jeekers Christ,' Doan exploded, hammering his open hand on the mantel. 'Those state cops aren't about to let go of this one now. They were pushed aside just like the Santa Fe cops when De Sales was killed, with all that federal whitewash and cover-up, and they are just like hungry pups with a fresh bone on this. Where in heck was that fool kid taking my truck and that kachina doll? It doesn't make sense. Heck,' he pointed out the window, 'it would at least make some sense if he was driving up my driveway—then we'd know he was mad at me for something—or driving into the company yard, but he was going off in the direction of nowhere.'

Emily sat with her hands clasped between her knees, looking from one of them to the other. 'Doan, don't say that. Why would Jimmy Lathen want to blow you up?'

'Why the heck would he want to steal one of my trucks, Em? I don't know. Maybe he was mad at me because Timmy told him I kicked him out of the house or something. How do I know what those darn fool kids think? Jeekers, I'll have to call Tom Lathen; remind me, Em.' He looked more miserable at the thought of talking to the boy's father.

'How would that bunch learn to make a bomb, Barry?' Neil asked. 'I can see them owning rifles and learning how to shoot by the time they're twelve in the great American western tradition, but bombs?'

'God knows. Easy enough, of course, for them to get the makings. Plenty of blasting stuff around any big construction job. But someone would have to teach them.'

Barry turned to Linn tiredly. 'Linny, I'm afraid the first thing tomorrow we'll want a site-by-site, job-by-job inventory check on all explosives, and not just a computer run. Call every clerk of works and get a signed statement of eyeball inspection and hand count, and compare it with the printout yourself. If they got those explosives from FiFoChi, we'd better know that too.'

CHAPTER 8

Slater turned up again while Neil was having a drink with Dan Michaels Monday noontime at the Staab House, on the sunny, white and green porch off the main lounge.

Neil was weary and discouraged at the prospect of ever making sense of what was happening and, without standing, he introduced the psychiatrist to the spy, using just those precise terms. 'Dan Michaels, this is John Slater. He's a spy. Dr Michaels is a psychiatrist.'

Slater was not apparently disturbed. 'May I join you for a drink? You live here in Santa Fe, Dr Michaels, or are you at the conference out at St John's?'

'Frankly, I'm surprised that anyone, even a spy, would have heard of our little conference of specialists. Just for that,' he leaned forward confidentially, 'it's not a very good meeting, I'm afraid. I wish now I'd sent my paper in by mail.' He had an afterthought and added, 'but then, of course, Professor Kelly and I would never have met, so maybe it was worth it.'

Neil said, 'We have been discussing the trickster as a psychological type, Mr Slater. Do you know the type?'

'Ah,' he accepted his drink from the waitress and sipped it, 'do I not, Professor Kelly? They put on funny hats, they duck out side doors; they perform all kinds of tricks. It happens even right here in River City.' He lifted his glass to Neil. 'Being a spy is no bed of roses, Doctor.'

Michaels unbuttoned the straining front of his wash-and-wear jacket, loosened his tie luxuriantly, and slumped deeper into his peacock wicker chair, giving every indication that he was settling in, not moving out. 'Are you spying on Professor Kelly?' he inquired blandly, beaming over his drink, his guileless blue eyes magnified by the thick lenses of his glasses.

'Actually, I've simply been trying to get Neil's attention long enough to have a friendly conversation with him. He looks mild-mannered and sedentary but, believe me, Doctor, he's the Scarlet Pimpernel when he wants to be.'

Neil thought he had been polite long enough. Slater, after all, had barged in on their conversation, and if he was intent on mildly malicious chit-chat, they could do it some other time. 'It's too bad you can't stay, Slater, but I know how busy you are.'

Slater turned a suddenly hard face to him. 'I have

another headache cure for you, Neil. Em's Linn. With two n's. It took a little while, but I finally found a place where they have it. Ever hear of a place called FiFoChi?' He drank again, slowly, savouring the tang of the lime juice and watching his companion's face. 'Right here in River City, you say, but not so. Not in the first instance, anyway.'

He knew that he had Neil's attention now. Dan Michaels sat back and watched both of them. 'We know that Em's Linn is Emily Mitchell's daughter Linn, and therefore the niece of Barbara Lacey. We know that she works for a construction company owned by her father, the company from which the truck which blew up mysteriously yesterday was taken. Now, listen to this one. Az-Zauiah. Got it? An Indian deity, you guess? Wrong. A friendly greeting in Navaho? No. Try Africa. Try Libya, specifically a place called Tokra, a satellite town of another place called Benghazi and you are getting warm. Az-Zauiah is the pride and daily joy of Colonel Moamar al Qaddafi, beloved father figure of Middle Eastern terrorists; it is his training camp, the best damned training camp for saboteurs and assassins in the world, probably, run almost entirely by Cuban instructors, and most recently in the news because it was proven to be the training site for the IRA Provos who blew up Mountbatten's yacht.'

'Aren't you getting a bit far afield, Slater? Weren't we interested originally in a small, ugly incident in Santa Fe, involving no Cubans, no Provos—'

'Are you sure, Neil?' Slater cut across him. 'Listen to this for a connection. Last month, an Israeli raiding party in Lebanon—I do apologise for the elaborate efflorescence of this conversation, Dr Michaels—'

'No, no, no, I assure you,' Dan Michaels said, lifting his pudgy hands to his chest, 'you are not boring me a bit. It is just like my business. In psychiatry also, one thing inevitably leads to another, and so on and so on.' When he smiled at the agent, his mouth made a small, wet flower.

Slater resumed his narrative to Neil. 'An Israeli raiding party picked up a whole stash of documents, most of which—ahem—' he coughed modestly—'we now have copies of. Our computers picked out one word or name or term from that list, all of the items apparently having originated at Az-Zauiah, which did not match up with anything else in the file, and it turned out to be the name of a construction company in New Mexico, USA.'

'FiFoChi?'

'Exactly. Now isn't that astonishing? Doesn't that make you just yearn to get down off your goddam high horse, Professor Kelly, and stop obstructing this investigation of what the hell is going on that resulted in the death of your friend and the maiming of his wife?'

Dan Michaels could see that Neil was shocked and for once not ready to rebut what had been said to him. The psychiatrist curled an uplifted finger at the waitress and made a circle in the air for another round. 'Isn't it a bit beyond the norm, Mr Slater, for you to be saying these things in front of a mere citizen like myself? I'm not sure if you are automatically enjoining me under some implied official secrets act—'

Slater was in command now, and he glared steadily at the fat man. 'When I walked in here, Doctor, you were told that I am a spy. There was no need of that, but there it was. I thought you should know the sort of thing that you, as a citizen, are getting from your spies for your tax dollar. Actually,' he paused as the new drinks were put on the table and the empties cleared, 'everything you just heard except the last detail is public knowledge. You could have read about Az-Zauiah in detail in the *Sunday Times Magazine* last month, complete with details about the IRA Provo unit training there. If I exceeded the limits of professional discretion at all, I'll just ask you to observe your own professional silence. Consider me a little crazy if you wish, and treat it as a patient's confidence.'

'That will be seventy-five dollars, Mr Slater.'

They all smiled differently at the psychiatrist's witticism.

'Now, now, Doctor,' Slater said, admonishing him with a finger, 'when you directed the personnel psychiatric review for us at Langley in '78, you were cleared and given a classification rating as high as my own, *n'est-ce pas?*'

Michaels bowed like a rug salesman, with a small bunch of fingers inserted into his belly below the sternum. 'I'm just a girl who can't say no. It's not a particularly deep secret, is it, since I list it on my *curriculum vitae*—to the dismay of some of my colleagues.'

'You were first identified when you were photographed, along with everyone else who was spotted coming from the airport with Neil Kelly on the shuttle bus.'

'The nun too?' Neil asked.

'The nun first. So far as we know, your meeting with Neil here was strictly chance, but I am rather fascinated by the close tie that seems to have developed so rapidly between you two.'

'Take another picture if you must,' Dan Michaels said, posing in profile with his hands spread. 'This will probably be the last time anyone sees us together. Neil doesn't want to write a book with me.'

Slater spoke behind his hand to the psychiatrist, in mock Bogart tones. 'Just between you and I, Doc, were you two really only talking about psychological types and all that jazz?'

'My oath on it, sir,' Michaels wheezed back in his best Sidney Greenstreet manner. 'I was explaining to Neil that even the Catholic church in the High Middle Ages had ceremonies in the great cathedrals designed as fools' masses. Donkey braying, and all sorts of shenanigans. The feast of April Fools itself probably descends lineally from those rites, although they are banned by the church now. Nietzsche parodied the event in the asses' mass in *Thus Spake Zarathustra*. Pure blasphemy, of course.'

Neil was the first to speak again after they had all taken a drink. 'I have no idea why FiFoChi turned up where it did, Slater. I do know that you'd find out a lot faster by asking Doan Mitchell, and not me.' He had been remembering something that made him feel better. 'Since Doan's construction company has contracts in the Middle East, isn't it possible that his projects have been marked for sabotage by terrorists?'

'We are looking into that end, Neil,' Slater said pleasantly. 'And I am also asking you to arrange for a talk with Doan Mitchell. Away from his home and his office. I think you know that our, ah, brother service in Washington has some doubts about the correct jurisdiction in this matter, and so we are in the ridiculous position of having to operate clandestinely here.' He turned to Dan Michaels. 'You have no idea, Doctor, since Watergate and all that nonsense, how many ways politicians have found to impede the conduct of my craft. As a concerned citizen, you might like to write to your senator and complain; every letter counts, they say.'

'Why should I?' It was Neil answering him.

Slater looked frankly disgusted. 'Are we back to petulance and suspicion again, Neil? Don't you trust me? Haven't I put all my cards on the table, even beyond the bounds of propriety and good sense? Don't you realize that my spy's licence might expire if Mr Big even finds out I'm sitting here telling you two uncircumcised—sorry, Doctor—civilians all the secret passwords and everything? Because we need to talk to him, Neil. Either him or his daughter Linn, whose name also turned up in the Libyan materials just yesterday. As *Emslinn*, no less.' He had saved that until last.'

Neil expelled a slow breath and tried to absorb this new

fact. 'Hazlitt was right. He once said, "What stubborn things are facts." Perhaps you and I and Doan Mitchell could meet this evening. I know he went to one of his job sites somewhere this morning. Eight o'clock? Where?'

'Eight is fine. I'm at Bishop's Lodge, over at Tesuque. Where that boy had that nasty accident yesterday, nearby.'

Neil thought he understood the answer to another question now.

Dan Michaels now got up and excused himself. 'You won't believe this, maybe, but I have a date. Have I got a date! With a rich, thin, divorced *shiksa*. I owe this all to you, Neil. Until you told me they were here, I never noticed. She's not old, she's reasonably nubile, lubriciously mobile, and not the least bit hostile. She is jocose in her liquor, but neither lachrymose nor bellicose. I think I died and went to heaven last night. Why am I standing here? A lovely evening to you both.'

Neil checked the bill and paid for the drinks with more of his traveller's cheques. As he and Jack Slater rose and walked toward the courtyard, he asked the CIA man the question that had been irritating him.

'Perhaps you'll think I'm slow to catch on, but why can't you people and the FBI just communicate with each other? In the old-fashioned sense of exchanging information? We concerned citizens who pay your salaries do rather expect a certain minimal degree of cooperation among all you public servants.'

Slater laughed ironically. 'Have you met Agent Cady, Neil? Federal Bureau of Investigation Regional Representative Russell Cady?'

'Briefly.'

'Then you know that he's an ethnic policeman, finest kind of ethnic policeman.'

'My own immediate immigrant ancestors included a number of ethnic policemen. I don't see the point.'

'You're talking about Irish policemen, Neil. The Irish expect to grow up to be policemen, so when they do it doesn't unbalance them. Agent Russell Cady is a Native American policeman. They *never* expect to grow up to be policemen, so when one of them does, especially a Native American anus like Cady, it makes him temporarily insane. Agent Cady has taken some anthropology courses—cultural anthropology you can be sure—which is practically virulent for them. He has probably read the collected detective stories of Tony Hillerman. Agent Cady thinks he is Joe Goddam Leapinghorse, the inventor of interracial suffering. Agent Cady is the person you always thought I would turn out to be, Neil, a dyed-in-the-wool stereotype. Did he tell you about his goddam heart beating for the buffalo and the antelope?'

'I'll tell Doan you want to talk. Eight o'clock. If not, I'll call.' Neil walked away without waiting for a reply. Jack Slater was a bit of a shape-shifter himself.

CHAPTER 9

Neil had not seen Will since he had pedalled away the previous day and then come back with the news of the second bombing. When the boy drifted into the living-room about five that afternoon, Neil put aside the Mitchell family photo album he was leafing through to ask him more about his school.

'I was looking at some of your climbing magazines this afternoon, Will. Do you do a lot of climbing up at your school?'

'Hi. No, not exactly. I mean, a few kids are into rock climbing, but it's not a credit sport.' He exhaled a mild vulgarity. 'I figured if I transferred to Colorado, for Pete's sake, there'd at least be more climbing than in Massachusetts.' He threw himself on the other end of the sofa, putting his feet up on a pile of *Outdoor* magazines. 'The guy who wrote that article there, in *Outdoor*? He teaches back in Massachusetts. He's even from Colorado, and he's written about a million books about climbing, and he's back there. I might have to go back east to college just to get some good instruction. If I go at all. I'd like to just ride my bike all over Europe for a couple of years, see everything.'

Neil knew undergraduate restlessness when he saw it. 'Are you having some doubts about whether school is worth the effort?'

'Not really. Yeah, I guess. It's worth it, if you know what you want to do, but I dunno.' He grimaced. 'I'm supposed to be doing a term paper for old Folsom in English this vacation, but I can't even read the dumb book he assigned. He'll burn me, too. His name's not really Folsom; it's Fulton, but we call him that because it's the name of the oldest man in North America. He's about a million years old. His grandfather knew Lew Wallace, for cripes sake.'

'Ah, then you're just the person to tell me something I want to know. Is the Lew Wallace who was the territorial governor out here the same one who wrote *Ben Hur*?'

'Boy, would old Folsom love you. Yeah, he didn't only write it, he wrote it down in his office in the Palace of the Governors. Because Billy the Kid was supposed to be after him, so he went in there and pulled down the shades, whatever good that did, to write. At least that's what Folsom says. Billy the Kid must've seen the stupid movie and wanted to kill the guy who wrote the stupid book.' He laughed self-consciously at his own joke, and said, 'I guess we're not exactly supposed to be making jokes about killing people right now, sorry.'

'That's what humour was invented for, Will. Christopher Fry says laughter is the surest touch of genius in creation, so I guess cracking a few jokes isn't going to do any harm. Lots of fun at Finnegan's Wake.'

'You think they're going to arrest Tim?' The boy scrunched down in the cushions and studied his running shoes intently. They were yellow and blue, and broken through in ten places, but Neil knew they didn't need all that attention. It was as good a way as any to keep from crying.

'They're certainly going to round up everyone in BG&E and take them in for questioning.'

'Poor Jimmy.'

'Indeed. Was he a friend of yours too—I mean as well as a friend of Tim's?'

'Not really. Well, sort of. I wouldn't say a friend, but he wasn't really solid with BG&E; he was sort of a rookie with them. He was pathetic, always trying to please those older guys, trying to impress them, you know, drinking hard stuff and smoking pot and all that.' He chewed his lip and studied his shoes from a new angle. 'They used to get him to do all kinds of crazy stuff for them, errands and driving them around. He was a wild driver. He said he wanted to drive stock car races as soon as he was eighteen. I don't think he stole Dad's truck, though, you know why? He was real honest about stealing, because he was a Born Again Christian. Those other guys don't care what they take, but this preacher from California who converted Jimmy was really death on stealing. I guess he did time in jail for it. That and sex stuff. Timmo used to tease him, call him Preacher Lathen.'

Neil saw two possibilities in that anomalous fact and thought about both of them at once. Obviously, one or both could be at the bottom of Will's misery and roundabout rhetoric. Since Will appeared to be unable to broach the real subject, Neil thought it time for another direct question.

'Do you think Tim told him it was all right to use the

truck—lent it to him on his own authority, as it were?'

Will groaned. 'Isn't that what the cops think? And if he did, doesn't that mean he knew about the bomb and where Jimmy was taking it? Does that make him an accessory to manslaughter or something?'

'Do you think you know where Tim went, Will?'

'I dunno. Maybe. Who knows. The cops already found Alfie Dunne and Dougie Jamison and Foo Foo Gene—that big guy; I never knew his real name, I guess he's a retard—they were all up in their cabin near Taos that Foo Foo's old man gave them. At first, I figured Tim would be there too, but him and Dally—Dickie Dally—weren't there. They're the ones the cops are still looking for. They thought they might've come here to hide because Mum told them he didn't take any clothes and stuff with him when he left. That Indian FBI guy was here with some damn search warrant or something when you were downtown. I think that car up in the Lillienthals' driveway up the hill is another FBI guy on stakeout in case Timmo shows up here. I saw them talking to Mrs Lillienthal, and I guess she gave them permission. She would. Every time I go out, I can feel them putting the binocs on me to see if I've got red hair.'

'Listen, Will. I want you to not let this thing get to you. If you do, you'll either lose the ability to think straight or you'll start being an additional problem for your mom and dad. Perhaps both. I know that you think I'm here as some sort of detective. The fact is I'm as bewildered and confused about what's going on as you are, but I shall keep trying to think logically, and if I can help discover who killed your uncle and Jimmy Lathen—assuming their two deaths are indeed connected—and put your aunt into the hospital and blinded her, I'm going to do it. Now, given that, shall we pool our intelligence and try to figure a few things out?'

The boy shrugged without taking his hands from his

pockets. 'Sure. I guess. But what if—'

Neil knew what he was trying to blurt out, and cut across his question. 'No matter what we find out, if it's true, it's worth knowing. Let's just say that we're out to discover the truth about as many parts of this puzzle as we can.'

'Does that mean the facts won't hurt anyone? 'Cause if they do, I guess I don't believe them.'

'Not the facts. Facts can hurt all kinds of people. Crashed trucks and toys that blow up in your face and all sorts of things are facts, but collecting facts and arranging them into endless patterns to see what they mean is what detection is all about, what inquiry is, scientific or any kind. When the police have their pattern, they will have the answer to their problem, which is who killed whom, and when and where. But let us be concerned with the question behind all that and ask ourselves why. That's the truth of it, the why. Not just motive, mind you—an impulse of anger can be a motive—but the deepest reason X did this to Y, that's the farthest truth we can know on earth. Are you with me?'

'Yes.' There it was again, the simple, admirable answer. 'Mr Kelly, do you think people can really be evil? You know what I mean?'

'Yes, Will, I know what you mean, and it's a terribly important and profound question. Yes, I do. I know it. People can choose to do what they know will bring unhappiness to others; can even choose deliberately to make themselves unhappy; can choose their own eternal misery over the opposite.'

'Then I guess you believe in hell, huh?'

'If I were God, Will—and every teacher, as you well know, likes to think that occasionally—I'd give people free will, but I'd warn them that if they choose to use it to be unhappy and to make other people unhappy, to make the world wretched, then they will get exactly what they chose as their result. I think heaven and hell are the result of our choices, not the rewards or punishments for them.'

'Wow.'

'Wow is for fireworks, Will. Or other mysteries of the beautiful, like pretty girls in summer dresses. "Wow" might do as a response to Mozart, if you can't jump up and down, but not for ideas. Never for ideas.'

It occurred to Will for not the first time that their visitor was interesting, but a little weird.

As if he might have been reading the boy's thoughts—or as though after thirty years of teaching boys, he knew what they thought—Neil added his own afterthought. ' "Wow" is for what's weird. The three witches, those rump-fed runyons in *Macbeth*. It's an old English word for what they thought the whole universe was like before St Augustine told them about the logos. Sorry, Will, end of class.'

He stood and walked over to the mantel, where a number of family photos in small lucite blocks were stacked in a small pyramid. He studied the picture of Tim at fifteen, about Will's age, still grinning in rather a shy, winning way, his mop of red hair down over one eye, wearing a t-shirt celebrating the Beatles. 'Who is actually leader or president of the BG&E, Will?'

Will was looking over his shoulder at the picture showing the whole family clutched in a group, arms around each other, hamming and laughing. 'That's us at the lake. We haven't been there for about five years. I guess Tim is. BG&E—the name? That was Tim's idea. They used to be the Hawks, and some of them were the Space Flyers before that. Tim thought those up, too. He's pretty good at convincing people to do things the way he wants to.'

'I was studying your family's album. You took an awful lot of pictures that summer at the lake.'

'That was the greatest time we ever had. Dad stayed down for about a month—we hardly ever used to see him during the summer because it was his busiest season – and we had a blast.'

'If you were hiding-out Tim, where would you go?'

'You mean if I were me or if I were Tim?'

'Either.'

'I would've bet Timmy'd go up to Taos, where they race their bikes and have the cabin and all that stuff. Me, I'd go down there, to our old place at the lake.'

'Might Tim go there? If he thought Taos was too dangerous for him? Remember, the last time you were all there, he was just about your age, and even if he's different now, he doesn't seem all that different from you back then.'

'Yeah, he might. He knows it's empty in spring 'cause the people who rent it now sent us a cheque last week and said they'd be there in July. Tim asked Dad why he didn't sell it to them if we weren't ever going to use it again.'

'How far would you have to travel to get there?'

'I dunno exactly. Two hundred miles? Down toward White Sands, I guess it's actually in Cloudcroft. We made it in three hours in Dad's Chrysler once when he wanted to go fishing.'

'What's the farthest you've ever ridden your bike, Will?'

'My bike?' The excitement of realization was making his face shine. For an instant, Neil was saddened by the vulnerability, the accessibility of the young. A skilful adult could really manipulate any of them if he chose to.

'When Boyd and I went camping last week, we did eighty miles a day both days. I've got a Fuji with special hubs. Twelve speeds. And a really beautiful French derailleur.'

Since Neil's own bike was a sturdy, venerable Rudge with three speeds, black and bent, he didn't have the slightest idea what Will was saying, but it sounded impressive.

'Now listen, Will. If I, or anyone from the family, were to leave here in the company car with your father's logo on the side, that gentleman up the hill is simply going to follow us all the way to White Sands or anywhere else. But if you pedal out of here with a daypack on your back, and perhaps a sleeping bag rolled under your seat, no one is going to bat an eye. Leave off your helmet, at least until you're away, so that he'll know it's you, and just ride away as though you were heading for a friend's house. Are you willing to try? To see if Tim is down at the lake?'

Will nodded wordlessly.

'Good man. Here's what I want you to do . . .' For the next half hour, Neil outlined to the nervous, skinny boy what he wanted him to say and do if his brother Timmy, with or without his friend, was down at the lake house. He helped him pack sandwiches, gave him fifty dollars for emergencies, and slapped him on the shoulder. 'If you break your own record, you might be there Wednesday night. I'll explain to your parents. Watch yourself, and call me—don't be impolite to anyone else who answers, but tell them I want to get your message personally. Call whether he's there or not, okay?'

Watching the casual wave Will gave as he eased out of the yard, and knowing how hard his heart must be pounding against his ribs, Neil recalled what it was to be a young athlete starting out at the sound of a starter's pistol, all nonchalance, inner tension, and adrenalin.

The car in the Lillienthals' driveway flashed binoculars at the window briefly, then stayed where it was.

Emily and Linn had gone to the funeral home where the autopsy had been done on De Sales and where his remains had been kept since, until their official release that morning.

Fortunately, De Sales's brother Connell had called from Chicago at about nine o'clock in the morning to say that he was flying out, and with the usual confusion of purposes and good intentions common to complicated inter-family rites, had been forestalled. It was finally agreed that he would turn around and head for Philadelphia, where De Sales's attorney was going mad trying to answer questions and fend off company officers who wanted to stop the slide of DLC stock, which was down six points since the market opened. Con, who was a modest edition of De Sales, no tycoon but a solidly successful insurance man in downstate Illinois, agreed to handle affairs in Philadelphia and see to the interment. He had been as confused as could be expected under the bizarre circumstances surrounding his brother's sudden death.

Before they left, and while Emily was still up in the bedroom getting dressed in something suitable for her errand, Linn sat down across from Neil in the chair cornered with the sofa and surprised him.

'I've been deceiving you, Neil, and I'm sorry.'

'How on earth? Are you really a redhead?'

'I'm serious. It's about Tim. We're pretty close, you know, the way twins are. We used to be like that.' She twined two fingers. 'But now we're more just touching.' She put the tips of two opposite fingers together. 'He was such a sweet boy, like just a little while ago. Now that gang of nuts he hangs out with—' She took a deep breath. 'I sort of implied that we were out of touch. Well, that was kind of a copout. We had a really good talk just about two weeks ago, one day when he was feeling he didn't have anything to prove, I guess. Actually, he had some really good grass—Mum would kill me if she could hear this—and we both had a couple of joints between us, and he got nice and relaxed and started to joke around. It makes *me* feel stretched out, you know? Like I feel skinny, as if I'm a mile long, but all it does to Timmo is sort of get him back to his nice, natural self; he's so tense now.'

Neil thought of all the things children do, thinking their parents would keel over at, and then of the casual horrors they entertain without ever imagining that anyone rational would be concerned.

'He wanted to talk about going to work at FiFoChi.

You could have knocked me over with a feather, and he made me swear I'd never tell Dad, at least until, you know, he had a long time to think about it, but he wanted to know about the new computer system. He thinks maybe he'd like to get into computers, and when I explained how we used it, and how we can link up with other people's computers and run everything from payroll to inventories, he really got excited, you know, the way he used to about stuff when he was a kid. He used to love gadgets.'

'I suppose most people who love motorcycles and that sort of thing think of them as gadgets.'

'I really think they are to Timmy. He's really gifted at figuring out how things work. Once he worked out a way of playing taped musical notes into the telephone, and he and his friends called Paris free. Dad found out, though, and I thought he was going to murder him. Ugh. Nice going, Linn.'

'Was that all there was to it, just Tim asking about a possible job at the company?'

'Not quite. The next day, Barry and Dad were both flying down to Tonepah for some conference about a contract, so Tim came to the office and I showed him the set-up. Naturally, after ten minutes, he begins to sound as if he knows more than I do about it. He had some dumb course in high school, and I had this special seminar at IBM.' She paused, as if trying to frame a delicate remark. 'For a test run, I showed him how to locate a piece of equipment that wasn't tied up in repairs or on a job, you know, as an example of what the programme could do.'

'And you think he might have had an opportunity subsequently to utilize that knowledge?'

'That's what worries me. I let him sit there in my office while I went over to the canteen truck and brought back coffee.'

'When he decides to show himself again—and I think

he will, honestly—he's going to have to explain all that.'

'If Barry could talk with him for ten minutes, he'd be better off. Barry told me he's willing to go anywhere to fetch him if he gets in touch with the family by phone or anything.'

Neil tried to recall whether he had told Will to speak only to him or if he had simply said not to tell his mother or father about Tim. For the life of him, he couldn't remember how he had phrased the instruction, to his immense self-disgust.

'When you and Barry marry—oh dear, let me phrase that again—when you two are married, that's better, will you both still keep on working for your father's company?'

'Can you keep a secret? Barry wants to start his own company. Don't tell Daddy, please, because Barry wants to finish up this big Tonepah project first and have his manager trainee ready to replace him before he announces that. He's an Iranian. I'm so proud of Barn because all during the hostages thing everyone gave Maimandi a terrible time, but Barn stuck up for him. He says he's really brilliant, and he hopes he can convince Daddy to move him up to project manager. He's this year's MVP, a sort of Moslem Barry. Oh, I know I sound gaga about his nibs, but honestly, Daddy's company, big as it is, isn't enough to keep one-tenth Barry's mind occupied full-time. Sometimes I think he's going to burn out a fuse just sitting around waiting for something to come up that's too complicated for him to do easily.'

'And you'll go along with him, is that it?'

'Well, like they say, for better or for worse. As if there could be a worse if I'm with him. Oh Neil, I wish I could explain to somebody what it's like to be in love with a genius who loves me—that's the frosting on the cake, with the candles and the writing that says "and they lived happily ever after," so help me!'

'Is he good to you?' Neil was startled to hear himself ask

the question, but he knew immediately what place in himself it came from. His mother would sometimes characterize the persons she knew, for good or ill, by summing them up in that phrase: 'he's awfully good to her,' which was her highest praise, or 'he's not good to her, and I'll have nothing to do with him.'

'Isn't that an odd question? Do you mean, does he give me things?' Linn seemed more puzzled than offended by the query.

'Not at all. I mean, is he good to you?' Sometimes the only way to make a student understand a question is to repeat the question so that she will know it means exactly what it says. Cummings was asked once after reading one of his poems to explain it; he patiently read it again.

'We're awfully compatible. We like the same things. We both love Fellini; we both hate spaghetti.' She seemed to be struggling to satisfy him without answering him. 'Philosophically, I guess he's a lot more sophisticated than I am, of course. He's much more educated. I'm a sort of a vague Unitarian, I guess, and he's, oh, I don't know, an existentialist? Sexually, we're very compatible, if that's what you want to know. Neither of us is exactly old-fashioned. Oddly, I think I've had almost as much experience as he has, and I'm not exactly Madame Récamier. Was she terribly promiscuous? I always thought her name sounded promiscuous. Now, is that frank and revealing enough?'

She had, he could tell, worked herself up into a state of mild resentment, if not incipient rage, and by the end of her little aria she was flushed.

'You mustn't think that the middle-aged are just sitting out here, safe in their decrepitude, judging you, you know. It's just that—this is really a ghastly presumption on my part—you seem to have such finely drawn feelings, to touch the world so much in terms of its value to you, while Barry is so much the intellectualizer, the abstractionist—a bit of a juggler?'

She sniffed. At his naiveté? 'If you mean I'm a sentimental slob and he's completely lacking in sentiment, that's true. He says I'll grow out of it, and I'm sure he's right. I'm already less of a knee-jerk bleeding heart than I was before we met.'

'May I ask you a further personal question without losing your tolerance completely?' 'She watched him from the corners of her eyes. 'Yes? Then tell me, if you could change one thing about Barry, what it would be.'

'I'd marry him tomorrow instead of two or three months from now. I guess that would really be changing me more than him, because I'd end up being the one with the new name, but even if it sounds corny, I think he's about the most perfect man possible. I'd be his mistress or his after-hours girl-friend or his damn scullery maid if that's what he wanted, but fortunately for Linn, he wants what I want—for me to be Mrs Barry Keeney.' She put an arm through his arm, as if wanting him to feel the reality of her words through her. 'With Barry, I know how men must feel with women. I want him to open up and take me inside his life and hold me there. He's good to me if he does that; there's nothing any better.'

By the time Doan and Barry had flown in from Tonepah in the company Learjet and been driven to the house, it was past the dinner hour. Emily had been home just long enough, after an exhausting day of attending to the details of De Sales's body being shipped off east, to prepare steaks on the gas grill, served with shoestring potatoes from a bag and a quick green salad. She, Linn, and Neil ate from the kitchen counter. When Neil explained to her that Will had wanted to do something useful, so he had encouraged him to take off on his bike to search their old boyhood hideouts for Tim, Linn looked sceptical and Emily looked relieved.

'At least he'll have the sense he's doing something. That poor boy, he's not having much of a spring vacation, and he doesn't know which way to turn with all this,' his mother commented.

Neil thought it worth an effort to calm her scarcely covert fears about her older son's whereabouts. 'I don't think Tim's likely to run very far for very long, Em, and so it seemed to me that having Will sort of on the lookout, asking around their friends, you know, wouldn't do any harm and might turn him up. I think he's a scared young man, and that being frightened has probably confused his thinking.'

'Tell me honestly, Neil. I don't know. Do you think Timmy and that gang of his are somehow mixed up in these bombings? Oh God, I hope not.'

'One of the problems with wearing any uniform, of course,' he said as lightly as he could manage, 'is that if one person wearing it does something notable, everyone wearing it gets noticed.' He could see that he wasn't helping much.

Grim as it was, he changed the topic back to the legal procedures she had been involved with since morning: the forms that had to be signed and the bills accepted before the transfer of the remains had been effected. In the middle of that, Doan and Barry arrived.

They both ordered a real drink, took Scotch over ice, and dropped like exhausted runners on the sofa.

'Goldarn it, Emmy, you wouldn't believe the problems they've got. I thought FiFoChi had some problems, but they make me look like a piker. That night security watchman we had to fire last month for drinking on the job? Heck, he could get a job as a colonel in charge of that secret installation up there. You never saw such a sideshow as those Army boys.'

Barry drained off his drink and wiped his beard on his hand with relief. 'They've turned up more than thirty cases of soldiers on duty using drugs—marijuana mostly, but hash and pills too. Mind you, Neil, we are talking about one of the most sensitive installations in the country, the place where they test-fire new missiles.'

Doan ran his hand through his hair in disgust. 'They're ready to run polygraph tests and loyalty oaths and hang new electronic badges on every contractor and civilian employee who goes in and out of there. They'll believe anything before they accept the fact that a rag-tag, illiterate army recruited from a bunch of reform school kids and city punks isn't some elite military force that can be trusted with this country's top military hardware and secrets. I don't know if I'll even bother to bid for any more business up there after we finish this new installation. Ain't worth it.'

'I've been telling Doan all the way back that if FiFoChi backs off from this Army investigation, it's going to look a wee bit like taking cover, isn't it, that the thing here with the truck—'

Doan waved a hand in the air. 'Ah, let's drop it, Barry. These people don't need our business griefs on top of what this family already has. Em, I'm sorry to come home here like a bear with a burned tail and not even ask about Babs. Any news?'

'No change, if that's news,' his wife said. She sat beside him and took his hand. 'Jane called about half an hour ago; she's still in a coma. Oh Doan, they don't know if she'll ever come out of it. Jane says she could wake up tomorrow and start talking, or she could lie there for six months.'

'Any word from Tim?'

Neil answered for Emily. 'None. Will is out looking around in different places they hung out at, you know, places where only boys would know to look for each other.'

'That darn FBI, or whoever he is, is still up there at

Lillienthals' watching us. Gives me the creeps,' Linn said. 'Oh Barn, have you men eaten at all?'

'We had hot box lunches from the Army on the plain. Really, not bad at all. All we needed was a stiff drink. It would have been easier, I gather, to get drugs up on that base than to get an honest drink. The Army is always efficient about the wrong things; it's almost comic.'

'Well,' Doan said, heaving himself up off the soft cushions, 'it's no joke they can't find one of their goldarn missiles. Would you believe that? I need a long, hot, deep bath, Em.'

'Are they really missing an entire missile?' Neil asked, astonished.

'They are.' It was Barry's turn to answer and stretch. 'A shower, my love. May I leave you all here without the courtesy of further conversation, and get myself to my own place and wash off the travel dirt?'

'Did someone just walk out the gate with a missile? How big is it? Is it some miniature supertoy missile?' Linn seemed exasperated that the Army's incompetence to manage their own affairs had left her man so bone-weary. She rubbed his back, and he stretched against her luxuriantly.

'This one they're after is eighteen feet long, fully mounted, so no one walked out with it under his arm,' Doan said.

'If I were hiding a missile, I suppose I'd hide it on an Army base,' Neil said. 'Have they looked there yet?'

'Probably be the last place they look,' Doan said.

'Barn, let me get my coat and go over with you. It's only out in the back.' Linn ran out through the hall.

Doan circled Emily's shoulder with his long arm. 'In this family, the women are expected to scrub the men's backs, Neil, so excuse us.'

Barry stood yawning, with his hands crammed into the pockets of his jeans, rocking on his toes as if to stretch his cramped muscles. 'Apparently, those dimwit soldiers up there have a computer system paid for by the innocent taxpayers of this land, and so modern that the bird colonels can't even manage it. They've got sergeants and lieutenants running programmes they can't read, and other horrors too complex and sad to contemplate. Someone from outside, it would appear, has been cutting into their computers and simply moving things around without the Army realizing it, and then, they think, sending in transport to carry off the stuff. Now isn't that ingenious?' He grinned admiringly as he thought about it.

'I'm afraid I don't know much about computers, but Linn was telling me how that could be done with just one truck if you wanted to locate it.' He paused. 'She says she showed Tim how to do that.'

'Oh, did she indeed? Well, it's simple enough logistically. I showed the Army on their own programmes, in half an hour, how anyone could do it to them. I think the only one who understood me was a bright young woman named Corporal Veletti. Now get this, Neil. They took the mini-programme I wrote out for them, ran it up, mind you, on the spot, and they are going to have what they call an Intensity-training Seminar tomorrow morning for all personnel over the rank of captain.' He laughed delightedly. 'They'll find when they get to the end of it that I left a piece of verse it will print out for them: I HAVE MET THEM AT THE CLOSE OF DAY, COMING WITH VIVID FACES, AND CORPORAL VELETTI AND THE BASE COMMANDER SHOULD CHANGE PLACES.'

'Ah, a little Yeats and a little mischief.'

'He's from my hometown, man.' He glanced out through the doorway. 'You must be enormously important to Linn, Neil, if she'd lie to you.'

Neil was startled by the passion and the abruptness of the remark. 'Does she do that?'

'You're close to her family in some important way. I can see that for myself. You are, I can only gather from her rhapsodies on the subject, the Mitchells' idea of their wisest old friend, some sort of father confessor to everyone. Linn wants like mad to impress you—she does me too, you know, so I'm familiar with this, ah, habit of hers from experience. She'll exaggerate, she'll embroider, she'll move a small fact around like a housewife with an odd piece of furniture until it fits in where she thinks it will impress the most.'

'Can you be more specific?'

The Irishman looked grim. 'I can. This stunt with showing Tim the computer terminal at the plant—when was all that supposed to have been done?'

'Two weeks ago. The last time you and Doan flew up to Tonepah.' He watched the Irishman's face closely.

'Now why on earth would she tell you that? Neil, man, that day—it was a Tuesday, because the logbook in the plane shows we were up there Tuesday and Wednesday that week—Tim and his mob of leatherjackets were up near Taos at Red River Pass, racing their dirt bikes. It's easy to recall because Doan asked me to go up there on Monday, right in the middle of a problem with the hundred-foot crane on a building in Albuquerque we're putting up. The union pulled their man off the crane, don't you know, until some rigging was changed because they said we violated their contract specs—ah, Christ, anyway, I went up there the next morning, specifically at Doan's request, to try and persuade them none of them was good enough on a bike to make the climb they were planning to try. We really thought some one of them would get killed up on that mountain.

'Well, they wouldn't listen to me, that's the sum of it, and Doan picked me up there that morning in the jet for the Tonepah trip. They survived, of course, God knows how. Anyway, Tim was there in all his glory, not here or down at the plant with Linn.' He lowered his voice. 'I've heard, and I'm sure you have, that twins have a relationship with each other that's different. Do you think that could be it, then? Do you think Linny's trying to convince herself that Tim couldn't be the sort of fellow'd steal a truck for a joke, or that he might do that, but he'd be a trivial kind of rascal if he did, not a murderer?'

Neil looked sceptical 'The logic of that is a puzzle, but I suppose it's possible. The real question seems to be whether young Tim learned to operate the computer from *anyone*.'

'But isn't it conceivable? Linny's too young to be profound, Neil, but she's quick and ingenious. I know, I know, two like us have a special relationship too, and I could be reaching for a way of explaining her out of this.' He looked stricken, confessing that. 'It hurts, you know, the way whisky hurts with the shock of the warmth, to be abruptly loved as I was when I met Linn. Love is a bit Irish, has a saint's face and a soft tongue with a curse in the mouth. It's lucky; it fills feeling; it makes a man reel. And real too. I suppose I need to believe her even if she lies.'

'And would you lie for her, Barry?'

'I don't know how much I'd be willing to do, but it would be a great deal. She's half my age, y'know, and sometimes I try to tell myself I'm a complete fool. But some other times, when I'm alone without her, I'll remember something—her pulse punching at the skin of her throat that was quiet at an inch distance in bed, and I'll *hear* it, as a runner might see, running his third hour of a marathon, the cold, coloured taste of water. Then I know I need her, need her there.'

His eyes shone and his face was suffused with blood above his beard in the emotion of his words. Neil knew that swelling of feeling; his memory only had to go back a very short time to when each skin inch of himself sang because some she touched him, and he would have balanced his whole life along the fine wire of that connection.

'Ready?' It was Linn, back completely changed and carrying an overnight case. 'I'm really becoming the portable Linn Mitchell these days. God knows where she'll sleep tonight.'

'Ach, sure,' growled Barry, taking her in a bear hug. 'We all know that one.'

It was an Irish saying too, Neil knew, that the fact there are counterfeiters is the proof there's such a thing as real gold.

CHAPTER 10

The guidebooks have warnings in them about spring in Santa Fe. It can be fickle and chill. A playful quick switch of the wind from dry west to wet east, or sometimes only a sudden malevolent blast with real sleet and an icy edge to it, will turn the day around.

The weather turned nasty that evening, and Neil felt a pang of remorse for having sent Will out with a sleeping bag and a ground sheet to spend a couple of nights in it. Perhaps if it could change one way this fast, it could change back just as quickly.

As he and Doan drove out to Tesuque, sharp bits of sleet began popping the windshield.

'We got in just ahead of this front in the plane. Skinny Campbell, our pilot, said this was coming, and he just wanted to set down, take off, and get back into Albuquerque just before it hit.' Doan looked satisfied to be wearing a leather coat and baseball cap he kept in the truck. Neil shivered a bit in his Harris tweed jacket.

'I felt like a very low form of life telling you I'd made this late meeting for you, Doan. I rather thought Emily might prevail on you not to come when she saw how tired you were.'

'Em's used to it. What the heck's going on, Neil? You didn't exactly say the CIA was tangling lines with the FBI in this thing, but that's the way I read it.'

Putting his words together as quickly and deliberately as he could, aware that each allegation of any connection between Doan's company and the bombings was also a hint of connection between them and his family, he spelled out how he and Slater had met, and met again. He told him too what Barbara had said, or not quite said, about Slater, but still could not quite bring himself to include what she had scrawled on the paper: his daughter's name.

'It's a red-eye missile that's missing, you know, Neil,' Doan said, 'and that means every federal agency from here back to Washington is bound to be falling all over each other out here even if they weren't before.'

'My knowledge of weaponry is mostly from Shakespeare and World War Two, Doan.'

'Heat-seeking ground-to-air missile. Some of those terrorist boys would love to get their hands on one, I guess. The old models you can buy on the open market, if you can get clearance to ship it out of the country. Heck, General Dynamics has ads for them in the trade magazines, surplus. Make a big difference if the friendlies or the unfriendlies get 'em, and what kind of encoding hardware, computer directors, and so on go with 'em. And, of course, what's in the darn warhead.'

'I hope the Army's not missing some nuclear warheads.'

Doan wrestled the pickup around a skiddy turn and glanced at him. 'You kidding? It's one of the worst-kept secrets in the world that there's weapons-grade uranium missing in cargoes of tons of the stuff for the last twenty years. No question at all, I guess, that the Israelis got their nuclear weapons programme started with materials they stole from us. That's what the general says. Army knows for a fact that a lot of people have been shipping secret industrial tech stuff and even explosives out of Dallas on commercial flights, packed as solvents, for two years. They can't stop it, though.'

'Why on earth not?'

' 'Cause they can't search every cargo, cut open every steel drum, can they?' He grunted and peered hard through the windshield. 'Besides, there's a thing called an end-user certificate. We got tangled up with them plenty of times. If some classified stuff is headed for one of the NATO countries, say, that's okay. But if the same stuff was headed for Libya, or Chile, or Brazil, or somewhere like that, no go, no way.'

'Therefore?'

'So the stuff goes out with some German company listed as the end-user, and when they're outside American jurisdiction, the papers get shuffled and, bang, the stuff lands in some Ayrab's backyard, postage paid.'

'You're quite an expert.'

'You don't deal in big contracts with the Middle East without getting an education, Neil. Especially heavy machinery and high-tech stuff.'

They drove in silence for five minutes before slowing to pull into Bishop's Lodge. The flurry of sleet had ended, but there was a smell like cold metal in the wind. They walked fast, bent against the wind, the twenty yards from the parking lot to the Lodge, where Slater was waiting for them, in the cocktail lounge. In his Cardin navy cashmere jacket, ascot, and tasseled loafers, he looked every bit a tourist taking his expense-account leisure.

Doan and Slater appeared to like each other reasonably well immediately, which, given his expectation of tension between them from the start, surprised Neil. They sat amiably around a corner table, away from the scattered half dozen other solitary and paired drinkers staying in out of the weather.

'I'll tell you right off, Mr Slater, I don't want to sound as if I'm King Bird, but I think both those so-called bombings were intended somehow for me.' He turned to Neil. 'That sound nuts to you, Neil? That's the first time you've heard me say that, isn't it? Am I getting paranoid, do you think?'

'Tell me your hypothesis, Mr Mitchell, before we decide if you're schizo or just maybe seeing something the rest of us are missing.' Slater was being his sincere self, Neil saw. 'Hey, if I call you Doan, for Pete's sake, will you call me Jack?'

'Heck yes. Sure. Well, after spending today talking with the Army up in Tonepah, it seems to me that there has to be some connection between the fact that they're missing a red-eye missile and that FiFoChi has been having a run of our high-tech equipment getting lost in transit between here and there, missing trucks—heck, all kinds of things.'

'But why send the first bomb to De Sales, Doan?' Neil sipped his Heineken slowly; this might be a long, drawn-out conversation. Doan seemed ready to unburden himself, and he knew that Slater would skilfully exploit the opportunity.

'Don't think it was sent to De Sales at all. Think it was sent as a warning to Barbara. Look—' his blunt hands drummed on the table impatiently, and he folded them self-consciously around his glass. 'Barbara arrives in Santa Fe from back east. What's the first thing she does? She calls up my house to talk with Em. They are a lot closer than just half-sisters, you know. Heck, closer than most real sisters. Barbara says they'll be coming over as soon as they settle the house. They talk about—oh, heck, everything girls talk about: how the kids are, how their husbands are—all that stuff. Now here's the part where maybe I'm all off; suppose someone is tapping my telephone right then. Is that too far out?'

Slater shook his head slowly and pursed his lips. Tacit agreement or pity. Whatever, it encouraged Doan to go on.

'Whoever they are, they are looking for a way to get me, my company, to cover their tracks with the Army—warn me off, you know, or just kill me off to keep me from pushing this investigation of my missing stuff too hard. Now I know you can read that just backwards to the way I'm reading it, Neil; you don't have to tell me that. You could say the last thing in the world they want to do is call attention to themselves. But, darn it, that's assuming they're brilliant. Even champion chess players make stupid moves. Catcher I had, he's got ten years' experience and I'm a rookie? Calls for me to throw a fastball to Hank Aaron, bases loaded once. *I* shouldn't have known any better, but *he* should. Boom. I think the first bomb was a warning for yours truly. That's my so-called hypothesis.'

Having said his piece, Doan looked around uneasily, obviously embarrassed by how thin it sounded to him.

'And the second one?' Slater was leaning back, his eyes hooded, polite almost to the point of appearing indifferent—an academic pose Neil knew well.

'I think the kid was on his way to Los Alamos. We've got a project there—nothing important, nothing to do with the Army, just a mobile construction office in a trailer and a few pieces of equipment for a road-widening job. I think they were going to blow the trailer up, in case I hadn't got the point from the first one.' He subsided and took a long draught of beer. 'That's it. Amen. I had my say.'

Slater took the floor before Neil might. 'It's not at all impossible, Doan, but let me tell you why it strikes me as improbable. First, my friends tell me there's no tap on your phone.' He held up a hand as though staving off a protest. 'Naturally, we checked.'

'Which doesn't mean there couldn't have been one

earlier,' Neil felt obliged to interject.

'Correct. There certainly could have been one earlier, but right now there isn't. Second, since that second bomb went off half a mile from here, in a truck pointed at this Lodge, you'll forgive *my* paranoia if it seems more logical to me that the Lathen boy was in the act of delivering it to me this time. Somebody must know I'm here in Santa Fe and why. I'm not invisible and, to some people, I'm not welcome.'

Neil thought rapidly of three persons beside himself who could know that Slater was in Santa Fe and who either knew or might know that he was an agent.

Doan traced the wet circles on the table into spirals with a thick finger. 'Yeah, well, as I said, I could be wrong. But do you know I'm starting to suspect everyone? I'm talking about my family, their friends, the people I work with in the office. Heck, I thought, coming here to-night, why shouldn't I suspect this Jack Slater, even if he's some kind of government? Wouldn't be the first time someone went both ways. No offence.'

Slater grinned delightedly. 'If you lived and worked in Washington these days, Doan, you'd be right in the main-stream, suspecting my firm of being the enemy. It's ab-solutely the height of intellectual fashion.'

Doan seemed only a little sheepish. He signalled for more beer, which arrived while Jack Slater was asking him if he had ever been in Washington.

'Took the kids there to see the sights when they were small. It's awful impressive to me—heck, I'm still a country boy, remember—all those places like the White House right there. I mean that's where the centre of half the world is, the good part of it. But I sure as heck wouldn't want to live there and try to work there. Doesn't look like there's anyplace to live until you get over into Virginia somewhere, and commuting isn't zip down the highway, it's that goldarn bumper-to-bumper inch-along one mile an hour. That would eat my gut.'

'Do you do much travelling at all, Doan, for your company?' It was a skilful segue, but not a seamless one, Neil thought.

'Me?' The waiter brought a dish of peanuts over to the table, and Doan nodded thanks and took a pawful. 'Used to. When you're young—like when I was first with the Cubs, Godalmighty—you think it's heaven to check into one of those fancy hotels, order anything you want in the restaurant, walk around looking at things you had seen in your books in school. Some train travel still in those days; then it got to be mostly planes, but by that time I was out of the Bigs anyway. Then I got so I'd fly to contract meetings and job conferences about jobs, but most of that was in New Mexico. Oh, Em got me to take her to Hawaii once on some goldarned construction convention I wished we never bothered going on, and we'd take the kids east to see their kinfolk every once in a while, but I'd guess you could say I'm not much of a traveller, Jack.'

'Then who does the travelling for FiFoChi, Doan?'

'Barry Keeney. Irishman who heads up my operations and planning for me. Loves the damn airlines. Goes all over for us when we need someone.'

'He went to the Middle East for you last year, didn't he?'

'Middle East, Germany, England; heck, all over. It was him worked out this exchange programme we're trying out with those people—' It finally dawned on him where Slater was leading him. He confronted it bluntly. 'You saying maybe Barry Keeney's making some deals for himself on the side, maybe using our set-up to move his own pieces around the board, sort of in between mine?'

Slater raised his hands, palms up, and lifted his eyebrows. He had, Neil noted, let Doan say it. Now he was letting Doan reflect on what he had said.

'Neil, does that make any sense to you?' Doan turned

back to Neil, who knew that what he'd say in answer would probably reinforce Slater's implied thesis.

'If you start with the question, who does the travelling for your company, Doan, then you arrive where you just found yourself. But suppose you begin with a different inquiry. Suppose you ask first who in Santa Fe has been supplying the Lathen boy with explosives and the technical knowledge for making small bombs. And suppose you proceed from there not to your idea about your army contracts and the missing hardware, but to the assumption that the first bomb was aimed directly at Barbara—sent to De Sales, but intended as a warning to her. If that were the case, then it would indicate that someone knew, or suspected, that she knew something dangerous to them. Then the question becomes, what could she have known—especially, what could she have known that she might have passed on to Mr Slater here?'

'Did the members of your family, Doan, any of them, know that Barbara Lacey had done some work for my firm in the past?'

'Jeekers K. Christ, Neil,' Doan said, glancing at Slater, but pushing the bowl and glasses aside to put his arms on the table to talk directly to Neil, 'would that mean Timmy *is* involved in this business? Of course he knew; we all knew. It was a family joke, having an aunt the kids called "the Spy" for laughs.' He drained his glass and signalled impatiently for another. When it came, he took a thirsty swallow and said to the waiter, 'You see me empty, you get another one here, understand?'

Slater drank off his beer neatly and took another. Neil let his half-finished glass sit there. He wasn't going to try to keep up with these two.

'Sorry, Doan. I'm at the age where I need a piss break to keep up this pace,' Slater said, edging out of the table. 'Be right back. I think maybe you two might have some things to say to each other that you wouldn't want an outsider to hear anyway.'

As soon as he went through the door, Doan groaned. 'Hell's fire, Neil, what are we getting into here? This guy has me going backwards and forwards at the same time.'

'Do you think you ought to be talking with your attorney, Doan? There are some legal questions here that are way beyond my capacity to advise you on.'

'Those lawyers? Neil, I swear to you, they are no darn good for anything but dotting the i's and crossing the t's on contracts. Most of them are useless as tits on a bull.' He rubbed his face, the fatigue of the long day beginning to tell after he had used up his second wind getting to this meeting.

'You said yourself, Doan, that with all that's happened, with the killings and all the rest of it, everyone tends to get itchy and suspicious. It's ugly, but it's natural. That's the way human beings are made. I'll tell you something I've never told anyone else. When Pril Lacey was killed last year, right there on campus at Old Hampton, I got confused, so confused and anxious to find out who'd done it, that one night I woke up in a cold sweat absolutely convinced for three seconds that *I* had done it—that I must have done it in some kind of a fugue or blackout or something. I thought I even had a motive, that I was afraid to marry again. Anxiety can be the worst basis in the world for logical thinking, Doan, and I think what we need more of, and not less of, right now is logic.'

'Just tell me this, Neil. You think anyone in my family *could* have done these killings? Me? You think I could've? Barry? He's practically family . . .'

'If I say no, is that going to relieve your mind? Or would you just think I was trying to patronize you with some easy, cheap assurances?'

Slater appeared in the doorway again, paused coolly to survey the room, and went over to the bar where an elderly male in evening clothes, with a huge turquoise sunburst on a cord for a necktie, was sitting alone. He patted the man on the back like an old friend and told him something, and both of them burst out laughing. He came back to the table red-faced, still chuckling.

'That fellow looks so much like the senator from Connecticut that I had to ask him. He wasn't a bit offended, told me his wife thought he looked like Wallace Beery, so he'd tell her other people had better eyes. Good old boy.'

Doan said to Slater with a laugh as he slid back into the table, 'If you thought old Harry Bell was a senator, you can't be much of a spy, Jack. Old Harry just sits in some bar every night, all dressed up with his squash-blossom tie on, waiting for some widow woman with blue hair from the east to ask him if he's an artist. Runs a broken-down gallery on Canyon, sells stuff for ten times what he pays for it, not that anyone buys it much. Even tourists can't be fooled all the time.'

Jack Slater gave a self-deprecating shrug and leaned back, arms crossed. 'Did you two decide between you what you think is the most plausible explanation of what's going on while I was off watering my tree?'

Neil answered for them. 'We were discussing the distorting effects of anxiety on perception.'

'Now that's a special interest of yours, isn't it, Neil? It seems to me you lectured in Boston about my tendency to see the world through a glass darkly, given my terrible prejudices in favour of thinking that if a bomb goes off, someone must have set it off.'

'Neil and I naturally have a harder time than you, Jack, in suspecting anyone in my family.'

'Leave the Mitchell family out of it completely, Doan. Consider the other possibilities.' He paused significantly. 'For example, you have some foreign nationals working for you at FiFoChi, don't you?' He made a circle in the air with a pinch of peanuts and put them into his mouth, looking at Doan.

Neil felt something like a lurch of distaste and a twinge of admiration. If Slater had wanted to soften Doan up for suspecting his foreign employees, what better way to have done it than to let him think about the possible guilt of his family first?

'Yeah. Three. One in the office. Couple more out on jobs. So?'

'So, why don't we consider the possibility that there's a connection right there?'

Doan pulled his nose and snorted angrily. 'Jeekers Crow, I thought some of the local people were bad. The minute we took on those fellows, about a week after, there was a fire in the big storage shed. Goldarn Jensen kid smoking out there when he was supposed to be loading pipe, but everybody immediately starts saying what about the Jordanian you got out there? What about that Iranian or that Ayrab? Same dang thing they'd do if it was an Indian. We got a Navaho draughtsman in the office? People treated him like dirt when he first came. Good draughtsman, too—fast, neat. He's different from them so he must be some kind of damn fool. These people are just afraid of losing their jobs, is all.' He took a drink. 'Whew, and some of them think they're educated.'

'Are you saying it's impossible?'

'Heck no. I'm not saying anything's impossible. But why go off saying "what about him"? just because somebody's a foreigner? You got any evidence you can lean on? Show me, I'm reasonable. It's just too darn easy to crucify some outsider.'

'Just for my education, Doan—now don't think I mean any more by it than that—just who is this foreign national you say works in the office?'

'Well, just one's in the office all the time; one's in and out. The one works there is Maimandi Nejad. He's the Iranian. Darned good engineer. Had him out on some field projects, too. Started out as a roughneck in the oil fields over there and got himself to school by himself. Poor bugger's family're half of them still in jail from the Shah, the other half everyone thinks is skunks because they're for this Khomeini. All Maimandi wants is to be an American citizen; he'd give his eye teeth for that. Hassan, he's got an American name now, changed it legally to Joe Hassan; he's from Jordan. No family at all, got himself a scholarship from some American missionary outfit. Catholic boy, straight as an arrow. Married a Zuñi girl. Heck, my whole family went to the wedding, right down in the cathedral. Works like a goldarn coolie and never cuts a corner. Not as smart as Maimandi, but he works so hard, y'know, that he knows more about FiFoChi than a lot of fellows been there three times as long. Both those old boys been to my home, met my family, et dinner with us—'

'Did they come to you as the result of recommendation from someone you knew, or how?'

'FiFoChi lend-lease, that's how. We've got this exchange arrangement with some people specializing in desert construction over there, Saudi Arabia and so on. Now, wouldn't it be a heck of a note if every time anyone set off a bomb over there, they blamed one of my people working there? I can just hear them. Let's arrest that American; he must've done it.'

'No one's talking about arresting anyone, Doan, you know that. Do you mean those people over there picked the men to send here, and vice versa?'

'Of course! You think I'd let them take their pick of my men?'

'Why couldn't it be possible—' Slater held up a forestalling hand—'just possible—that one or both of them are using your computer access to do some industrial espionage and maybe a little bit more?'

'Because neither of them ever gets near our computer, that's why. The computer is locked in a private office off the main business office, and the only one works it is my daughter, Linn.' Doan sounded triumphant.

'Em's Linn? Is she the one they call that?'

'You must've heard Neil here call her that, yeah. Now you're not going to tell me my little girl is an industrial spy, are you?'

Again Slater simply sat and lifted his hands, widening his eyes helplessly. The facts weren't his fault. Doan stared at him, then called for the check and paid it without saying another word.

The wind cutting across the parking lot was still wintry, out of the east. They climbed back into Doan's four-by-four and sat for half a minute in silence. Neil knew that his friend was thinking how many ways the CIA man had made him look foolish just by letting him talk. Finally Doan gave a grunt of annoyance, at himself probably, and turned the key.

The noise, the smoke, the dull glare—music?—were suddenly all around them. Both men cried out and threw up their arms against the blast and a rain of glass from the windshield, or whatever was tearing at their faces for a millisecond, then they crashed headlong out the opposite doors, acting on instincts as primitive as two blasted, half-deafened animals in a panic bolt from a forest fire.

There were feet running, and a hand reached down to the blacktop and helped Neil to his feet shakily. His hands were skinned and black. A flashlight gleamed over him, then switched over to search the lurching figure of Doan, who was groping around the front of the pickup towards him. Neil's right arm ached; he remembered landing on it.

'You all right?'

'He's all right, Mr Mitchell—just singed and scraped.' Neil recognized the voice of Joe Goddam Leapinghorse Cady of the FBI. Someone was playing 'For He's a Jolly Good Fellow' faintly. Neil shook his head to clear it. He looked at Doan and the truck. Wisps of smoke were still curling out of the cab, but that was all. He felt his face. He could see Doan was doing the same thing.

Cady spoke again, inspecting the cab of the truck with his light. He reached in and shut off the engine. 'Some joker put a little smoke bomb in there. In a goddam music box, from the sound of it.' They could all hear the final strains of 'which nobody can deny' winding down. Neil watched the agent gingerly lift the partly shattered toy from under the dash and hold it up for their inspection.

The noise had been insufficient to arouse anyone in the Lodge, apparently, because no one appeared in the door. Thank God for that, Neil thought, just as Doan spat and enunciated the same thing aloud.

'Doan, this is Russell Cady, from the FBI.'

'Cady? You watching us? You see who did this to my truck?' The big man was sucking the heel of his hand where he had gouged out a chunk hitting the ground.

Cady spoke bitterly. He was hunched against the wind in his tan suit. 'I followed you here, yes. And I've been watching you, yes. I wanted to know who you were meeting out here, seeing as how that kid got himself blown up out this way yesterday.'

Neil knew with a sure sense of frustration what the next line would be. 'But you didn't see anyone put anything into our truck, right?'

'That's right, sir. I got here maybe two minutes after you, and I went twice to see if you were still in the bar. I could see you through the side window, but only if I went around the corner from the parking lot.'

Neil's face felt peppered and stung in the cold. He asked Doan if his eyes were all right.

'Feel like someone threw dirt in 'em, but I can see okay. Sheeit, now who do you suppose that special delivery for old Doan was from?'

'If you move your paranoia over to the side for a minute, I think this one is mine,' Neil said.

'Well, Cady, whoever, you weren't much use to us, were you? So why don't you just go in there and have a nice talk with Jack Slater, 'cause that's who we are talking to, and he's not much use either,' Doan snapped. 'Lemme see that flashlight there for a minute.' He took the light and searched under the truck until he found his Cubs baseball cap, then he returned the flash to Cady, hit the hat against his leg to clean it, and jammed it on his head. 'My lucky hat. About as lucky as the darned Cubs, I guess.'

He climbed back into the truck and slammed his door. 'You coming, Neil, or are you and that jackass going to stand there talking all night?'

Neil almost felt sorry for Cady. Almost. The truck cab smelled of burnt powder. They drove out with a roar of their own making this time, and spun onto the highway.

CHAPTER 11

Doan flatly refused to notify the police of the music-box bomb incident, since the only damage was a small piece out of his hand and a rip in Neil's jacket sleeve. 'What am I supposed to tell them, that I had six beers and fell out of my truck?' Damage to dignity cannot be assessed as easily as other kinds of injury.

At breakfast the next morning, when he explained at greater length than his anger had permitted the previous night, Emily was distraught. While Doan and Neil had been away talking with Slater and becoming victims of the joke bomb, Jane Wheeler had called again and said that Barbara was showing signs of imminent recovery. Since Emily had been struggling all along, torn between representing the family at De Sales's rites and going to see her sister in the hospital, and staying right in Santa Fe while the police hunted for her elder son, she was now more divided than ever.

Taking his cue from Doan's big foot against his ankle under the table, Neil had encouraged her leaning towards Boston and Philadelphia. Between them, they persuaded her that there was no real case against Tim, hence no need to worry about what would happen when he showed up. Neil pointed out to her that if anyone wanted to injure Doan through her, they'd all be better off if she got away soon. It was clear to Neil that Doan's chief motive, now that the toy bomber was getting closer, was to get Em out of there before someone planted a real bomb in the house or in her car.

'Tim shows up, heck, you could turn around and be back here in a few hours, Em. It isn't as if you were going to the moon,' Doan told her. 'Go on, get yourself to Albuquerque with me this morning and get on that plane.'

Neil nodded reassuringly when she glanced worriedly at him. 'Doan's right, Em. There's nothing you can do here, and if there's reason for you to be here later, a phone call takes one minute and a plane ride just four hours. Do it.'

'I'll feel an awful lot better the rest of my life if at least one of us is at Morgan's funeral, I know that for a fact,' she said firmly, and her husband knew she was convinced. He didn't give her a chance to change her mind.

'Shuttle to Albuquerque leaves thirty minutes from right out front, ma'am, better hop it. Guaranteed no joke bombs, no problems. Heck, I think I can guarantee an FBI escort all the way. I'll call for your ticket.' He paused after she had left the room and turned to Neil. 'No, I won't. Call. Anybody wants to know she's flying to Boston today, let 'em come along and watch me put her on the plane.'

By eight-thirty they had driven out, with Emily saying in a distracted voice as she kissed Neil goodbye, 'You'll think we really live in the wild west if this is what happens when you come for a visit. Promise you'll be here when I get back.'

'Promise.' He kissed her and waved them off. The car in Lillienthals' driveway was a green Chevrolet this morning. It pulled out after them and stopped in front of the Mitchells' gateway. The driver, a pleasant young man in a zipper jacket, said, 'Morning. Where they going?'

'Morning. Albuquerque.'

'Thank you. Have a nice day.' He waved and drove off using his radio. A gold-tone Datsun came down the hill and disappeared in the wake of the Chevy, and then a blue and white pickup went down the hill five seconds behind the Datsun. Neil realized that it was possible that cars C and D were both following cars B and A, but also that a man could go mad trying to outguess ordinary morning traffic. He looked ruefully once again at the ripped sleeve of his good sports jacket, tucked it together in a fold that immediately came untucked, and went back into the house.

Over a second coffee in the kitchen, he recalled that Doan's version of the meeting with Slater last night had rather skimped on the details of Slater's implications that if some members of the Mitchell family were not responsible for the events of the past several days, then the prime suspects were the FiFoChi employees he preferred to call 'foreign nationals'.

Neil knew that for his whole adult life Doan had been a relentless supporter of civil rights causes and a bitter enemy of all the self-serving practices that had discriminated against Indians and Hispanics in his native state. He also knew, from what had happened at the College, that the federal government had been systematically finding excuses for cancelling visas, especially those held by Iranians, and shipping their holders back to an uncertain fate in their homelands whenever some office in Washington got into a panic about foreigners who were not bona fide anti-communists taking political refuge.

Looking out over the hills, he wondered vaguely, with his easterner's wildly insufficient sense of southwestern geography, where the camps had been in which thousands of loyal, intelligent Japanese-Americans had been locked up during World War Two. Somewhere out here. And somewhere a few miles from here, he thought, we had also developed, with immense energy and ingenuity, the first atomic weapon—called, as though it were a huge toy, 'Fat Man'—and made the decision to drop it not on our white cousins in Europe, but on our racially distinct enemies in Asia.

No matter with what speculations or possibilities he busied his mind, one question recurred and would not be ignored. Why Em's Linn? Why had Barbara written that down as one of the key phrases in this mystery? Em's Linn was obviously in love with Barry Keeney, to a degree which any student of Shakespeare, or indeed of Harlequin romances, would recognize as classical infatuation. Not incompatible with eventual deep, lasting love, but not its mature flowering either. Would she protect Barry if she knew or suspected that he was evil? Perhaps. No—probably. Would she do something she herself knew to be deeply wrong if she thought it was what Barry wanted? Possibly. One knew that she would lie in small things, and those who lie in small things have the necessary practice at self-deception to rationalize large lies when they are wanted. But why say she taught Tim to use the computer terminal in the first place? It could only make him a more obvious suspect in the theft of the truck in which Jimmy Lathen died. Was that kachina doll and its bomb being delivered to Slater out at the Lodge when it went off? Lathen had delivered the bomb that had killed De Sales—there was no doubt of that—but did he know then what he was doing? He was, after all, simply the delivery boy for the toy store where the jack-in-the-box came from, and therefore the natural agent for its delivery. Had he simply been in the store when Barbara Lacey came in and made her purchase, overheard the transaction, then told someone about it offhandedly, as a joke—*these rich people are nuts; she buys him this toy for an April Fool's present, she says it looks just like an old friend of theirs, guy with a big schnozz*—and thus given someone else the idea for the bomb and been allowed to deliver it unknowingly? If so, perhaps he wasn't delivering that second toy bomb anywhere. Perhaps he was simply carrying his own death in the cab of that stolen truck, timed to kill the only witness who might connect the first bomb with its sender.

But then—Neil put his hands over his eyes wearily at the endless unfolding of logical possibilities in every direction. Someone had actually told the Lathen boy where to locate that missing FiFoChi truck. Tim? They both wore the BG&E colours, both belonged to the same reckless, rowdy, possibly dangerous gang of hooligans with their *Beyond Good and Evil* philosophy one inch deep. But it was scarcely conceivable that a pack of antisocial teenagers were responsible for the disappearance of an army missile. One could picture them stealing trucks, even explosives, if they thought they were going to arm the Navaho nation for some romantic retaking of the West from the whites, but not a ground-to-air missile. The one truck they had taken would, according to Doan, not carry much more than a small automobile, and one didn't drag such a weapon on an open flatbed trailer down Highway 25.

Who had planted the joke bomb? 'For He's a Jolly Good Fellow', indeed. To how many people had he used the word 'joker' or 'trickster' in describing the person they were after? Had the bomb been an additional nudge to Doan to get out of the army contract business? And if so, why? And by whom? A competitor? There were millions, even hundreds of millions of dollars at stake, but Doan refused even to name potential rivals who might be responsible, dismissing the idea as fantastic. Had it been a deliberate nose-thumbing at Neil himself, a reminder that schoolteachers who get themselves involved in large affairs can be removed at any time? Was it purest coincidence that he had met Dan Michaels on the shuttle from Albuquerque, and that he had been able to suggest only the same hotel he himself was staying at? How many psychiatrists were there who were experts in the analysis of the trickster complex and who also, coincidentally, worked for the CIA? Had the entire chance meeting between Michaels and Slater on the Staab House porch been carefully orchestrated? Were Slater and the psychiatrist working together?

Neil realized that the sole person his meandering recapitulation of the situation did not implicate was the FBI man, Cady.

The phone rang. Lifting the receiver, he realized that his arm still ached when he raised it. It was Russell Cady.

They met, at Cady's suggestion, just half a mile away, in the parking area of the museum complex halfway up the old Santa Fe Trail. There was a different impressive view from this side of the hill, and some sort of botanical walk, glorious with flowers.

Waiting for the agent, Neil forgot about trying to locate and identify a bird just once and looked at the masses of brilliant flowers down the path. Someone in one of Iris Murdoch's novels once remarked that if an alien from a planet without flowers ever came to earth and saw them, he would think we'd all be constantly mad with joy. Mad, yes, he thought, but how often is it with joy?

Cady pulled up in a brown Plymouth and walked over and put his foot up on the fence beside Neil.

'Morning.'

'Are you ever mad with joy, Cady?'

'Am I ever—? Is that a literary reference?'

'Are you?'

'I was loco on peyote once.'

'I was drunk on Gallo wine once, but I don't think either of us was ever mad with joy.'

'I thought this would be a good place to meet.'

'Museums are closed Mondays.'

'That's why. I gather you and Doan Mitchell didn't notify the local cops about your adventure last night.'

'Hmm.'

'You really think that was your song they were playing on the music box, Dr Huffam?'

Neil had completely forgotten about Dr Huffam and laughed aloud when he heard the name again. 'You're thinking of someone else. That's Charles Dickens's middle name.'

'Ah. The office will not be too thrilled to hear that the man I told them was apparently using the alias "Neil Kelly" is not Dr Huffam. They told me you were from a rival firm, but they seemed confused about the name. Are you Neil Kelly?'

'Are you Joe Leapinghorse?'

'Where'd you get that one?'

'A CIA man, who is probably back up there somewhere watching our rear ends with an infra-telescopic sight on a laser beam spyglass, told me you think you're the Navaho Eliot Ness.'

'Would that be Mr John Slater?' Cady picked up bits of gravel and threw them at a brown bird, one at a time, missing by a mile.

'That would be, as you guess, the inimitable Slater. Who is himself the CIA's answer to a painful case of haemorrhoids, I'm beginning to think.'

Cady actually smiled thinly. He put his hands around his mouth and whistled an intricate, delicate call. The brown bird, who had ignored his throwing, cocked his head and made a beeline off over the hill.

'What did you say to him?'

'Her. I told her that her kids were fascinated by that snake on the branch over her nest.'

'I'm being put on again, I suspect.'

'Would Joe Leapinghorse do a thing like that?' Cady brushed off his hands fastidiously. 'I don't like amateurs doing my business any more than you would if I tried to do yours for you, Doc—Kelly. What is it, anyway?'

'I teach college students literature.'

'Would you mind if I came to your college and walked into your class and said, "Listen, students, this expert here knows only the formal stuff, but me, I know with my heart, see, I'm the one who should really explain Tennyson to you?" You're the one who's coming out here like the intuitive man from outer space with powers far beyond those of mortal men, you know, not me. I do this for a living, and I have been doing it well for a long time, and I resent like hell when some civilian, or some other professional who's off his goddam turf for that matter, sets up shop in my college.'

'You are right. I would resent you, and so I do apologize if I have given you reason to resent me.'

'Fine. Now let's share goodies. Maybe you've heard something about this Tennyson I haven't read in a book; for all I know, he and your Aunt Tillie slept together. Where does Dr Dan Michaels fit into all this? I thought, when I heard about him, that since you two were in the same trade, maybe you were a team. Slater thought so too, apparently, because he called his Boston people about it.'

'As far as I know, the fat doctor is here purely by chance.'

Cady sniffed.

'We met in transit. He's here to read a paper at a conference, and as far as I know, he's gone back by now. To New York.'

'Wrong. He's shacked up with a lady who lives over in Tesuque, that artists' colony. Are you ready for this? She runs the toy store on Canyon Road where the jack-in-the-box came from.'

'That could be coincidence too.'

'It could be coincidence that all the birds happen to fly south every winter too, but I don't think so. Mary Dowd doesn't think so either.'

Neil was getting more data than he could file, and too fast. 'You did say Mary Dowd.'

'Yes.'

'Mary Dowd, square and ungenial, of the very same CIA we were discussing?'

'Yes.'

'I think another bird just flew south. Does winter ever return in these parts about mid-April?'

Cady smiled, wider this time. 'Oh, to be in Boston, eh? Mary Dowd is in Santa Fe right now, did you know that?'

'The tourists and Indians are going to have move out to make room for all the cops.'

'She and I had a nice chat last night, about an hour before you got your surprise package at Bishop's Lodge. She doesn't like you, by the way, so we got along fine, since I told her I had the same feeling about this Dr Huffam who was using your name. A professional.'

'The KGB is full of them, I understand.'

'I think you're unconsciously prejudiced against dykes. Mr Kelly. Now, Mary Dowd and old Leapinghorse get along just fine, partly because we're both gay. It's a bond, like being black or liking lots of vermouth in your martini. We happy few.'

Neil looked at him a long few seconds. 'She works for Jack Slater, you know that, don't you?'

'I don't think so.' He turned his back to the view and leaned against the fence, looking past Neil's shoulder over the museum buildings. He glanced for the first time at

Neil's face, and what he saw there made him happy. A bewildered civilian. 'Fleas have little tiny fleas that bite 'em, do you know that one?'

'Oh yes. And so on, infinitum, up and down the entomological and cosmological scale. Do you think Mary Dowd is Jack Slater's flea?'

'I don't know. Honest Injun. She might be Dan Michaels's flea. You're right; there's someone up there watching your ass this second.'

'Should I turn very slowly with my hands in plain sight on top of my head or assume the spread position? I'm afraid I don't know the protocol.'

'Hell, why worry? Just don't lay lascivious hands on my body. It could be my people, who aren't entirely convinced that I'm a good risk, watching to see I don't feel up any male suspects in the course of my crafty investigations.' The FBI man scratched his crotch conspicuously. 'I think, if you want to know what I think, that Mary Dowd thinks that Jack Slater is a baddie.'

'Now, that's all we need. Another suspect and another suspicion. And I think, Agent Cady, sir, that she thinks that Slater and Michaels are in some kind of cahoots, but she can't possibly know what kind. You know there's a large army ordinance matter mixed up in this?'

'You know enough to *be* a spy. I know that, but you're not supposed to.'

'Cady, I have learned enough about army ordinance and computer access in the last two days to more than satisfy my secret desire for information on those subjects. You are not giving away any national secrets if you admit you know it, too. I also know that a lot of other assorted high-technology industrial stuff is getting mislaid and probably stolen and shipped out of the country. I can even tell you how the end-user certificates get altered; how's that for inside information? I even hear that there's a remote possibility that the people doing the mislaying and the stealing and the shipping out might have some weapons-grade uranium and the means for making it into a big, dangerous snowball to stick on the end of their new missile to point somewhere like the White House or Tel Aviv or some other tempting target.'

'Well, except that it's a ground-to-air, and that we are chiefly concerned at this time not with missiles at all, but with several thousand digital remote-control detonators, that's all very interesting.'

'Remote control as in setting off explosive charges from a distance?'

'Even so. As in setting off a tiny little bomb packed in a little box like a toy.'

'We are getting into what the humanistic psychologists call some really good sharing here, isn't that so, Mr Cady, sir?'

'Oh hell, yes, Professor. So tell me, since that's so, who the hell or what the hell Emslinn is. Besides your friend's daughter, if anything.'

'That's a question which has been perplexing me, sir, since a blind lady in a hospital many miles from here wrote that down on a piece of paper and gave it to me with every indication that it should not be shared with friend Jack Slater.'

'You want my guess?' He spoke rapidly and incomprehensibly. 'That's an invitation to go do something terrible to yourself in Navaho. I wonder if those turds up there are trying to read my lips. My guess is that it was chosen as a code name for something else.'

'Hmm.'

'You know that my people arrested a fellow last month who tried to kill a Libyan student not far from here? Guy was an ex-Green Beret, gun for hire, and Qaddafi's people gave him a contract on this student, who was leading an intellectuals' movement against Qaddafi. You see that in the papers back east?'

'In the papers, on TV—but I'm afraid I didn't pay much attention.'

' 'Course not. But I couldn't tell you who won the Pulitzer prize in poetry this year either. Well, that merry soldier of fortune belonged to a sort of fraternity of unemployed infantrymen who have a cell, a cadre, here in New Mexico, and another one in New Orleans—you read about them?'

Neil remembered the TV news picture, and the photo in the *New York Times*: men manacled, being herded into police vans in the rain. He thought inevitably of Tim's adolescent storm troopers. 'Ah, the people in the *Times* and *Newsweek* who were going to capture some island in the Caribbean and turn it into the world capital of gambling and narcotics. Notable if only because they were a mixed bag of Klansmen and Black Power types.'

'Right again. See, your FBI *is* out there, cleaning the streets and putting the shit away in tightly covered containers. It's not all just propaganda.'

'I want to thank you personally, but what has all that got to do with all this? It's getting damned cold out here.'

'You cold? That hairy jacket looks warm, so I figured you were as warm as toast. I'm freezing my ass, but I wasn't going to admit that to you. These bulletproof vests we wear don't really keep you warm, you know.' He looked at Neil, who knew better than to believe him, but suppressed a shiver anyway. Nice thought.

'I'd say let's sit in my car and finish this talk, but hell,' said Cady, 'you might make free with my body, now that you know my Achilles heel is in my ass, so let's just talk faster. What that has to do with this, Kelly, is that in both cases the Bureau confiscated materials including the code word EMSLINN.'

'Oh my.'

'Oh your? Oh *our*, Mr Kelly, I think. Our big, sloppy, national, probably international conspiracy to steal and ship high-technology secret equipment out of the United

States. With local chapters in selected cities and towns.'

'So Santa Fe is just one piece of a very large puzzle.'

'This whole region, not just Santa Fe, is just one piece. I told you I had a prior and well-developed interest in this case. This just happens to be where some people live who have the contract for constructing the firing platforms for the newest version of the red-eye missile up at Tonepah.'

'Did De Sales Lacey have any connection with this at all?'

'None we know of. His wife did, though, as you well know. She was doing some kind of surveillance for Slater's people, and we theorize she came across EMSLINN and made the connection with FiFoChi and the Mitchell family.'

'So whoever stole the missile probably works for FiFoChi.'

'Not necessarily. It might not be that neat. Let's say that FiFoChi—what the hell does that mean, anyway? It's not any Indian language.'

'Fifty-four, Chicago. Doan Mitchell used to play for the Cubs.'

'I'll be damned. You know, during World War Two, the Marines trained a lot of Navahos as communications specialists because then they could speak Navaho to each other over open lines and the Japs couldn't break the code. Did you know that?'

'An Irish poet once said that a language is not a code to be broken, but a mystery to be entered into.'

'Well, let's say that FiFoChi is just a sort of terminal, that maybe someone is using their trucks, their access to the base, their moving equipment, even their office computer, to move the stuff all over the world.'

'Would they have to be able to get into the company office regularly to do that?'

'Hell no. They could do it by phone if they had a set of the right computer code keys.'

'You think that EMSLINN might be a computer programme?'

'Now you've got it. That's the whole Navaho Mystery Theatre theory in a nutshell, Mr Kelly, sir. I think someone has a master computer programme channelled through the FiFoChi computer somehow, and I think they've started using it to steal and ship stuff which goes out to Europe, but which has its eventual end-user in Libya.'

'Az-Zauiah?'

'Again?'

'Az-Zauiah. Colonel Qaddafi's terrorist training centre.'

'Ah, so. I thought it was another baseball code. That's a new one on me, thank you.' He jotted it down while Neil spelled it. 'Oh, by the way, here's my card. Phone number. We don't use smoke signals any more; too easy to tap.'

Neil started back towards the road. He had walked the half mile from the house, and he needed another brisk walk now to get his blood circulating again.

'What are you going to do now?' The FBI man called after him.

He stopped. 'I'm going to sit down someplace warm and think about all you just told me and wait for Mary Dowd or Jack Slater or Dan Michaels or some other mysterious, familiar stranger to show up and tell me that Russell Cady is really the heterosexual cousin of Colonel Qaddafi.'

This time Cady laughed aloud. 'Ride back? I wasn't joking about the bulletproof vest, you know.'

Neil felt a sensation he remembered from the distant days when he had found himself in war for the first time, eighteen, and realizing that actual other people were pointing actual guns at his mother's actual youngest child and firing them with actual intent to do him bodily harm. The feeling began with a clutching large colon and rapidly spasmed up into a lurching gut and sudden cold sweat everywhere. Since he was next to Cady's car anyway, he sidled in.

Cady came in the other side. 'Relax. I don't go for older men.'

CHAPTER 12

The first to call was Dan Michaels. 'Neil? Wonderful. Afraid you might have fled these western precincts for the sane, predictable East. How about us getting together for dinner, a leetle talk about the book you and I are going to do together, meet Margo—Neil? You still there?'

'I'm still here, Dan. What book? Never mind Margo.'

'That's what I want to explain to you, of course. Met a wonderful drunken publisher at the conference. Published three of my books, thinks I'm as drunk as he is. Told him you and I are going to do a whole new treatment of the trickster figure in literature and psychology, thought you'd want to hear about it. I'm smiling, are you smiling, Neil?'

'No. I guess I don't see the joke.'

'Oh hell. Let me explain. I've got a table at the Pink Adobe. Wait till you taste the Creole cooking there. Margo took me. Listen, about Margo. This is the thin, rich, divorced lady with the upturned tits? That was you I told about her, wasn't it? Well, she has a medium zaftig friend if you're into non-thin, slightly masculine women, heh heh. Listen, I said I'd ask; we can make a nice foursome. You haven't got something better lined up, have you?'

'Dan, why are you giving me this borscht? Do you know that Mary Dowd is in Santa Fe?'

'Well, you do get around. As a matter of fact, Mary

Dowd is your blind date for tonight. We think maybe the time has come for you to tell us frankly what you know. You know, sharsies time, show and tell. Although if Mary starts showing, I might have to leave. God.'

'And will Slater be there? Cady? The director of the CIA? Who the hell is the director of the CIA now, anyway? Is it a secret?'

'Search me. We need you, Neil, my literary friend and collaborator. We need you because I think something very large is going down at this point in time, as our lost leader used to say, and there is the centre of the board where you have ingenuously placed yourself, you hold many of the pieces that answer many of the questions the rest of us have. If I were the bad guys right now, I would feel that I definitely had to kill Neil Kelly.'

'I feel safe.' Did he? 'At least three federal agents from at least six federal agencies are watching each other watching this house even as we speak.'

'Consider this, Neil, my friend, then plan to meet us at the Pink Adobe. At least one of those *federales*, maybe two, and at least one local who knows you by sight and whom you might trust enough not to suspect just might be the one or two or three planning to do the killing. If I were you, Professor, and I intended to collaborate with the distinguished psychiatrist from New York on a terrific book later, I would find a cool spot in the cellar and lie there very still until dark. Then I would sneak the hell down to the Pink Adobe, perhaps disguised as a Navaho Indian. Wear a blanket and a black hat with a feather in it. Eight o'clock?'

'No joke?' Neil realized as he asked the question that, given the context, it made no sense.

'About the book? Guaranteed advance in five figures, pop-psych best-seller list for twelve months, national tour, talk shows, champagne, all the Holiday Inns you can eat, bimbos, you name it.'

'Goodbye, Dan.' He hung up thoughtfully.

The house seemed suddenly very small and very transparent. If hostile persons, armed with large-calibre rifles and telescopic sights and/or remote-control detonators for small packages possibly already in place within the house, were out there in various strategic locations, then any good persons watching might just see a house blow up. That made it seem the better part of wisdom to leave the house and go somewhere else. The house would only be safe for the Mitchells if Neil Kelly moved out of it. Which left only the tactical problem of getting himself elsewhere with all deliberate haste and without getting shot.

While he considered the problem, he wrote a note for Doan Mitchell, saying that he was taking a side trip and would be gone overnight. He didn't know where the family left notes for each other, but he propped it against the Johnny Walker Black with some sense of reassurance.

He could not walk out of the house, not if someone were drawing a bead on him as the front door opened. He could not drive out. He had been away long enough for any vehicle to be booby-trapped. He couldn't call an armoured car to come and get him. He remembered again, with an acute physical sensation, his earlier sense of imminent disaster from the war and the sphincter that makes us all social animals when it is under control. It was like being once again back in a slow convoy, sitting in line, and waiting for the kamikazes to peel off and pick out one ship for the suicidal moment. God, he had prayed, hating himself for praying so basely, let them pick out someone else; it's a big fleet. The idea of being one of a fleet seemed a good one, but in his own case it hadn't worked at the time. Yet the odds were that something like that would work because the shooters he feared were not on a suicide mission, just after Professor Neil Kelly. *And if mine enemy maketh of me a laughingstokke, thought the Greene Knight, then him will I make to smile on bothe sides of his hed*. The line from the absurd senior play of the Lit. Majors ran through his head.

He dialled the cab company and ordered six cabs. Yes, he assured them, he needed six. Immediately. Yes, he supposed five would do if they had only five free. A tight squeeze, but send them. No, it wasn't a wedding party; it was a going-away party. Yes, the address is . . .

Five cabs arrived in a convoy after he had waited about ten minutes, sitting conspicuously away from all windows. The driver of the first cab came to the door and asked him if he was the party. He assured him that he was indeed the party and suggested he ask all the drivers in for a glass of Johnny Walker Black. Hell yes, man. The living-room filled up with two girls in jeans and work shirts, two Indians, and a hairy, middle-aged man as wide as a barn door.

He explained that he wanted to give each of them a ten-dollar tip before they started. Then he wanted to drive one of the cabs downtown himself while the real driver rode on the floor in back. Then he explained that no, he wasn't whacko; he had just made a bet that he could leave the house without being seen. The bet being with his neighbour, who was whacko. Through the living-room window, he pointed out to them the person seated up in the Lillienthals' driveway watching them all with binoculars. As a matter of interesting fact, they would notice that he was now standing on the roof of his car watching them with binoculars. Neil explained that the person riding on the floor of his cab would receive an extra fifty dollars. He realized that he was squandering his sabbatical spending money at a rate that would have made him weep a week ago. But his sphincter was holding firm again.

He poured another round of JWB. The drivers conferred among themselves and looked at him again. Their representatives asked for twenty each. He agreed. They looked angry at themselves, as though they thought they could have got more. Neil was looking at their hats. One Indian was wearing a black high-crowned hat with a feather. One girl wore a cap with 'Caterpillar Tractor' written on it. The barn door wore a Greek fisherman's cap. Neil wished that he had brought his secondhand Stetson into the house.

They agreed. Barndoor would ride on the floor of his own cab. They discussed strategy and agreed that if all the cabs backed into the yard and the three that would fit into the garage backed in there, then they could all barrel out together, taking pole positions, Sadie on the inside, Doc number two, then this guy with Albie on the floor, then Loomis, then Long, down the hill to fan out in the Plaza—one to La Posada, one to Loretto, one to the Capitol Building, one out Guadalupe five blocks, and one to the Palace. Okay? Okay.

Money exchanged hands. Doc copped an extra shot of JW. Neil went out through the side doorway into the garage and watched them manoeuvre their cabs in a cloud of dust into their agreed starting positions. As fast as they could make it, he and Albie switched places. He grabbed Albie's hat *en passant*. For half as much, he had got a perfectly good, used Stetson. He tried to remember his position. Third. They went off like an insane stock car race, five cabs racing down the old Santa Fe Trail. Eat your heart out, Billy the Kid, the mad driver of cab number three thought. They want tricks; we'll give them tricks. Please God, no shooting. Past them, going uphill, a sixth cab came flashing, waving and tooting madly, arriving just too late to carry their surplus passengers. Neil signalled him with an arm out the window to turn and follow. Bless him, he did, or at least he tried. Just hard enough to stall across the road sideways while a tan Dodge coming downhill with an FBI man driving it braked precipitously and made a fuss.

In five minutes, they were fanned out all over Santa Fe. Neil put Albie's hat on the seat, disembarked with a silent nod to the large man sitting on the floor smiling, walked casually into the Palace of the Governors, and sat down in a quiet spot under a portrait of Lew Wallace.

Perhaps the entire episode had been a panic, literally. In ancient Greece, that name had been given to the frenzy of fear in which men raced blindly through the woods, trying to escape the spirits, never seeing or hearing what they fled. Now, inside the low, vast, rambling old palace, which had stood on the north side of the Plaza since 1612 and had served the Spanish Empire, the Pueblo Indian Confederation, the Mexicans, and the Americans—Confederate and Union—as a capitol, with tourists quietly drifting through the old rooms whispering and joking, Neil was overtaken finally by a sense of complete foolishness. He had succumbed to a mindless moment of terror that had infected him with the irrational energy of pure panic, as a rat running a maze might finally bolt and break in any direction.

He breathed slowly, and walked along with a small family group who were being shown the governors' work-room by some knowledgeable local relative. He heard again, in greater detail this time, of how Lew Wallace had sat in that room with the shutters closed, writing his book while the venomous outlaw Billy the Kid had prowled the Plaza outside.

The trickster, Dan Michaels had said, is essentially a psychological reversion phenomenon; a throwback from rational, logical thought to an earlier level of collective evolution; an ancient child being summoned with a retinue of poltergeists and fairy folk, triggering off primitive fears and infantile terrors in the brain.

Neil stood alone for a while, studying the maps and drawings of early Santa Fe which illustrated the enormous difference the railroad had made in the shape and character of the town.

He had been rattled, he realized, like a child watching a shaman by firelight—the bird mask leaping in the shadows, the rattles ringing in his ears, shaken down to some level of his oldest fears, perhaps of his species' oldest fears. He remembered what he had told Will—that laughter is the genius in creation—and what Joyce had told us all—that the grandest answer to a universe which terrifies us is a great cleansing gust of laughter, not a snicker but a roar. The grandest answer is the question of the great Krazy Kat standing cocked against his lamp post: 'Izzat so?'

Calmly reconsidered, it was certainly possible that his life was in danger. He had accumulated in his hands, by one means or another, a number of threads that, if he could find the design, might show clearly the pattern of events and their causes. Barbara Lacey, it now seemed obvious, had come to this same point, had somehow put together the threads in such a way that whoever was behind the mystery thought it best to eliminate her. He should not return to Doan's house, for the Mitchells' sakes, he was sure of that. He would call Cady and have the FBI sweep it for explosives and electronic bugs, too. If the phone was tapped, who else knew he was supposed to meet Dan Michaels tonight? And that Mary Dowd was in town?

He walked into the gift shop of the Palace and looked over the Indian dolls and Indian silver and turquoise, at souvenir aprons and gewgaws. The three women behind the counter smiled absently in his direction and kept discussing the price of the dress Nancy Reagan had worn to some dinner. One woman said she had read twelve hundred dollars, but another said more, much more.

Although it struck him as an odd question to ask in a three-hundred-year-old building, he asked where the nearest phone was. Lobby entrance. He called Dan Michaels at La Posada, assuming that 'shacking up' with Margo was not necessarily a full-time activity.

'Dan, you alone? Can I talk?'

'Hello, Neil. Alone I am. Margo just left me. Am I an insatiable vulgarian, Neil? Be frank.'

'Listen, I'm not in the house now.' He felt like a fool pronouncing the words he had heard spoken in so many films. 'I think the phone might be tapped, and I want to change the place we'll meet.'

'Where are you? Of course the Mitchell phone is tapped, but it's my people who are tapping it. The only ones who know about our meeting tonight are you and I and Mary Dowd.'

'And Margo.'

'Well, actually, Neil—' he could hear the fat man belch quietly, 'that Mexican food is murder on my digestion—Margo I never got around to telling about it. We got involved in a discussion of sexual eccentricity, and it turns out that Margo is, in her heart of hearts, quite a puritanical person. Did I tell you we had a falling out?'

'I'm also told she's the woman who sold the first explosive toy. Is it pure coincidence, Dan, that you ended up in her bed?'

'Of course not. My zeal to find out what was going on, artfully inserted between my zeal for getting my paper applauded and my zeal for getting our new book published, led me to her shop. Charming, talented woman. I'm convinced she could have made it big on Madison Avenue: smart little shop up near the Whitney, gigantic prices for one-of-a-kind toys. Alas, she lacks urban attitudes; New York would destroy her. Anyway, she seemed copacetic at the time, so I moved in. Gone.'

'Am I being unrealistic to think I might be a target? No humour, just a straight answer.'

'I told you the truth. I think certain persons would prefer

to eliminate you. I don't think they will choose to do that in public or in any way that would set the police in pursuit of them but, as with the others, in some way distant from the perpetrators and hard to trace. The one I think is in the greatest danger is your host, Doan Mitchell.'

'Why? He's the least informed person in the whole cast of characters.'

'Yes, but I suspect that our trickster friend is directly connected somehow with FiFoChi. And in his stubborn, thorough, and uncompromising way, Doan Mitchell will start taking that company apart piece by piece until he finds out who that is; I do not think they will let him get that far in the dismantling process before they stop him. By the way, do you know where the scion of that clan of junior Klansmen is hanging out, the redoubtable Timothy Mitchell?'

Neil did not have to dissemble. 'No.'

'Has anyone else noticed that the younger boy, Will, has disappeared? Neil, are you still there? Now, that could be a kidnapping, in which case I'd think everyone would be sitting around talking with the FBI, or it could be that someone sent Will on an errand, like to talk to his brother and, if so, that person knows something my employers would like to know.'

Neil had put in two extra dimes and had only two left. 'I'll see you and your butch girlfriend at eight.' He hung up and dialled again, taking the number from the card Cady had given him.

No, Agent Cady wasn't in. Yes, he would receive the message Mr Kelly would leave. Yes, he understood that Mr Kelly wanted Mr Mitchell's house searched for explosives and swept for telephone taps this afternoon. Yes, he was taking this seriously. Agent Cady had given them Mr Kelly's name in case he called. He hung up again and walked out into the Plaza.

The long portico of the Palace was lined with Indians

displaying and selling their silverwork and crafts. By tradition, they had the right to positions there, and knowledgeable tourists, as well as those just curious to see live Indian craftsmen and women close up without going all the way out to a Pueblo, crowded past each other studying and buying what was on display.

Neil walked leisurely down the line, looking at silver and turquoise jewellery and Indian faces. The silverwork ranged from tiny rings set with chips of blue turquoise to great silver conchos of the sort he saw everywhere in belts and hatbands, the old horse trappings of the conquistadors now decorating tycoons from Akron and bar jockeys from the other San Francisco. He wore no jewellery himself, but it occurred to him that he might buy a silver ring for Barbara, for luck. We do not buy presents for the dying; perhaps our faith in their lives adds some sort of spiritual guaranty. He asked an Indian woman selling rings why one of her turquoises was green, not blue. He touched it. It had tiny birds delicately carved around the entire band.

'It's an old stone. Turquoise must be stabilized or it always turns green. Some people prefer that.' She spoke in the unaccented American speech of everyone else in Santa Fe. Had he been expecting a mixture of grunts and hand signs? 'It would be nice for someone who loves the birds.'

He bought the ring for eighty-five dollars. He knew a lady who would remember the birds when she touched them.

The day had warmed. A dry west wind had cleared the sky, which was now a Fabergé enamel blue; the vendors on the portico put off their blankets and ski jackets, and the tourist traffic became more leisurely.

He was suddenly hungry, almost weak-hungry. He walked east along the Palace, which became another structure without losing the line of the long portico, and found a narrow door through the wall into a courtyard. Within was a small restaurant. The sign on the door said forthrightly that if he was looking for fast food or junk food, he'd better go away; that they took their cooking seriously, so it might take a little time to get waited on. He silently cheered the policy, despite his hunger, and went in. He was taken through low rooms to a table down back, and given the coldest, best Mexican beer he had ever drunk, followed—in good time, as they had explained—by some Mexican food that he had ordered after the waitress described the contents of each dish carefully, as though she doubted his ability to understand what he was doing. In a way, she was right. The food—light, hot, even fiery—was entirely new, made his eyes weep, curled his tongue, and entered some place in his soul, bringing calm and deep satisfaction. He felt he had discovered soul food in some original form. It was one of those moments of personal discovery, even better for being wholly unexpected, in which our tastes and sometimes even our values are transformed permanently. Neil fell in love with Mexican cooking in that little restaurant with the dignified sign out front. He ate slower, drank deeper, and savoured the hour.

By the time he had left the restaurant, visited seven galleries of southwestern and Indian arts, sat in a tiny church which reminded him disconcertingly of Sainte Chapelle until he found it was a miniaturized copy built by some homesick French nuns, visited the oldest house in the United States—a mouldering adobe structure across from the oldest mission church—had a long slow gin-and-tonic in the La Fonda bar, and sat in the Plaza for an hour just watching tourists watching Indians, Neil felt ready to face Dan and Mary Dowd, if not dinner at the Pink Adobe.

CHAPTER 13

The restaurant was close to the mission church he had been in earlier, in the section of Santa Fe that had been settled earliest. He found the jovial psychiatrist and the expressionless Dowd seated at a table at the end of a low passageway, partially obscured by the bulge of a kiva fireplace in which the inevitable piñon blaze was flaring, perfuming the small room.

'That table's permanently reserved, so no one's going to sit there,' Michaels said, waving at the unoccupied table between them and the entrance. 'Private room, practically. You know Ms Dowd, I believe.'

'We've met.' Neil nodded to the imperturbable woman. 'Are you here because you began to miss your father, Ms Dowd?'

'Can we cut the crap and talk business?' was her opening remark, before Neil had quite seated himself.

'I see what you mean about your father's type, Mary,' Michaels said to her, patting her hand, 'but we mustn't be rude to our guest.' Neil fully expected her to clout him, but she simply withdrew the offended hand to her lap with dignity.

'Neil, I took the liberty of ordering for all of us, so you'd better like it or it's fifty bucks down the tube.'

Chilled white wine arrived in an ice bucket stand. Its label was inspected by the psychiatrist, its contents sampled, its purveyor approved, and finally it was actually poured into their glasses. A quite ordinary white Rioja.

Dan Michaels's attempts at leading the discussion while leavening the heavy dough of loathing with banter and offhand chat didn't matter one iota to Mary Dowd. She brushed aside his pleasantries as if she were waving away an unpleasant odour.

By the time the onion soup and salads were on the table, she said, 'Now can we get to the goddam point?'

The psychiatrist tossed his roll in the air and caught it weakly. 'Oh, all right, Mary, if you have no soul, I guess you have no soul.' He sighed gustily and ate his soup as if he resented it.

'Good.' She put her meaty arms on the table and swept things out of her way. 'Kelly, I know what you've been doing. Dan has brought me up to date. Now you know that I don't like you, but I think you don't know why, so I'm going to tell you.'

Neil forestalled her, feeling at some risk, but feeling even more that enough was enough. 'Unless I've developed some new personality flaw in the last few days, Ms Dowd, I think I know exactly why you dislike and resent me. Because damn near everyone else in Santa Fe has taken a turn at telling me why they dislike me, and it seems everyone has the same basic reason. I'm butting into your business. I'm the tenderfoot teacher from the effete East who has wandered into the OK Corral at high noon, waving his weapon, which turns out to be a wooden sword, just when all you professionals were set to have a shootout. You hate me because I'm a goddam interfering amateur.'

She nodded. 'That's close enough.'

'But I'm an amateur you all need.'

'So Dan says. I doubt it, frankly.'

'And finally, this *fricfrac*, whatever the hell it is going on, which has killed a friend of mine and a harmless boy and put another friend of mine in the hospital, somehow involves one or more of your professionals, and you resent like hell having this amateur seeing your soiled laundry, Ms Dowd.'

She eyed him bitterly across the small table. 'And maybe I'm just a little afraid that if we have to depend on a creepy amateur in a crisis, it will be your jockey shorts that get soiled, Professor.'

Dan leaned back and wiped his lips fastidiously with his napkin. 'Jesus, you two certainly know how to make good food taste better.'

The waiter cleared and brought plates of seafood in thick, caramelized red sauce. Neil was reminded instantly of the French Quarter of New Orleans, and with that his appetite revived.

'What do you know about computers, Kelly?' Mary Dowd asked him bluntly, scooping the food into her mouth, apparently without taking time to chew it before swallowing. It was like watching a machine feed itself.

'Nothing. Bread?'

'No, this is enough trouble. We think someone's rigged the Army's computer up at Tonepah, and we think it's being manipulated through the terminal at FiFoChi.'

Neil kept eating the delicious shrimp daintily.

'And we think we know who's doing it. Are you interested, against my better judgment, in helping us find out?'

'You mean, am I interested in helping you prove your guess? Why should I be? The person you suspect might be someone I know personally, *and* your guess might be quite wrong. I'd be conspiring against a friend, and because I am—as you say without saying, Ms Dowd—relatively naive, I could be giving aid and comfort to your cause without really knowing what I was doing. In other words, I would be your puppet.'

'Mary is right about one thing, Neil. You are either in or out of this *fricfrac*, as you call it. If you are in, you have two choices. You can cooperate with us—that is, with your government—or you can obstruct us, which, in effect, means you are cooperating with criminals.' He lifted his hands in his 'is it my fault?' gesture.

From the main dining-room on the other side of the wall, they could hear a table of celebrants shouting 'For

He's a Jolly Good Fellow' and applauding. Neil had a fleeting memory of exploding red smoke and the instant of believing that his face was being shattered. He took a long drink of wine and looked at Mary Dowd, who was studying him like a large bird eyeing a disgusting bug.

'I'm sorry, I didn't hear what you said.'

'I said, if you don't cooperate with us, they might kill you anyway, to prevent your doing so eventually.'

He felt helpless and tired. He was rapidly changing sides to feel sympathy with those who believed this was no game for middle-aged literary scholars. 'What do you want me to do?'

'Find out fast for us who—everyone—who has access to the computer terminal and codes at FiFoChi.'

'Isn't that just a question of finding out who works at the terminal? And isn't that just a matter of checking personnel records?'

'Uh-uh, look.' The big woman leaned forward over the table, and Neil knew that she felt completely at home talking about computers because she started to speak from the authority of her intelligence for the first time, with the unselfconscious assurance of a teacher.

'Anyone can use a computer to steal. A cashier in a New York bank who never had an hour's instruction used his own bank's computer system to steal two million dollars. He was only caught because his name turned up in a police raid on the bookie joint where he was betting ten times his salary on the horses. A student in California taught himself not only how to use computers, but how the telephone company uses theirs to order equipment. He set up a dummy company, called it the Los Angeles Telephone Company, for Chrissakes, ordered equipment charged to the real phone company, and sold it out of a warehouse. He's a computer security specialist now; one of his biggest customers is the phone company. He got out of it with a fine.'

'But isn't the Army computer system a lot more secure than those in ordinary company offices?'

'Balls. Less, because assholes run it. The Army spent three years developing a foolproof Univac up at MIT. Two Army specialists who did know what they were doing broke into it by phone in two hours and stole the whole memory system. They were hard-wired into the system they were stealing from, which meant it was a closed-circuit theft, and the Army itself was paying them to run the test because they were so sure they'd fail, but two hours it took. There are *no* foolproof computers; they all have a flaw.'

'Like us poor mortals.'

'And,' Dan said, clearing his throat and glancing at Mary Dowd as if for permission, 'this might be a good place to bring up this other thing. There is at least a reasonable suspicion that whoever at FiFoChi is doing the breaking and stealing from the Army computer is connected with someone—how shall I say it—?'

'Oh, for Chrissake, Dan, one of us. Just say the goddam truth and get it over with. Someone in our firm, Kelly.' She appeared to be grinding her teeth, but she made the admission.

'Slater?' Neil pronounced the question to make it sound like a statement, and it gave him some satisfaction.

'That's possible.' This time her teeth were firmly clenched.

'By the way, does Slater know you're here, Ms Dowd?'

She blew her nose into her napkin. 'Slater is up at Tonepah tonight.' The subject seemed closed.

'And inside FiFoChi?'

'There are three possibilities.' Dan Michaels spoke abstractedly, as if he were trying to remember the odds on drawing a third seven. 'Linn Mitchell. Barnabas Keeney. Maimandi Nejad.'

'Anyone else would be absolutely impossible?'

'No, not absolutely. Remember, anyone who could get the keys and codes—from those three, probably—could do it. But those three are unquestionably the best bets.' He emptied the wine bottle evenly into their three glasses. 'The girl because she is Em's Linn, as you could have told us in the first place, if you had chosen.'

Mary Dowd intensified her glare.

'Her boy-friend, the Irishman, because he is not one person, but several. First off, he changed his name to Barnabas Keeney; he was born Bernard Koenig of German parents in Ireland during World War Two. They were there quite legally, working in some clerical capacity for the German government in a neutral country, but at the end of the war they disappeared, along with their young son, and were never seen again. He apparently changed his name quite openly in this country, in Massachusetts, years later. *After* spending an unknown amount of time in Germany, possibly in East Germany under at least one other alias, Willi Schmidt. He is a graduate engineer with expertise in electronics.'

Neil accepted coffee from the waiter and put sugar and cream into it while the conversation lagged.

'And finally, the Iranian. Although Mr Nejad prefers to have it believed that his family are half old-regime supporters and half revolutionary Shiites, they are in fact well-identified members of a leftist group opposed to both factions and connected to a pan-Muslim movement outside Iran. Their group, in fact, seized the Grand Mosque in Mecca last year and tried very hard to start a new all-out holy war against everyone at once. Nejad is a brilliant technician.'

Neil was without any adequate reply. He drank more coffee and tried to absorb what he was hearing.

'You see, Mr Kelly, don't you, that there is a great deal you need to know that you don't know?' The rhetorical question from Mary Dowd had an edge of rotten sweetness to it; she was gloating.

'And, oh yes,' Dan added as an afterthought. 'That Jordanian who flits around there is not what he pretends to be either. He puts it out that he is a liberal, leftish Democrat, but he is in fact a registered Republican, and boasts to his close friends that he voted for Reagan.'

'Isn't there a Navaho Indian in there you missed?'

'Don't come all over liberal-bitter, Kelly,' Mary Dowd said in the same whore's caressing tone. 'The Indian would like to support AIM, but he's basically scared shitless for his job, so he keeps his mouth shut, even among *his* closest friends.'

For the next twenty minutes, the two agents briefed Neil on what they needed to know from inside FiFoChi. He was being recruited by the CIA. If anyone had asked him a week earlier of the possibility of that happening, he would cheerfully have bet his sabbatical against it. Now he was listening to the odd couple tell him how to listen and what to ask when he visited Doan's plant tomorrow.

'What makes you think I'll be asked to visit there tomorrow?'

'You'll see that you are. It shouldn't be too difficult to ask your friend to let you have a tour of the plant, should it? You'd probably do it on any extended visit, and now there are a hundred reasons why he might want you to anyway—the wise old friend, shrewd old Professor Kelly.'

Tension and anger were taking their toll of Neil's energy. 'I need a place to stay tonight,' he said abruptly.

'My place or hers?' Dan asked, his lips pursed in a Kewpie smile.

CHAPTER 14

Neil's late evening with Dan Michaels was lacking in most of the desirable qualities of a memorable social occasion. The psychiatrist's wit didn't seem so effervescent now that it was clear that the mind behind it was calculating each witticism with some unsettling effect in mind. Neil refused to let himself be drawn into a discussion of the psychology of the trickster or to take seriously his host's repeated assertions, as he laid out towels and made up a bed for his guest on the couch, that they were potentially the greatest comedy team since Masters and Johnson.

He showered luxuriantly in the slamming hot spray and towelled himself viciously, reviewing in his mind the variety of turns in the maze he had been led through. There was just one question he still had to ask Dan Michaels before he could go to sleep.

'Which one of the three do you really suspect?'

'I thought you'd never ask.' The fat man was eating a sandwich composed of several layers of leftovers from his refrigerator. 'But if I tell you that, won't it prejudice your objectivity; clutter your keen, untrammelled vision; fuck up the dispassionate detecting?' He was grinning cherubically. He had the compulsive talker's need for conversation, and the true trickster's love of games. He was clearly delighted to have finally tempted Neil into an exchange.

'Which, goddammit, Dan?' Neil was furious and unwilling to play.

'Well, aren't we touchy late in the evening? You and Margo would have got along fine. Have you ever thought of talking to a shrink about this unwillingness of yours to engage in social intercourse after ten o'clock at night?'

Neil felt beyond reason and decorum. The lamp would

do nicely if he had to hit the munchkin sitting before him. 'So help me, Dan, I'll clobber you with this,' he said flatly.

The psychiatrist's clinical experience had taught him to recognize when the client had edged up to authentic violence. He shrugged eloquently, as if relinquishing a cherished sweet, and said, 'Keeney, the ersatz Irisher. We think he just entered the girl's name into the computer—EMSLINN—as some sort of routing key or trapdoor to cut off any trace. Would you like to know what a trapdoor is in computer talk? It's a very playful device—all right, all right, don't get nervous with that lamp; I just thought you might be curious.'

'Why Keeney? What is there that makes him *the* prime suspect? Is there something, or are you just guessing?'

'Why not go to sleep, Neil, and let it rest until morning. Aren't you tired? Don't you want a nice beddy-bye? Want a trank? I'm a doctor, you know; I have candy make you sleep like a baby.'

Neil lifted the psychiatrist's glass of milk and poured it sadly over the owner's foot.

'Now, that's terrible.' The fat man jumped to another chair and shook his foot finickily. 'Okay, okay, so we know a few things. Starting with what you already know. Keeney was a German national, born and raised in Ireland until he was five, six. He and his parents later disappeared, probably into Germany, from which he came out, but not they. Came over here, went to school, changed his name. We think he was trying to establish a clean identity and a clean life for himself, but he knew there was always a chance he'd hear again from his folks—you know how families are. And when he did hear, we wanted to know why. We picked up a signal from East German sources. Bertha and Harry suddenly surfaced.'

'His parents?'

'We don't know. We think maybe. Or at least the code

signal for them. Things suddenly began to move rapidly here. Our Irish friend decides to get married, right? His residency papers are a leetle funny; he didn't tell the truth and nothing but truth when he emigrated. He wants suddenly to be married to an American citizen.'

'They're in love. I've seen them; it's not an act.'

'Wonderful. Bless them both. But still we are interested in the timing, which could be pure coincidence, but which we Jungians think is synchronous in the larger sense, you know, connected. It will be simple to find out, and that's what you can do for us better than anyone else.'

'Am I to go up to him and ask if he's an East German spy on detached duty, some sort of mole, waiting for his father and mother to join him?'

'Something like that, but subtler, you know, with a little more finesse. You should tell him—or anyone else who's listening—that Bertha and Harry have decided to go into the umbrella business if they can get a light-industrial permit.'

'I'm going to bed.'

'No, I swear. There are three phrases which appear to be significant as some sort of trigger for a German agent over here. We don't actually know if they are for someone named Joe Schwartz in Buffalo or Bemis in Atlanta, or Keeney, or Joe Schmo from Chicago. But we know they mean something. The names of the aunt and uncle, the umbrella business, and the light-industry permit. We have people all over this wonderful country wandering in and out of country clubs and McDonald's and God knows where else, muttering about this wonderful couple trying to get a foothold—a handhold, I suppose—in the umbrella business if they can only get an industrial permit.'

'And I am supposed to mention that tomorrow?'

'You are if you would like to prove or disprove our thesis that Keeney is our man.'

'Good night, Dr Michaels.' Neil lay down on the convex

sofa and turned his back to the lighted room.

Dan Michaels sighed and turned on the TV to watch a movie about an endless horse race across the West in the old days. Gene Hackman seemed to be winning, but Michaels rooted vocally, ignoring his recumbent guest, for Candice Bergen.

'I love that girl's uvula,' he announced, 'ever since I saw it for the first time in *Carnal Knowledge*.'

When Neil left Dan Michaels's casita in the morning and walked across to the Staab House for breakfast, the day was already warming. Two small kids in cutoff jeans and their mother, a bony woman in a lime green bikini, were already using the pool on the grounds.

Before he went in for breakfast, he used the public phone behind the souvenir shop to call Doan.

Yes, he had got his note all right, but he was a little worried about how much Scotch Neil had apparently imbibed. His chief interest was in what came next.

He told Neil that all hell had broken loose at the plant the previous day because the Army and the FBI had both descended in force, with a court order to shut down the terminal on their computer until it could be examined by some people flying out from Washington. A bunch of experts in computer espionage. They thought the darn thing was being used to break into the Army computer up in Tonepah, and that his daughter Linn had something to do with it.

'The fertilizer has really hit the fan, Neil, and how in heck I'm supposed to run a business I don't know. Poor Linny is in shock. They want her to appear at a special inquiry or hearing or some darned thing at the FBI office.' He sounded distraught. He wanted to know if Neil thought he should call Emily back home, no matter what.

Neil advised him not to decide anything yet, skipped breakfast, and took a cab out to the house. He was almost completely convinced that matters had gone past the point now where anyone cared to eliminate Neil Kelly, and besides, if Cady had kept his promise, the house was safe.

The two men stayed in the kitchen while Doan cooked some eggs and made coffee, then ate standing at the counter.

'Doan, I don't *know* what's going on, but I've learned enough in the last twenty-four hours to know that it's a lot bigger than a few trucks being stolen or even the Army losing a missile. Someone has been using the FiFoChi computer to steal from the Army computer, and beyond that I'm as ignorant as you are.'

Then, with great care, and going step by step, he told the big, worried man across the counter from him that the CIA thought Barry might be an East German agent.

Doan Mitchell almost went through the ceiling. 'Well, Jesus God Almighty Christ, Neil, are they nuts? Why that man—'

Neil interrupted him to tell him everything he knew: the name change, the residency problem and, finally, what he proposed saying later with Barry present. 'If he doesn't just tell me I'm mildly eccentric, talking about Harry and Bertha and the umbrella business—if he makes any dramatic move to respond to that signal, Doan, we're going to have to believe them.'

Doan's moan of angry and confused rebuttal was cut off by the phone. Doan grabbed it viciously off the hook. It was Will, asking for Neil.

'This is your father, goldarn it, Willy, you okay? Can't you talk to your own father? You over at Boyd's?'

'I'm fine, Dad. But I really need to talk to Mr Kelly. It's really important.'

Doan gave up the receiver with a black look at it.

'Hello, Will. This is Neil Kelly. Listen, I'm with your father, but he's going to go out on the patio for five minutes.' He waved Doan out the screen door, and the big man went, taking his coffee cup and looking more puzzled than mad.

'Okay, we can talk now. Is Tim there?'

'Yeah. He's right here.' Neil gave the thumbs-up sign through the door to the peering Doan. 'He wrecked the wheel on his motorcycle doing jumps, and he sprained his stupid ankle, but he's here. Alone.'

'Good boy. Now listen. We are really pressed for time, and there are a lot of things at stake in this—more than a stolen truck. Let me talk to Tim.'

'H'lo. Yeah, this is Tim.' The familiar, sullen voice, sounding at least a little chastened if not sincerely contrite, came over the phone. Doan made the name 'Tim?' with his lips, head stuck in through the kitchen door, and shook his fist at the phone.

'Tim, this is Neil Kelly. Has Will explained the general situation?'

'Yeah, I guess. If I come back up there and admit I stole the truck out of the yard at FiFoChi and all that, the FBI won't be on my back about Jimmy Lathen getting killed in it.'

'That's correct. Will you come back with Will?' Doan was edging inside the door and getting into listening range. Neil held the receiver so that they could both hear. Doan started making whirlybird signs with a finger over his head, a question mark on his face. 'Your father will send the chopper for you.'

'Okay, I guess. Listen, what about the backhoe?'

Neil shrugged and asked Doan with his eyes, but got a shrug back.

'Sorry, Tim, nobody said anything to me about a backhoe.'

'Boy, that's really wild. We ripped off one of them, too, see? To grade the dirt trail up at Red River. I just said to the guys one day, "Let's do it!" You mean those assholes don't even know it's missing yet?'

'Forget it, Tim; the point is, they did find out about the truck, and you are going to have to meet with your father and face the music on that one.'

'Ah shit, I guess.'

'Tim, this is crucial, so answer carefully and truthfully. Did Jimmy Lathen tell you about the toy your Aunt Barbara bought to be delivered to De Sales that evening?'

'Yeah. Well, like he mentioned it, y'know? Like he thought it was weird for grown-up people to be giving each other toys for presents. She told this lady in the store, I guess, and he sort of overheard.'

'And did you tell someone else about that?'

There was a perceptible pause along the line.

'Well, Chrissakes, only that FBI guy.'

Neil was entirely nonplussed. 'You told someone from the FBI?' Cady? he wondered. Or one of the others, behind a false FBI beard? 'Anyone else? Anyone at all?'

'Nah. Why would I? But this guy was like leaning on me. Listen, he came into Pinto's when I was having lunch that day, and he sits down with me, and he says he's with the FBI and he's checking out the Laceys. At first I thought it was a gag, y'know? But, well, like he knew some stuff about us—the BG&E? We had this kilo of really good hash this same guy sold us the week before, and he says he'll come down like a ton of shit on us if we don't cooperate, and if we help him out he'll lay off. So I told him some stuff about the Laceys, like she's really into photography and all that, and Jimmy Lathen comes in in the middle of it, and he tells us about this toy thing. I figured maybe they were after old J. P. Morgan for taxes or something, so what's the difference, y'know? Then, after we heard something really bad went down up there, and my old la—when Mum said this FBI guy was around the house, I figured I better bug out. Will told me about Jimmy—Jesus, that guy do it or what?'

Neil found he was unready to respond to this unanticipated complication. He said nothing for several seconds before answering. 'We don't know yet, Tim. But tell me just one more thing before I hang up. Who taught you to use the computer terminal at FiFoChi? That was how you got the truck, wasn't it?'

'Will she get in trouble? I don't see why they should give her a hard time, like she didn't actually help me rip off the stuff. Linny, of course. A couple of days when Dad and Barry were up in Utah.'

'Barry told me you and your gang were up by Taos that time, at Red River, racing your bikes.'

'Yeah, well, we were. And he comes up there early that morning and gives us all a bunch of shit about danger and how we'd break our necks on that slope—the grade's kind of hairy there—and all that stuff. Then he left in my old man's plane, and we kind of talked about what he said. Some of the guys went on practising jumps, but I got on my bike and headed south back down to Abbacue—Albuquerque, y'know?—and I went down to the old man's plant. And Linny started talking to me, bragging like, about her computer. So I go, "Hey, I could learn to run that thing in about five minutes," and she says, "Oh yeah?" and so I sit down there and she shows me how it works and I just tried it out. A baby could do it.'

'As simple as that.' Neil shook his head at Doan, who looked on the verge of exploding at his son. 'Stay put. The chopper will be down there in, what? Three hours, maybe a little longer.' Doan held up four fingers, mouthing, 'Where?' 'Now, don't answer the phone again; just sit tight.' He hung up and wiped the sweat from his own forehead. 'Thanks, Doan.'

'Where's he at, anyway?'

'Cloudcroft. Your cabin there.'

'Dang me. I'll bust his goldarn butt, that brat. And where the heck's my backhoe? I'll bust that Los Alamos foreman if it's not on his job site where it's probably supposed to be, bigod.'

Then, as if he had suddenly remembered he had other concerns, Doan looked sheepish for a second and grabbed the phone to dial Emily in Philadelphia. After two calls, one to her family's number, being told she had left an hour ago to fly up to Boston, and then another to his sister Jane, who wasn't there, he gave up in disgust. Then he tried one last time, calling his sister at the Boston City Hospital, and fighting his way past an officious operator to have her paged. They tracked her down in the doctors' lounge having coffee.

Yes, she knew that Em was coming up, and they had plans for dinner back at Jane's apartment. She thought Em would be staying at the Copley Plaza, but she wasn't sure. Doan told her that he wanted to talk to Emily urgently, to get her to call home, and left it at that.

'Lord knows what she'll think when she hears that. That Tim has got himself shot by the FBI, probably. Last thing in God's world she'll expect to hear is that they think Linny and Barry are some kind of spy team.'

Neil broke the silence that followed his friend's unhappy observation by saying, 'Are you going to call Barry, or should I?'

'You can't call him. Why would you want to call him? No sir, I'm the Judas goat for this one, Neil. And if he's guilty—if, mind you, and it sours my stomach to say that—I'm not going to feel bad I done it. But you'll have to convince me with a lot more than some wild stories the CIA got out of some other computer.'

When Barry did drive up in the yard in his scarlet car that still looked to Neil like a giant toy, the two men were sitting in the living-room going over the whole affair again, starting back with Barbara's injury and Morgan's death.

The Army had called Doan to tell him he was going to be needed back at the main office in Albuquerque for a general inquiry starting at one o'clock. Until the moment Barry arrived, Doan kept shaking his head and picking at the callouses on his hands.

'It was Barry showed them colonels how easy it would be for someone to bug their darned computer. He didn't make any bones about it; he just sat down there at the terminal and showed them.'

After he had made the comment, he saw that it could be heard two ways and winced. 'Everything's backwards and upside down, Neil, I dunno.'

Barry came in and threw himself into one of the big chairs and started talking without any small social niceties.

'Did Doan tell you what the FBI did? They didn't exactly arrest Linny, but they all but have the girl in custody! They think she's been breaking into the Army's goddam computer and stealing their codes and God knows what else.' He seemed wild with strain, his hands and eyes jumping. 'I slept about twenty minutes last night. What's going on, anyway, do you know, man?'

Neil started in a low key because he assumed that the conversation would get high-pitched fast enough. 'We all slept poorly, Barry, I think. I had a meeting last night with some people from the CIA myself. They asked me if you were German, and not Irish.' He let the statement hang there as a question.

Barry put his hands over his face. 'Glory be to God, wouldn't you know they'd come up with that now? It's not something I've gone around telling the world, mind you. Anyone can look up the records in Boston and see that I changed my name when I was at Northeastern. Look, man, I *am* Irish by birth, as much as you're American. Linn knows all that— ' He waved the idea away from him irritably.

'You never told us.' Doan's tone was mournful and accusing.

'Ach. I would have eventually. I'm not exactly thrilled or proud, you know, that my parents were Nazi clerks in Dublin during the war, or that they were stupid enough to try to get back into Berlin afterwards and apparently got caught up in somebody's security net.'

'Do you actually not know where they are?' Neil watched him. The man was obviously in a state of acute nervousness. There were purple circles under his eyes, and he hadn't combed his hair or beard.

'Oh, I'm reasonably sure where they are, or were. The last time I saw them, remember, I was six years old. I was taken out of Berlin by friends of theirs who left me with an aunt, who shipped me back to Ireland as fast as she could. One more mouth to feed was no joke then. Thank God the Irish take hospitality for granted. It was the Coughlins, where I went then, who raised me.'

'Did you have any token, or souvenir, or picture, or anything from your parents?'

'No, nothing, it was a clean break. They either got taken away or decided to stay for their own reasons, and I was back in Ireland so fast I have trouble remembering the journey at all now as a real event.'

'If someone were to contact you now with news of your parents, what do you think you'd do?'

'Mother of God, how do I know? How old would they be now?' He hammered the arm of his chair morosely with the flat of his hand. 'Go to them? Walk away from it? Anyway, it won't happen.'

'What were their names, Barry?'

'Wilhelm was my father—a big, stout, blond man, I think.' He smiled at some inner joke. 'I used the name Willi on a visit to a whorehouse in Berlin once, to see what it felt like to be a Willi. And Edwina was my mother. She smelled of something sweet, and she had ginger hair, frizzy, like a cloud around her head. She called it her cloud of glory.'

Neil leaned easily against the mantel, kicking at a piñon log sticking out of the basket. 'Is it true you had an Uncle Harry and an Aunt Bertha who were in the umbrella business?'

The Irishman looked astonished. 'Who in God's name told you that? Harry and Bertha, you say? Where would you hear a thing like that? I suppose there is such a thing as the umbrella business, but it sounds crazy.' He did not seem to be able to let it alone. 'Crazy.'

Neil waved it away with a movement of his fingers. 'They are actually the ones who mentioned it. A foreign couple staying at La Posada phoned me there last night and said that they were your aunt and uncle, and that they needed an industrial permit to get started in the umbrella business out here, and wondered how to reach you to see if you could help them with the red tape and so on.'

'Completely nuts. God, people get crazier all the time.' He jumped up. 'Listen, Doan, I can't sit here while everything's going around in circles and the FBI is trying to convince Linny that she's a spy. I'm going to get over to her place and see how she is.' He moved towards the door.

'The Army wants you and me back at the plant at one for some meetings with people from Washington, Barry. Don't miss that, or they might send a search party out for you.'

The departing figure waved stiffly back through the door. 'I'll be there, have no fear.'

They watched him get into his red sports car and drive off.

CHAPTER 15

'Now what?' Doan asked, watching the disappearing car.

'Now we wait, I suppose, and see what happens.'

'You think Linny's in any danger from him, Neil? Think I oughta call her, maybe tell her to be out?'

Neil thought a moment, knowing how hard the question was for Doan to frame, and gave him the only answer he could. 'There's no harm in taking some precautions, Doan. Why don't you just ask her to visit the supermarket for the next half-hour, perhaps bring you a few groceries over here? Tell her we two old bachelors are starving to death here without a good woman to take care of us and feed us right.'

He listened as Doan called his daughter and asked her if she'd be good enough to do some grocery shopping for her old daddy, maybe bring over some ribs that he could barbecue tonight after they all got back from Albuquerque. Linn told him she didn't want to go out right then because she was expecting Barry to call, he told her that he'd already talked with Barry and told him to come by here this morning, so she'd probably run into him if she came over.

'Lie to my own child,' he growled disgustedly after he hung up.

After they had both had another cup of coffee and stared out the window a while, Neil noticed with idle interest that no one was sitting in a car up in the Lillienthals' driveway any more.

Doan remembered with a start that he had promised Tim and Will a helicopter ride home from Cloudcroft, and called his pilot in Albuquerque to dispatch him. He laughed for the first time all morning. 'That darn old cabin. Neatest little place we ever had. Down by the national forest. Kids loved it. So that's where that little peckerhead went.'

Three minutes after he had hung up from talking with his pilot, the phone rang again.

Doan didn't go to it immediately. He said, 'Well, it sure is more interesting to stay home and answer the phone these days than ever it used to be. You take that, Neil?' It was the first time Neil had ever seen naked fear in his friend's eyes.

'Professor Kelly? Dr Michaels here. We've just had a visit from your friend Mr Koenig-Keeney. A large acquaintance of mine is standing over him as he sits in my chair, even as I speak. He inquired at the desk, it seems, for old Bertha and Harry, and so was sent here, as I had suggested to the management. I think he's our man, Neilo, and I think we have him cold. You tell your friend Doan Mitchell that. It won't take all the heat off his daughter, but it will lower the temperature a degree or two.' He hung up without waiting, for once, for any repartee.

Neil sat down slowly. 'Barry walked into the CIA trap, asking for Harry and Bertha.' His body and mind felt numb with disbelief and anger in equal, paralysing mixture.

'Well, sheeit me for a dummy! He sure had me fooled. I am goddammed for a fool, Neil. Poor little Linny.' He looked sharply over at Neil. 'He say she was involved at all?'

'No. So far he's said nothing, I gather. What will you tell her?'

Tears welled up in Doan's eyes, and he wiped them away with the tips of his big fingers at the corners. 'I don't know.' His voice was a big whisper. 'I don't know, Neil. Tell her they've arrested him, I guess, and wait and see. Oh my God, Neil.' He looked as if he had been beaten; his face hung in folds, and he sagged in his frame, all the energy and fight gone out of him.

When Linn arrived with two brown bags of groceries in her arms an hour later, she was met by two men each trying to be more solicitous than the other in helping her.

'Hey, you guys, I'm not pregnant or anything—as far as I know. All of a sudden, Linn's getting more help than she needs. Is that because the stupid FBI thinks I'm a master spy, or a mistress spy or whatever, and you two are trying to ease the pain?' She set the bags on the kitchen counter and efficiently started to unpack and shelve the contents. 'I got some really good ribs, Dad. Aw, Daddy, cheer up, I didn't steal their darn old missile.' Her animated face froze.

Neil had walked around the counter with a pound of oleo in his hand and put it back on the counter. Her father lifted a green cardboard oblong packed with a row of tomatoes under plastic, and stood holding it.

'Was Barry here?'

'Linny, he was here, but—he was here, but—'

'He's been arrested on the same suspicion, Linn, of breaking into the Army computer.'

'Oh my God, that's so damn stupid!' She left the remaining packages on the counter and went to the phone. Once she picked up the receiver, she became unsure. 'Who? Who arrested him? The FBI or the cops?'

Her father took the receiver from her hand and hung it up and put his arm around her. 'Come in here and sit, and we'll tell you what we know, Linny.'

'But this is crazy, Daddy. Neil, this is crazy. Why Barry? He didn't—' She turned on her father as though he were the cause of her anger. 'They found out he was a German, didn't they? So? Big deal.' She took a pack of cigarettes from her coat pocket and lit one. 'I'm sorry, Daddy, but I need this. Is he supposed to be a spy just because his goddam parents were Nazis?'

'You knew all about his parents and all that, Linny?'

'Of course I knew. Oh Christ. Do you think he was keeping secrets from me about his childhood? He was a little boy! Oh Christ, the CIA, the goddam stupid FBI, everybody else knows that. I'm sorry, Daddy, but I'm really pissed off. He told them all that crap a long time ago. Little Bernard Koenig and the Coughlins and the whole bit. We were going to tell you all eventually, but it hardly seemed the time this weekend. Barry didn't want to make a big deal out of it. What do they think he did, anyway?'

Her father was holding hands with himself clumsily, waiting to comfort his daughter, but not knowing quite how to soothe this spitting, swearing hellcat. 'Now, Linny, if you'll just settle down . . .'

'Oh my ass, Daddy! They've arrested Barry. Do you expect me to sit here and wait for them to call me up and tell me they've exported him or deported him, or whatever they call it, to Germany just because they don't like dirty little secrets like people having Nazis for parents?'

Neil cleared his throat noisily and entered the middle ground between distraught parent and furious child. 'Linn, so far as you know, did Barry ever expect to hear again from his parents?'

'Oh God. He used to say he assumed they were dead, or just as good as.' She squinted at the smoke of her cigarette and stubbed it out roughly in a saucer someone had left on the coffee table. 'Then about a year ago, just after we sort of started living together, he got some mysterious call one night. He told me about it because when he got it, I was at his place. They said they'd be calling back—maybe soon, maybe not for a long time, but eventually. And they said it was about his parents.'

'From Germany? Could you tell?'

'I couldn't tell. It wasn't me, it was Barry that talked with them. All he told me was—I remember he was as white as a sheet—that they said maybe there was a chance his parents could get out of Germany now, but they'd have to do it illegally and in complete secret. They said he'd hear from them, something about Bertha and the umbrella factory, God, I don't know, and he was supposed to go to them as fast as he could and not say anything to anyone, that maybe the American authorities might not be too happy, you know? That's all I know.'

'That signal came today, Linn. Barry was here when they called him, but it's more complicated now.'

Neil could see that what Linn had said made Doan easier. It appeared there might just be an explanation—a complicated one, but an explanation—for Barry's behaviour.

'I delivered that message, Linn,' Neil said.

'You? Why you? What have you got to do with it?'

'I was given that message, about Aunt Bertha and Uncle Harry and the umbrella factory, by a CIA man who said it was the trigger for setting in motion an East German espionage operation keyed to Barry. Barry said he didn't know what it meant. Then he said he was going to see you, but he went directly to the contact point and walked in on the CIA.' Neil watched helplessly as she started to cry.

Her father seemed relieved, and folded her into his long arms.

The doorbell must have rung at least once, but none of them had heard. Jack Slater walked through the door saying, 'Anyone here?'

Neil stood up. Doan held his daughter a little closer. Linn looked tearily past her father's shoulder to see who had arrived to witness her collapse.

'Did I interrupt something?' Slater seemed almost jaunty, in new fancy boots, fitted designer jeans, and a checked hacking jacket. 'Miss Mitchell, if you are upset because those cretins from the FBI have been harassing you, don't be. I can assure you that there isn't a shred of evidence implicating you in this mess, no matter what those goddam fools think, and after they question you today, they are going to realize very quickly that they have to leave you alone.'

She disengaged herself from her father and blew her nose. 'Are you the one who arrested Barry?' Her mother's pugnaciousness was apparent in the way she said it and in the way she pulled herself together, as if for a fight.

'I came here to see Barry. Why on earth should I want—Neil, is this some bright stunt by our friend Michaels?'

'Yes, it's Dan's doing. He called a little while ago to say that he had Barry in custody.'

'That moron. May I sit down? Can we see just what's going on here and sort this thing out?'

Doan Mitchell stood beside his daughter. 'Her Barry's in some trouble because of his being German, is the way I understand it, not that it makes any sense.'

Slater blew out his lips in a thin, disgusted whistle. 'And Michaels used that as an excuse for pulling him in? Believe me, he'll be back out of custody before sundown, and Michaels might be out of a job too. My firm will not like what the fat doctor has done, Miss Mitchell, and they will put his rear end in a very large sling for this.'

Neil spoke. 'There appears to be more to it than just his having German parents, Slater. Michaels seems convinced that when Barry reacted to a pre-arranged signal mentioning Harry and Bertha, which I gather has something to do with his parents getting out of Germany, he gave himself away.'

'Then Dan Michaels is a bigger moron than I thought the first time. Whatever this Harry and Bertha routine is all about, if Barry thought he was acting—even secretly—in the interests of his parents, no one is going to call him a spy for that. We know he was born German, sure, but that's about as relevant as the colour of his hair, for Pete's sake.'

Linn looked hopeful for the first time since she had heard of her fiancé's arrest. 'You think so? I mean, I don't know, what if they just ship him out as an undesirable alien or something? Does he have the right to a hearing, even if his citizenship papers aren't right?'

'I'll guarantee he'll get a hearing if he wants one, but I'll also bet even money he'll be back here this afternoon with all this behind him.'

Neil's prudence prompted him to hedge against Linn's euphoria building up again too fast too far, in case a new disappointment might be even more bitter. 'Michaels seemed to think they have evidence of Barry using the computer at FiFoChi to tamper with the army computer up at Tonepah.'

'Have they been giving you a crash course in computers and their misuse, Neil? Let me guess. Mary Dowd?'

'Let's just say I know more today than I did yesterday.'

'Do you know enough to understand the magnitude as well as the mode of this crime? Has anyone made clear to you not just what's being done here in Santa Fe, but how it links up with national and international terrorist activity?' He unbuttoned his jacket and stretched his booted feet out as if to put them on display, making himself more comfortable in the big chair. 'Great chair. We have been so lucky, my friends, so damned lucky, because this missile we have tracked down is, so far as we can tell, the first—get that, the first—of its kind to be stolen and shipped using the computer set-up named EMSLINN.'

'What do you mean, there's a "computer set-up" named for my daughter?' Doan looked stunned.

Neil passed right over his question. 'If the crime amounts to a single missile stolen, and that recovered in time, I fail to see, bad as it is, how you or anyone can talk so melodramatically of the magnitude of this, as though a whole arsenal had been taken.'

'First, Neil, magnitude isn't always measured in terms

of how many of X have been stolen. One Brink's truck missing might be a lot more important than twenty candy-store robberies the same day. Let me put it like this. In Korea ten years ago—I was there—a group of Korean civilians employed by the US Army set up an ordering and delivery system, using the Army's own computer, that allowed them to steal eighteen million dollars' worth of Army supplies and have them delivered directly to black-market middlemen. One scam, eighteen million dollars. This operation makes that look like peanuts from what we know of it, literally.'

'How?'

'Our Washington office has already drawn up a preliminary scenario. It's clear now that the word EMSLINN is at least two things: a code name for the whole operation, and what technicians call a trapdoor in a computer programme—that is, a coded anomaly deliberately inserted into the army computer so that the breaker—the person breaking in—could have access. It's called a trapdoor, gentlemen—I'm sure our computer expert knows this—because anyone trying to trace or audit through the system automatically falls right through, missing it completely, as they go. It's also evident that the breaker put in a so-called "Trojan horse", which is just what it sounds like. Under the guise of legitimate information, the breaker inserts bogus information and/or instructions. We think this breaker, over maybe a year's time, broke into the Army computer core, used their access to central records in Washington, and gradually created on paper a whole small Army unit of four or five men, supplied them with family benefits and leaves, serial numbers, the works, and assigned them to secret weapons-development projects at a nonexistent secret base, code name Holy Faith, in New Mexico.'

'Santa Fe.'

'Yes ma'am. Santa Fe in Spanish. It was pure accident

that someone came along—sorry, Doan, but we're sure it was your boy Tim—and used the FiFoChi computer to steal a truck.'

'And a backhoe. To grade a hill to race their fool bikes on.'

'We theorize that Barbara Lacey had come close enough at one point to the FiFoChi end of things because she knew that the EMSLINN signal was probably a person there. So someone tried to eliminate her, apparently hoping to create a suspicion that the real target of the bomb was her husband.'

'But how did the Lathen boy get involved in both situations?' Neil was beginning to believe Slater. Did that mean Barry was innocent?

'He was actually in the store when Barbara Lacey bought her jack-in-the-box. He told someone about it, possibly in an offhand, joking way, and that person either told someone else or took the opportunity to do what was already planned but still awaiting execution. Then young Lathen simply had to be killed to shut him up. It was his misfortune, and his killer's, that he was riding in a stolen FiFoChi truck when he died. That brought the police and us back to the point where we think Barbara Lacey was in her investigation when she was injured. From that point, it was simply a matter of discovering who at FiFoChi was using their computer access to break into the Army system.'

'And do you know that now?'

'I do; *we* don't.'

'Do you mean you just found out today? This morning?'

'No, Neil, I mean that I can't tell my colleagues on the scene because one or both of them are involved.'

Neil was giving nothing. 'Meaning?'

'Aw, c'mon, Neil. You know who they are because you met with them yesterday. For Christ's sake, do you think I went off on a wild goose hunt up to Utah without understanding someone was trying to get me out of Santa Fe for a reason? You were observed, Neil. Pink Adobe? Later, La Posada. Come on, give me the benefit of believing I'm not completely stupid.'

Neil felt himself standing in the middle of a Mexican standoff between Michaels and Slater, or perhaps between Dowd and Slater. He suddenly had new insight into the phrase 'one false move'.

'Then why did they take me into their confidence as far as they did? If they couldn't know what they knew except by being the originators of the information, wouldn't it have made a great deal more sense to eliminate me, just as they did the Lathen boy?'

'Is that what old Fatso told you the bad guys would do? Did he spook you out of this house yesterday by telling you the bad guys were probably drawing a bead on you through the picture window?' He laughed and wiggled his toes. Neil did not; after all, it had happened.

'They couldn't be sure I'd go to them for safety.'

'No? Where would you go? Take sanctuary in St Francis Cathedral? Hide out in the Palace of the Governors?' He looked at Neil slyly from the corners of his eyes. 'Let me guess the kicker. After hemming and hawing around and sticking his goddam fat toe in the hot sand and saying "oh shucks, fellers", Dan Michaels finally let himself be persuaded by your relentless interrogation to tell you that they suspect Someone Inside the CIA, right?'

'You, as a matter of fact.'

'Of course me! Now that presents me with a little problem, doesn't it, in reestablishing my credibility with you folks? It seems to me that if Fatso and Butch Cassidy—she *has* to be a double for the KGB; Christ, she looks exactly like Brezhnev—wanted to eliminate you, their star character witness, they would do it only after you had followed their carefully laid trail of bread crumbs down the garden path and identified the villain at FiFoChi as the person *they* want identified. Then you and he would perhaps be offed in one, a two-bagger, after your testimony was a matter of record. Presto: their man, or woman, stays in place here, and they let the whole schmear lie fallow and cool down until they are ready to start it up again, perhaps after moving it carefully to a new terminal location.'

'They are pretty sure they have a lot of circumstantial evidence on their candidate.'

'Keeney? Bullshit.'

'Proof?'

'It's Nejad, the Iranian. And I can prove it because I have got that fucker nailed. That's the son of a bitch those two want left in place. He's in Qaddafi's pocket, a Muslim fanatic and a trained terrorist, class of '77 at Az-Zauiah Finishing School for World Class Baddies. And, I can prove it.'

'Do it, then, for God's sake.' Neil felt as if he had been under fire steadily for a long time. His wits were exhausted, his sense of the intellectual pleasure of solving an infinitely complex puzzle was emptied, and he wanted only for it to end, no matter how it ended. He understood then why the speech of exhausted men is laconic; it is the rhetoric of spiritual capitulation.

'To do it, I'll have to take you to Nejad's place.'

Doan snorted hoarsely. 'And get us all shot if he's what you say?'

Slater held his coat open. 'I'm not armed, you know, and I don't expect that Nejad will be, although it's possible. What I really doubt is that he will be there at all. He received a call this morning. I know, because I made it. It said simply "EMSLINN is blown." A tape-tap on his phone will have that recorded. If that message meant nothing to him, then he should still be sitting there when we arrive, sewing his socks or reading the Koran or whatever he does for a hobby. Which should be about the same time the

FBI arrives, since I called them too.' He smiled sarcastically at Neil. 'You citizens want cooperation between your services; you got it. Once in a while, anyway.'

'My daughter's not going.'

'Come on, Daddy. If anyone goes, I go. Remember, the Army at least still thinks *I'm* the prime suspect here, and it's my future husband they've taken in.'

Neil said simply, 'Let's all go. Where is it?'

'Out on Sierra Vista. Not far.'

Doan and Linn went in his truck. Slater and Neil rode together in the agent's Camaro.

'I suppose we should all be grateful you showed up out here, Neil,' Slater said as they drove down the hill at a respectable thirty. 'Because this case needed a catalyst. Your arrival certainly provided that.'

'A policeman who doesn't especially like me once described me as a goddam lightning rod. He said it was a dangerous gift, but things seem to focus on me. Perhaps it's because I sit very still a lot and just wait for them to.'

'And let the buffalo hear your heartbeat, you mean?' Slater laughed. 'You and old Leapinghorse the wolf sticker.'

They turned out at Alameda and rode in silence until Slater pulled to a stop behind a familiar brown car in front of a low stucco frame house with a deep porch.

'This is it. Look who's sitting out front waiting for us.'

Cady stretched out of his own car and walked back to theirs. 'You know you have no licence to hunt here, Slater.'

The CIA man put his hands up in mock surrender. 'Just an honest taxpayer come to help the forces of good with their investigation, Cady. Who do you think called you guys?'

'You? Someone called and said Nejad was getting ready to run.'

'Is he? Did he? Will he? Do we have to tune in tomorrow to find out?'

'He ran,' the FBI man said drily. 'He got as far as Truth or Consequences.'

'Now there is an irony that titillates my risibilities, Cady. Which was it: truth, or is he going to pay the consequences?'

'We assume he was headed for El Paso, where there appears to be another link in this chain. He paid the consequences, Mr Slater. Someone planted one of those little bombs in his car. It appears to have been detonated. He's dead.'

Doan and Linn joined them, and all five now stood on the sidewalk as the agent finished his account. A woman neighbour wearing a flowered apron came out in front of her house and began sweeping the walk, watching.

'Why don't we all just go in there, Cady, and see what our Iranian brother left behind? I don't know what you fellows over at the Bureau call that, but we sometimes refer to it as "the evidence". That's a technical term, means—well, shucks, you probably know what it means.'

Cady looked sourly at him and led the small parade, Linn last, up on to the low porch. He opened the door carefully. It was unlocked and swung in without blowing up or providing any other surprises.

The four rooms of the tiny house, except for a back bedroom, were simply an open huddle of poorly furnished, discouraged-looking cubicles, their doorways either empty or hung with limp, faded green curtains. In the back bedroom, they found a telephone and a small computer terminal.

'My, my.'

'Maybe it was his hobby.'

'That's possible.' Slater lifted the phone and listened. 'It's working. Miss Mitchell, honey, how do you turn on this terminal?'

She started forward, but Neil held her arm firmly. 'Tell him.'

'The switch is right there on the side. It's set for paper printout, but on this one you can get a visual readout just by using that switchover button.' She pointed gingerly.

'Now let me tell you what I think, Cady, lady, and gentlemen,' Slater said in a pitchman's nasal whine. 'With this handy-dandy little desktop terminal, I think Nejad was patching through the FiFoChi terminal, using their codes, to break into the Army computer. I'm not expert enough to say how that's done, but it has to be possible. Then he was simply ordering the Army computer to order the Army to deliver the data he wanted to this station, which is probably listed in the memory core as Fort Riley, Kansas, or the Pentagon, for all we know. Miss Mitchell, explain to us what a data-base management system is, in computer terms.'

Linn did, in remarkably clear, brief terms. It was obvious why he had asked her. As she had pointed out before and did again then, the FiFoChi programme called BARNDOOR, designed to manage equipment inventory, and their payroll systems, was such a programme.

'Now, Miss Mitchell, if I wanted to cause a so-called "out-of-bounds" error in the army's computer memory core, how would I do it?'

'I suppose you'd place the bank of the core you wanted the main system to use either higher or lower than it should be—just put your management data out of reach, sort of.'

'They taught you well at IBM. Now, if a user, having put an error like that into the system, wishes to ask the system for the out-of-bounds data, do you know what happens in the world-famous Univac Exec Eight, which the Army insists on using?'

'No. You're way beyond me now. Barry told the Army something about the computer they were using being shown to be vulnerable back in 1974, but I didn't understand.'

'Neither does the United States Army, ma'am, but Barry was right. If I get my error back on the Army's computer, an error I deliberately placed there myself, that return opens up what technicians call an REP, a reentrant processor. In other words, my friends, Mr Nejad could call up the Army computer, dial an error he himself had put into the system, and automatically get an altered connection back into the system, by means of which he could go into the system to hunt for his lost data. Or go merrily through the memory of the computer hunting for anything else. It's exactly as though I gave you the key to my house and told you to get the tennis racket I left in the bedroom closet. If you prefer, you can go into my library and steal my first edition of the Gutenberg Bible.'

Cady listened closely, his eyes switching back and forth between the girl and the CIA man. 'Is that what EMSLINN is, an access programme into the Army computer's memory core?'

Doan shook his head. 'Why not just open the line up and let it copy every dang thing there? If they want to steal from the Army, why not steal all the information first, then sort it out and take what they want?'

'Too much, Doan.' Slater looked around the cramped room. 'Even a small computer's system—the Exec Eight isn't gigantic—can store a million items easily. That's three miles of paper printout. Mr Nejad would have had to run for his life a long time ago, pursued by miles of paper. No sir, selectivity is the key. Linn, would you be willing right now to punch your company's code into the Army computer, in the presence of a legally constituted and delegated federal officer, Mr Cady here, and, using the EMSLINN code key, see what you get? Me, I'll bet five million dollars we get an REP.' He stepped back from the table with the terminal and, with a gesture of his hand, offered her a seat.

'Don't you think we ought to wait until we meet the Army people in Albuquerque this afternoon, Mr Slater, before we run this test of yours?'

'The Army, Doan, has got hold of the wrong end of the stick, as usual. We all know that old Army term "snafu", don't we, and it wasn't a computer programme. Barry told them already what's being done to their computer, but the sad fact is they don't understand; not one bird colonel, not one buck sergeant knows what they are doing up there. I understand that he pointed out to them that a young woman corporal was their most valuable person. If the Army runs true to form, she will be transferred to fire brigade or kitchen duty. No, Doan, because Nejad would have programmed things to deliver the data here. The access codes are FiFoChi's, I'll guarantee you, but the computer will have been told to spit out data here. Linny?'

Doan's daughter left her father's side for the first time and sat at the little table. She switched on the terminal, picked up the phone, and dialled a series of digits. 'I've done this enough times this past year. For a while, I thought we weren't doing business with anyone *but* the Army.'

She listened, hung up the phone, typed rapidly on the keyboard of the computer, and sat back.

For a moment, there was nothing, then a visual display appeared on the green glowing screen above the typewriter.

EMSLINN IS BLOWN. SORRY ABOUT THAT. ERASED WITHOUT A TRACE ERASED. WE HAVE BEEN BETRAYED BUT THE REVOLUTION WILL GO ON. YOU LIVE IN A DOOMED CORRUPT CIVILIZATION. THE INEVITABLE VICTORY OF THE TRUTH WILL NOT BE FORESTALLED BY THE AMERICAN SATAN. ONE MAN UNDER THE

BANNER OF ALLAH BLESSED BE HIS NAME WILL UNITE THE HOLY ONES TOGETHER FOR VICTORY. SLATER YOU BETRAYED ME AND I NOW CUT OFF YOUR HEAD. YOU AND ALL YOUR CIA FILTH ARE NOT NECESSARY TO THE VICTORY OF ALLAH AND QADDAFI. I ABANDON YOU AS YOU ABANDONED ME SLATERSLATERSLATER . . .

The screen kept printing the same word over and over.

There was no struggle because Cady stood behind Slater holding a gun solidly against his spine.

'Now that is my idea of a Trojan horse, Slater. You know, we already knew it was going to say that. As soon as we heard Nejad was killed, we came here and went through approximately the same steps you just did. The last joke is on you, Slater.'

The CIA man turned to face him, ignoring the gun still against his body. 'You're not smart enough, Cady. Every scrap of evidence anyone could bring against me is classified national security. One of the nice things about working for the CIA, Cady, is that they can't put their people on trial without telling too many dirty secrets about themselves.'

'We'll see, won't we? It was Barry showed us what to do, Miss Mitchell. He's outside, along with a large contingent of my friends. We're surrounded by them, Slater, so if you are about to perform some miracle of karate on me, go ahead and get it over with because there are lots more waiting for a chance outside, all armed. And, oh, your car won't be there. Didn't you hear them drive it away while we were talking? You white men don't hear very well; *I* can tell a Camaro with one ear tied behind me. Open the front door, Neil.'

When Neil opened the door, he saw five or six new cars outside. Armed agents on either side of the door pulled him out and went past him into the house. Linn streaked out and jumped from the low porch directly into Barry's arms. Suddenly, everything happened so fast that the handcuffed Slater was hustled past Neil and down into Cady's car by two agents before anyone could speak again.

The Indian agent came out of the house looking, for once, satisfied. 'There are a lot more CIA and ex-CIA people than just Slater involved. We think a major international group, led by former agents who have formed a kind of military-industrial complex of consultants for sale to the highest bidder, has been selling US intelligence to Qaddafi. At least, he's usually the highest bidder these days. I guess the gas in all these cars here helps him out paying his bills.'

'Does that mean Qaddafi has the missing missile?'

'He would have by now if we hadn't found it in the Army's own backyard. You apparently remarked to Barry one day that if you stole a missile, you'd hide it on an Army base, and he said that to me. Once we knew that the computer was instructing Army transport to ship Army goods wherever these jokers wanted it, we guessed well enough to check back on invoices and found a cargo plane full of something labelled "spare parts" had delivered a large, unmistakable missile to Westover, Massachusetts where, still labelled "spare parts", it was ticketed for trans-shipment to West Germany. We know that several thousand digital remote detonators went that route, and an unknown quantity of encoding equipment. The instruction was our first Trojan horse—a simple instruction to send spare parts to Westover. Incidentally, it was Slater himself who named the thing EMSLINN. Smartass. Nejad knew you all called her that, and Slater thought it an easy way to point to her if it ever came out.'

'Which means,' said Neil almost wistfully, 'that the missing missile is about ten miles from my house.'

Linn and Barry came up on the porch and surrounded Doan, who had one more question for Cady. 'Can't you just run their programme through the Army computer now and pull it all back?'

'Never, Doan. The whole thing's erased. Ask Barry; it's beyond me. I'm sorry for everyone's sake that we had to go through that Harry and Bertha routine with Michaels, but it was our only hope that Slater would panic sufficiently to sacrifice his partner, Nejad, to prove his own innocence. We leaked it to him in plenty of time. We already knew the Harry-Bertha signal because Barry himself came to us a year ago and told us when he was first called. His parents had actually gone to work for the American occupation authorities in East Berlin under the Gehlen network. They did that on strict condition that we never tell their son, so that he could simply forget about his past life and have a normal existence. But Barry, unfortunately, had no way of knowing that his fiancée, Linn Mitchell, wasn't involved, so he agreed to act out this charade this morning.' He smiled thinly. 'He wasn't that sure about you, either, Neil. After all, you were apparently the messenger of whoever was trying to persuade him his parents were escaping.'

Talthubios again.

'And Slater did, *Deo gratias*, panic.'

Neil smiled. 'Panic. I've heard of that. A Greek invention, I believe.'

Cady grunted. 'Don't you believe it. A scared Indian invented that one.'

CHAPTER 16

For all of the long flight back, which ended with his watching the moon rise orange far below on their right side—the rim of the world so unexpectedly the edge of a distant, immense ball—Neil sat silently, reviewing and reordering the events that had whirled around him.

A safety deposit box in an Albuquerque bank had yielded six of the miniature digital detonators Slater had been using. Neil recalled him coming red-faced back in from the cold parking lot outside Bishop's Lodge, stopping to warm his hands by backslapping the old soak at the bar, laughing hard to appear naturally flushed. He had killed De Sales and blinded Barbara simply because she was a threat to him, and betrayed his Iranian partner in an effort to prove his own credibility when it was already too late to save them both. Tim had identified him as 'the FBI man'.

Neil had almost been convinced that the incurably prankish Dan Michaels had in fact been the puppet master of the whole horror show of death and mutilation, yet it was a fact that he had simply been in Santa Fe for a conference, and so the CIA had parked Mary Dowd with him and utilized his special understanding of the trickster to guide her in dogging Slater.

Everything came down, as the computer had shown, to Slater, Slater, Slater.

Sitting the next morning in the semi-darkened, pleasant room in a private hospital in Belmont, Massachusetts, Neil tried to adjust his feelings and thinking to this present reality, and away from that squalid conspiracy they had uncovered two thousand miles away, and only two days past.

Barbara Lacey had awakened on Wednesday and spoken with her sister Emily for a minute before falling asleep again for twelve hours. Her vital signs had stabilized, and her prospects of recovery from the mild stroke she had apparently suffered were good. She would probably be permanently weakened on one side, and her sight would never return, but she was alive, and she had spoken to Neil and reached out and touched his face just an hour ago.

He had put on her finger the green turquoise ring he

had bought that day on the plaza, and he had described to her the tiny birds carved around it. She touched them.

Doan and Emily had sat down with him to dinner in Locke-Ober's the night before and talked about their plans for their blind sister. She would never see Santa Fe again, but she would be feeling the dry, warm wind on her face soon, and she wanted to learn to walk through the Plaza she loved, and to hear the birdsongs she had only begun to know. She had whispered to them that she would be a listener if she could not be a birdwatcher.

His plane to England would leave in four hours from Logan. Devon was still green and wet with April, and John Donne was still not satisfactorily explained. He rose quietly and went back on sabbatical.